NOV 0 2 2009

W9-ANC-782

THE DEVIL'S BADLAND

**Center Point
Large Print**

Also by J. A. Johnstone
and available from Center Point Large Print:

The Loner Series
The Loner

By William W. Johnstone and J. A. Johnstone:

Fury Series
A Town Called Fury
Hard Country
Judgment Day

Sidewinders Series
Sidewinders
Massacre at Whiskey Flats
Cutthroat Canyon

**This Large Print Book carries the
Seal of Approval of N.A.V.H.**

THE DEVIL'S BADLAND
The Loner

J. A. Johnstone

CENTER POINT PUBLISHING
THORNDIKE, MAINE

WILLARD LIBRARY
7 W. VanBuren St.
Battle Creek, MI 49017

This Center Point Large Print edition
is published in the year 2009 by arrangement with
Kensington Publishing Corp.

Copyright © 2009 by J. A. Johnstone.

All rights reserved.

The text of this Large Print edition is unabridged.
In other aspects, this book may vary
from the original edition.
Printed in the United States of America.
Set in 16-point Times New Roman type.

ISBN: 978-1-60285-595-3

Library of Congress Cataloging-in-Publication Data

Johnstone, J. A.
  The devil's badland / J. A. Johnstone. -- Large print ed.
    p. cm.
  ISBN 978-1-60285-595-3 (library binding : alk. paper)
  1. Wives--Crimes against--Fiction. 2. Murder--Investigation--Fiction.
   3. Revenge--Fiction. 4. Large type books. I. Title.

PS3610.O43D48 2009
813'.6--dc22

2009027904

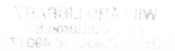

THE DEVIL'S BADLAND

Chapter 1

Thunder rolled over the mountains, and lightning clawed through the gray-black sky above the peaks. It would be a dark, violent night, the young man thought as he slapped the reins against the buggy horse's back. That was entirely appropriate, because dark nights of the soul were the only kind he knew.

The storm was still a ways behind him. He hoped he could reach his destination before it caught up with him. If not, he would have to seek shelter, which would delay him on his journey. That would be an annoyance, but not a major setback. The woman he was going to see would wait for him.

She had no choice. She was dead.

The approaching storm made the late afternoon gloom even deeper. The young man spotted a flicker of yellow light up ahead. Even with a new century only a few years away and civilization spread to much of what was once a lawless frontier, that part of southern New Mexico Territory was still sparsely settled. The ranches there were far-flung, isolated. The light had to come from a ranch house, or maybe a sodbuster's adobe shack, because there, as elsewhere, farmers were moving in on what had been open range until a few years earlier.

A hard gust of wind rattled the buggy's canvas

top. No rain was falling yet, but the young man could smell it coming. He sighed as he realized he couldn't make it to the mission at Val Verde before the storm overtook him. Better to head for that house where the light shone and see if he could spend the night there while the storm rolled through, then go on to Val Verde in the morning.

The light flickered again. Either the wind was blowing the flame, or someone was moving back and forth in front of it. The young man pulled back on the left rein, turning the horse and buggy toward the light. A few drops of rain pattered on the canvas. Thunder boomed again. Lightning cracked.

But those sounds didn't come from the storm behind him, the young man realized suddenly as he saw muzzle flame spurt in the gloom. That booming sound wasn't thunder. It was a shotgun being discharged. Those sharp cracks that followed came from six-guns and rifles.

A pitched battle was going on right in front of him. The smart thing to do would be to veer away, go around whatever the trouble was, and keep heading south as long as the weather would allow.

It had been a while since he'd worried much about doing the smart thing. He leaned forward, slashed the horse's back with the reins, yelled, *"Hyyaahhh!"*, and raced as fast he could straight toward the blasting guns.

. . .

Rory MacTavish blinked his eyes against the sting of powdersmoke and nestled his cheek on the smooth wood of the Winchester's stock. He peered over the barrel he had thrust through the rifle slit in the dugout's front wall and waited for a target.

He didn't have to wait long. A moment later, one of Whitfield's men darted across the open ground between the corral and the smokehouse. That took him right in front of Rory's gunsights. With the speedy reflexes of the young, the boy pulled the trigger.

The Winchester kicked hard against Rory's shoulder. Even though he knew to expect it because he'd been hunting many times in his fifteen years, he still had to bite back a yelp of pain. He'd always been scrawny, without much padding against such impacts.

"Good shootin', lad!" his father called from one of the other loopholes. "Ye downed the skalleyhooter!"

Rory looked through the slit and saw the gunman crawling back toward the corral, dragging a wounded leg behind him.

"Now kill 'im!" Hamish MacTavish roared. "Get 'im afore he gets away!"

Rory swallowed hard. His pa was right, of course. You couldn't pass up an opportunity to kill a Whitfield man.

But Rory had never actually killed any man, let alone one who rode for Devil Dave Whitfield.

"Ach, I shoods hae known!" Hamish said as Rory hesitated. The old muzzle-loader in Hamish's hands blasted, and even in the fading light, Rory saw the Whitfield man jerk under the impact of the heavy lead ball that blasted away a chunk of his skull. The man sprawled facedown on the ground near the corral as rain began to fall.

Hamish pulled his rifle from the loophole and started reloading. He was good at it, his motions swift and smooth. He'd carried a rifle just like that during the War of Northern Aggression, when he was a little younger than Rory was now, and to hear him tell it, he had used it to kill dozens of damn Yankees at a place called The Wilderness. For all Rory knew, it was true. By and large, his father was a truthful man.

And a harsh man in his judgments, as well. Rory had heard the scorn in Hamish MacTavish's voice just now.

He should have known that he couldn't trust his son to be a real man. That was what Hamish really meant.

" 'Tis startin' to rain," Hamish said as he slid the rifle's barrel back into the loophole. "I expect they'll be chargin' us now. They won't want to get wet, the bloody spalpeens."

"Let 'em come," Rory's older brother James said as he poked a long-barreled Remington revolver through a loophole. He carried the Americanized version of their father's name, since he, like Rory and their sister Margaret, had been born here, long after Hamish had immigrated to this country.

It had been James who had opened the ball by loosing both barrels of the old double-barreled Greener at Whitfield's men. The rancher's gun-wolves had shown up to accuse the MacTavishes once again of stealing Circle D cattle, and when Hamish and James argued, one of the gunmen reached for his Colt. That had been enough to make James's finger jerk the scattergun's triggers. The weapon had lived up to its nickname by scattering the hired killers and giving Hamish and James time to retreat into the dugout.

As he squinted over the barrel of the Remington, James went on, "Easier to kill 'em that way."

Ah, yes, Rory thought as he worked the Winchester's lever. James was a son after their father's own heart.

Margaret came up behind him and asked softly, "Do you need more bullets?"

Rory glanced over his shoulder at her. She was seventeen, two years older than he was and two years younger than James. There had been six children in the family, but the two youngest, a boy and a girl, had died of illness in childhood without ever reaching eight years old.

The oldest, Charlie, had been killed two months earlier in a shootout with one of Whitfield's gunslingers in Val Verde. The loss still put a bitter taste in Rory's mouth whenever he thought about it.

So he tried not to think about it, even now when they might all be on the verge of being wiped out by Whitfield's men. He hung on to the rifle with his right hand and thrust his left into the box in Margaret's hands. He took out a dozen cartridges and shoved them into his pocket.

"Thanks."

"Here they come!" Hamish called.

Rory leaned forward, put his cheek against the rifle's stock again, and waited to kill his first man.

It didn't have to come to this.

That thought went through his head as he saw men rush out from behind the barn and the corral and charge toward the dugout, orange flame spurting from their guns and splitting the stormy twilight. If his father and Dave Whitfield had been able to sit down and talk things over like reasonable men . . .

But the chance to be reasonable had vanished along with Whitfield's missing cattle. It had died with Charlie MacTavish. Hatred and the spilling of blood were all that was left.

Rory tried not to cry as he pulled the trigger, but the tears welled from his eyes anyway. The storm was suddenly right on top of the little ranch, with thunder rumbling so loudly it shook the earth, lightning flashing to compete with the muzzle flames, and rain falling from the heavens in drenching, sluicing waves. Rory no longer aimed his rifle at men but at vague gray shapes instead, shapes that brandished weapons of their own as they poured lead at the house.

Then something loomed out of the gathering shadows and cut through the attackers, scattering them again. Rory held his fire as he saw more muzzle flashes, but these shots weren't aimed at the dugout. Instead they sent Whitfield's men running for cover. Rory realized that a buggy had just raced into the yard, with a riderless horse tied on behind it. The vehicle wheeled into a sharp turn, moving so fast that for a second Rory thought it would tip over and spill the man at the reins. Instead, he kept his seat as the wheel that left the ground for a second came back down and bit into earth that was turning rapidly into mud. Amazingly, the man had only one hand on the reins.

The revolver in his other hand spat fire and lead.

"Who's that?" James shouted.

"I dinna ken!" Hamish said. "But he's on our side, so more power to 'im, I say!"

The stranger's unexpected attack had broken the back of the charge. Whitfield's men fled as the stranger's uncannily accurate shots broke arms and tore through legs. The man in the buggy wasn't shooting to kill, Rory saw, but he was inflicting plenty of damage anyway. Damage that had Whitfield's men turning tail and running, taking their dead and wounded with them.

James whooped gleefully and ran to the door. He flung it open and dashed out into the rain to throw some shots after their enemies. "Be careful, James!" Margaret called after him, but he didn't pay any attention to her. He was too caught up in the heat of battle.

Hamish went out, too, tossing aside his rifle and pulling an old pistol from behind his belt. "Pa!" Margaret said in exasperation. She turned to Rory. "I suppose you'll be chasing after them like a madman now, too."

"If they're goin' out, I can't stay in here, Meggie," he said. He had endured enough scorn from his father and brother for one day. Jacking another round into the Winchester's chamber, he hurried to the door and out into the pounding rain.

The force of the storm half-blinded him and almost knocked him off his feet. The wind wasn't blowing that hard; it was the sheer power of the rain itself that almost drove him to his knees. He struggled to stay upright and looked around for any of Whitfield's men who were still in range.

The only people he saw were his father and James and the man in the buggy, who had swung down from the seat and stood next to the vehicle with a Colt revolver in his hand. The stranger was hatless, but with the rain in his eyes Rory couldn't tell much more about him except that he was tall and dressed in a dark suit. The downpour had plastered the man's fair hair to his head.

"They're gone," Hamish roared over the rushing sound of the rain, "and we're much obliged t' ye for your help, mister. Come on into th' house, outta this storm!"

"I have to see to my horses!" the man shouted back. He gestured toward the buggy, where a big black was hitched to the vehicle and a rangy buckskin was tied on behind.

"Th' boy can do that for ye!" Hamish said. "Rory! Take the man's horses into the barn!"

"Aye!" Rory said. Unlike killing, that was a chore he could handle.

He handed his rifle to James, then grabbed the black's bridle and led the horse toward the barn. The buckskin followed along behind the buggy. Rory swung the big door open. It was a relief to step inside, out of the rain.

He was soaked to the skin. His feet squished unpleasantly in his boots as he walked.

Using one of the matches in a little box hung from a nail by a string, Rory lit the lantern. Quickly, he went about unhitching the black and leading him and the buckskin into a pair of empty stalls. Once, all six stalls in the barn had been full, but money problems had forced his father to sell off most of their horses. Only a couple of mounts were left.

Rory rubbed the horses down, then dumped grain into the feed troughs and filled water buckets from the barrel. With the animals taken care of, he walked over to the buggy and glanced curiously into the vehicle. He saw an obviously expensive saddle behind the seat, along with a fine new Winchester and a heavy-looking older rifle Rory thought was a Sharps. The stranger was well-to-do, plain enough. Rory couldn't help but wonder why the man had come along and taken a hand in their trouble. According to Hamish MacTavish, the rich didn't give a damn about anyone except themselves. They sure wouldn't care about a family of poor Scots trying to make a go of a hardscrabble ranch.

But this man evidently did. Rory left the barn and headed for the dugout, anxious to learn more about this stranger who had shown up out of the storm to rout Devil Dave's gun-wolves with a blazing Colt.

Built into the side of a hill, the dugout that served as the home of the MacTavishes was larger and less primitive than most folks might have expected. Hamish, Charlie, and James had used thick beams for the roof, then sealed it and the walls with pitch before mounding the dirt and stone over it again. It didn't leak even in a downpour like this, which was more than could be said for the barn. A chimney extended up through the hill from the large fireplace where flames now leaped and danced, warming the big main room. The floor was stone, but Margaret had put down rugs to make it nicer and more comfortable.

Except for the lack of windows, you'd hardly know that you weren't in a regular house.

When Rory went in, he saw his father, James, and the stranger standing in front of the fireplace, drying their clothes in its heat. Margaret was on the other side of the room, rattling pots and pans in the kitchen as she prepared a meal for the menfolk.

"Might I offer ye a drink?" Hamish was asking as Rory walked in. He glanced over his shoulder as the open door caused a draft. Rory closed it quickly. Hamish went on, "As ye might expect, I have some o' the finest Scotch whiskey ye'll find this side o' the highlands."

"That sounds good," the stranger said with a nod. He looked around at Rory. "Who's this?"

"Me youngest," Hamish said with a notable lack of pride in his voice. "His name's Rory."

The stranger smiled. "Hello, Rory. Thanks for putting up my horses." He held out his hand. "My name's Conrad Browning."

Chapter 2

The boy hesitated, surprised that Conrad had offered to shake hands with him. He took Conrad's hand briefly, keeping his eyes downcast as he mumbled, "Pleased t' meet ye, Mr. Browning."

Short and slender, Rory was a lot smaller than his big, brawny father and brother, but he had the same bushy red hair as Hamish and James, who had introduced themselves to Conrad while the boy was out at the barn tending to the horses. They had introduced Margaret as well, who shared the red hair and also possessed the same shyness as Rory. Conrad felt an instinctive liking for these people and was glad he had stepped in to help them.

He had faced a choice when he rolled up in the buggy just as the rain began falling in earnest. He had no way of knowing which side was in the right in this dispute, so he could cast his lot with the defenders inside the house built into the side of a hill, or with the attackers who were charging that dugout.

Conrad had counted nearly a dozen men attacking the house, where only two or three defenders fired back. When in doubt, take up for the underdog, he had decided. But he had shot to wound, not to kill, just in case he found out later that he had jumped into the fight on the wrong side.

Looking around at the MacTavishes, he couldn't

believe that was the case. They appeared to be honest, hard-working settlers—the salt of the earth, as the old saying had it.

The sort of people that Conrad Browning once would have looked down on with a sense of arrogant superiority.

He liked to believe that he had changed, that he wasn't that sort of man anymore, but it didn't hurt to remind himself from time to time just what a son of a bitch he had been.

Hamish MacTavish dug around in an old trunk and came up with a dark brown bottle and a couple of glasses. As he brought them over to the fireplace, his son James asked, "What about me, Pa?"

"Ye're too young for this," Hamish said.

"Old enough to fight, ain't I?" James challenged.

"Aye, but so's Rory, and ye dinna see me givin' *'im* a drink, do ye?"

"He ain't much of a fighter," James said, his lip curling in a sneer. "He didn't kill any o' Whitfield's men, as far as I could see."

Conrad glanced at Rory to see if the youngster would say anything in his own defense. Rory just kept looking at the floor and didn't speak up.

Turning back to Hamish, Conrad took the glass the man offered him. Hamish lifted his glass and said, "T' ye health, sir."

"And to yours," Conrad returned.

They tossed back their drinks. The whiskey went down like liquid fire and kindled a blaze in

19

Conrad's belly. He gave a little gasp for breath, and that brought a smile to Hamish's face.

"I told ye 'twas good," he said with pride in his voice.

"I never had any better in San Francisco or Boston," Conrad admitted. That made Hamish beam.

Conrad went on, "Why were those men attacking you?"

Hamish's smile disappeared. His broad face darkened with anger. "Because they're hired killers workin' for a no-good bastard called Devil Dave Whitfield!" he declared.

"The local cattle baron," Conrad guessed.

Hamish gave a contemptuous snort. "He thinks he is, anyway. He disnae ken that those days are over, that he can no longer run roughshod o'er the smaller ranchers. This is MacTavish land, and MacTavish land it will stay!"

It was an old story, Conrad thought, one that had been played out many times on the frontier. Despite what Hamish said, it nearly always ended the other way, with the richer, more powerful rancher triumphing over the owners of the smaller spreads.

In fact, by this point syndicates or corporations owned most of the large ranches, and companies always grew larger at the expense of individuals. At one point in his life, Conrad had believed that was the proper way for things to be, and he had enough experience in business to recognize the truth of the matter, whether he agreed with it now or not.

He smiled as he told Hamish, "I hope you're right." When he got down to it, though, this wasn't his fight. He had business of his own in New Mexico Territory. So he didn't ask any more questions, other than to say, "I wonder if you could put me up for the night? The weather's still pretty bad out there, and I'm not sure the storm is going to let up until morning."

Conrad could still hear the rain's sluicing rush. The MacTavishes must have done a really good job of sealing the roof and walls to keep the water out.

"Aye, we wouldna send ye back out in that deluge," Hamish said. "Ye'll be welcome to spend the night. Ye can have mah bunk."

Conrad started to tell the rancher that wasn't necessary, that he could just make up a bedroll on the floor, then he remembered that the man Conrad Browning used to be—the man Conrad Browning was still *supposed* to be—wouldn't have reacted that way. That Conrad would have expected to be accommodated in the best possible manner.

"Of course I'll be glad to pay you," he went on, his smile turning smug. That was something the old Conrad would have said, too.

Hamish frowned. " 'Twill no' be necessary to do that," he said, his voice suddenly cooler. Conrad knew that his offer of payment had just knocked him down a notch or two in Hamish's estimation, and that was a shame. Still, the game had to be played.

Not that he expected to win, Conrad mused. In the big scheme of things, he had already lost before he ever started, because no matter what he did, Rebel would still be dead. His wife was gone.

All Conrad could do was continue his quest to bring vengeance—and justice—to those responsible for her death.

The stew Margaret served for supper was hot and delicious, Conrad thought. When he complimented the girl on it, she blushed prettily. She was a nice-looking young woman, somewhere in her late teens, with thick masses of red hair tumbling down her back and a well-curved body in a homespun dress. Conrad recognized those things, but they didn't really affect him. He was still in mourning. Anyway, Margaret was the daughter of his host and much too young for him.

While they were sitting at the dinner table, James MacTavish said, "Whitfield's men will be back, ye know. We killed at least one of 'em, that gunman called Hardesty. I saw you put a bullet in his head, Pa."

Hamish gave Rory a hard look. "Aye."

Conrad didn't know what that exchange was about, but he felt a little sorry for the boy, who never lifted his eyes from his bowl of stew. Conrad could tell from Rory's attitude that he knew his father was glaring at him, and he felt a pang of sympathy for Rory.

He knew all too well what the tension between father and son was like.

Conrad couldn't stop himself from saying, "This fellow Whitfield must have quite a grudge against you folks to send hired guns after you like that."

"All over a bunch of blasted cows," Hamish said bitterly. "He claimed that we stole them, but that was just his way o' tryin' to get the law on his side, so he could run us off our land."

"So he accused you of rustling?"

"Aye," James said. He slapped a palm down on the table. "But we never did it! We never touched a one of his damned beeves!"

"James!" Margaret scolded. "That's no way to talk, especially at the dinner table."

"It's the truth!" James insisted. "What Whitfield said was a lie, and Charlie was right to tell him to his face."

Margaret paled. "All that did was get Charlie killed. Was it worth it for him to call Whitfield a liar? Was it, James?"

James scowled but didn't say anything.

These people had seen more than their share of hardship and tragedy, Conrad thought—but so had he. There was nothing else he could do to help them, not while his own mission was incomplete.

Anyway, if he tried to involve himself too deeply

in their problems, he would probably just make things worse, he told himself. He had a history of bringing trouble down not only on himself, but also on those around him. You could ask his wife Rebel about that.

Well, you could if she wasn't dead.

The strained silence lasted for the rest of the meal. When it was over, Hamish showed Conrad to a small room in the back of the dugout that contained little more than a narrow bunk.

" 'Tis no' much," he said, "but th' best we can offer ye, Mr. Browning."

"It's fine," Conrad assured him. "Thank you."

There was no door to the room, just a curtain, like the other two bedrooms, one shared by the boys and the other for Margaret. A candle on a shelf provided light. Conrad undressed by its flickering glow. The heat from the fireplace had only partially dried his clothes, and he was glad to get the damp garments off.

He wore a plain, black gunbelt while he was dressed in the dark, sober suit, although there was a different gunbelt coiled in his saddlebags. He curled the one he had taken off around an equally plain, black holster that held his Colt .45 Peacemaker and placed belt, holster, and gun on the floor next to the bunk, within easy reach if he needed the Colt. He didn't expect that to be the case tonight, but always being ready for trouble was a habit with him now.

Conrad wrapped up in the blanket that was on the bunk, stretched out, and tried to sleep. As usual, that wasn't easy. As soon as he closed his eyes, images began to whirl through his brain—awful images that he would just as soon never see again.

But at the same time, a part of him clung to them, reluctant to let go of the pain, because that would mean letting go of the past, too, and he wasn't ready to do that . . .

Rebel stood high atop the bluff that loomed over Black Rock Canyon. Behind her was the gunman, Clay Lasswell. Conrad had paid the ransom that was supposed to save her. The rest of the kidnappers already had their greedy hands on it. All that was left was for Lasswell to let her go.

But instead, the killer from Texas cried out, "Welcome to hell!" as the gun in his hand roared. The bullet tore into Rebel and knocked her off the bluff, so that she plummeted down toward the merciless ground below, falling, falling . . .

The image in Conrad's mind changed. Now he was standing over one of the kidnappers, pressing the barrel of a Winchester to the man's head. He saw the man's eyes widen in horror and disbelief, then bulge out from the pressure as Conrad pulled the trigger and sent a bullet through the bastard's brain.

That man wasn't the only one Conrad had killed in circumstances that might seem like cold-blooded murder to some people. He had killed

25

even more in fair fights. Their faces swam before him now as he tried to sleep, but always that image of Rebel falling, followed by the memory of cradling her broken, lifeless body in his arms, returned to drive everything else away.

Conrad dozed off and slept fitfully on the narrow bunk in the MacTavish dugout, jerking from side to side as nightmares haunted his slumber. No matter how much he tried, he couldn't get away from the ghosts who pursued him. All the men he had killed chased him, their bullet-riddled forms closing in on him, and in trying to get away from them, he ran toward the elusive form of his wife, still alive and vital, looking back at him with love shining in her eyes.

But, he could never catch up to her, and the dead men caught up to him instead, trying to pull him down like a pack of wolves. He fought against them, lashing out and driving them back until he had time to reach his gun. He drew the Colt and spun to face the grisly phantoms. The revolver came up, his finger tightened on the trigger—

A woman's voice screamed, "Mr. Browning! No!"

Conrad came awake and found himself staring into the terrified face of Margaret MacTavish over the barrel of the Colt clutched in his sweating hand, his finger taut on the trigger, only a hair'sbreadth of pressure away from blowing the girl's brains out.

Chapter 3

"Please don't shoot," Margaret whimpered as she stood in the doorway, one hand still on the curtain she had just pulled back.

"Dear Lord," Conrad said, horrified at what he had almost done. He took his finger off the trigger and quickly lowered the Colt. "Miss MacTavish, I'm sorry. I never meant to threaten you. I wouldn't harm you—"

And yet he almost had, Conrad thought. He had come within a whisker of shooting the girl, all because of the dreams that tormented him.

Heavy footsteps heralded the arrival of the male MacTavishes. Considering the words Margaret had screamed, Conrad wasn't surprised that Hamish had the shotgun in his hands and a furious look on his face. Under the circumstances, it was a father's natural assumption that the city slicker visitor was molesting his daughter.

Hamish wasn't the only one who was armed. James had his Remington revolver, and even Rory clutched his Winchester.

"What th' devil is goin' on here?" Hamish roared. "Is this the way ye repay us for our hospitality, Browning, by bein' free and easy wi' a poor, innocent girl—"

"Pa, no!" Margaret said. "It's not like that. I heard Mr. Browning thrashing around and thought

27

he might be sick from getting drenched by the rain. But he was just having a nightmare, and . . . and he . . ."

When Margaret's voice trailed off, Conrad said, "What your daughter is trying to tell you, Mr. MacTavish, is that I almost shot her. You have my word, though, it was unintentional."

MacTavish snorted. "A devil of a lot of good that would have done her if ye had pulled the trigger!"

"That's true," Conrad admitted. He picked up the holster, slid the Colt back into the black leather. He had become uncomfortably aware of the fact that he was sitting there naked except for the blanket wrapped around him. "I'll get dressed and leave now."

"That's not necessary," Margaret said. "You didn't mean it. You were asleep . . . you didn't know what you were doing."

Conrad shrugged. "Even so, I think it'll be better if I look for somewhere else to spend the night. I *am* grateful for the hospitality you've shown me, and I don't want anything to ruin that."

Margaret turned to her father and said, "Pa, you're not going to make Mr. Browning leave, are you? It's still raining out there. Pouring, from the sound of it."

"Aye, 'tis true," MacTavish admitted as he rubbed his beard-stubbled jaw. "And he *did* help us against Whitfield's men."

"They probably would have made it into the

house and killed all of us, if Mr. Browning hadn't shown up when he did," Rory said. Conrad was a little surprised that the boy spoke up in his behalf, when Rory wouldn't even defend himself, but he was grateful to the youngster for the gesture.

James scowled at him. "I ain't sure it's a good idea. This fella's a rich man, you can tell by lookin' at him, and you know they can't be trusted, Pa. Sure, he took our side against Whitfield's men, but that was because he didn't know what was goin' on. Now that he does, he's liable to turn on us."

Conrad felt a surge of anger. The accidental near shooting of Margaret was bad, he would grant them that, but he hadn't done anything else to make the MacTavishes distrust him.

He said, "I'm not going to turn on you, James. I don't have any interest in your dispute with Whitfield. It's not my fight. I just pitched in because I don't like seeing anybody outnumbered that badly. Come morning, all I intend to do is head on down to Val Verde. I have business there."

"Rich man's business," James said with a sneer.

"Being rich has got nothing to do with it," Conrad snapped. "I'm going to visit my wife's grave."

He hadn't meant to reveal that much, but once the words were out, a surprised silence fell over the dugout. Hamish and James frowned, while Margaret and Rory looked at Conrad with pity.

" 'Tis sorry I am to hear that ye lost your missus,"

29

Hamish finally said. "My own darlin' wife passed on five years ago, and not a day goes by when I dinna feel the pain of her passin'. I, uh, reckon I misjudged ye at first about what was goin' on with Meggie here."

"Nothing was going on," Margaret said. She turned to Conrad. "Forgive me if I'm prying, Mr. Browning, but the nightmare . . . was it about your wife?"

Conrad didn't want to hash everything out with these people, and he didn't want their pity, either. Pity didn't change a damned thing. He said curtly, "I don't remember. I'm just sorry that I almost shot you. If I leave now, we can all be sure that it won't happen again."

"But the storm . . ."

"I'll go sleep in the barn with my horses," Conrad suggested. "It won't be the first time."

"It won't?" James said. "You could've fooled me. I figured a fella like you would never have set foot in a barn, let alone slept in one."

"That's enough, James," Hamish said. "Mr. Browning has apologized for what happened, and he's offered to make sure 'twill not happen again. Ye cannot ask anything more o' the man."

James's glare told Conrad that the young man didn't like being reprimanded like that, but he didn't say anything else except, "I'm goin' back to bed." He turned and stomped off to the tiny room he shared with Rory.

"Ye don't have to sleep in the barn—" Hamish began.

"I'd feel better about it if I do," Conrad said. "The last thing I want is any sort of accident that might hurt one of you."

"Well, then . . . I've got an old piece o' oilcloth ye can hold over your head while you're runnin' out there. It'll keep ye from gettin' quite so wet."

"You're sure about this, Mr. Browning?" Margaret asked with a worried frown.

"I'm sure," Conrad told her. "Again, Miss MacTavish, I'm very sorry for what happened."

"And I'm sorry for your loss," Margaret said. "If you'd like to talk about it . . ."

Conrad shook his head. "I wouldn't."

"Come on, then," Hamish said to his remaining children. "Let's leave the poor man alone."

Poor man, Conrad thought. That was the first time anybody had called him that in, well, ever, at least that he could recall. And yet that's exactly what he was.

Because no amount of money could ever replace what he had lost.

Once he was dressed, he wrapped up in the blanket, draped the oilcloth over his head, and made the dash from the dugout to the barn. The rain wasn't coming down in torrents like it had been earlier, but it was still falling hard. Once he was inside, Conrad found the matches Rory had told him about and lit the lantern. The black and the buckskin nickered softly in greeting to him.

The barn roof leaked in a few places, but it was fairly dry inside. Conrad climbed into the hayloft and made himself a bed in the straw. He blew out the lantern, stretched out on the blanket, and discovered it was surprisingly comfortable.

Despite that, he didn't go to sleep right away. Too many nights in recent months had been spent drifting in and out of nightmares. Eventually, exhaustion would claim him. For the moment, though, his mind drifted back unbidden over everything that had happened to bring him to this time and place.

For most of his life, he hadn't known who his real father was. His mother was Vivian Browning, and so he had assumed that her husband was his father. He had been almost grown before he discovered that his real father was Frank Morgan, the notorious gunfighter known across the West as The Drifter.

No one knew how many men Frank Morgan had killed. Songs had been written about him, and sleazy, money-hungry scribblers had penned dozens of lurid, yellow-backed dime novels featuring The Drifter. He was a bloody-handed hired gunman, at least in the minds of many, including scores of lawmen who didn't want him in their towns.

That was the image Conrad had of Frank

Morgan, so it was no surprise that he was horrified when he found out that Morgan was his father. His mother had revealed that fact to him while they were on a trip west, checking on her business interests. Then, only a short time later, Vivian Browning had been killed by outlaws. Frank Morgan had avenged her death, but not before some of those same desperadoes had kidnapped and tortured Conrad. Frank had rescued him, but despite that, Conrad didn't want anything to do with the man. It was bad enough they had to be related.

But a day had come when Conrad needed Frank's help. Since they shared ownership of the businesses they had inherited from Vivian, it was only fair that Frank pitch in when there was trouble, especially when it was the sort of problem that was in his line of expertise. Someone had been raising hell with a railroad spur Conrad was building in New Mexico Territory, and he needed the services of a good man with a gun.

There was none better than Frank Morgan.

It was during that adventure that Conrad had come to have some grudging respect for Frank. Not only that, but he had met and fallen in love with a beautiful Western girl named Rebel Callahan during that dust-up. Rebel thought the world of Frank Morgan, and that had influenced Conrad to get to know his father better. Along with the respect had come some affection. Frank and

Conrad had come to be friends, even if they weren't as close as many fathers and sons were. After spending some time living in Boston, Conrad and Rebel had moved to Carson City, Nevada, and one of the reasons was so that they could see Frank more often.

It had been an idyllic existence—right up until the night when more than a dozen outlaws had invaded their home and kidnapped Rebel, holding her for the ransom that Conrad was to deliver in Black Rock Canyon. He had taken the money with him when he drove out to the rugged canyon northwest of Carson City, but he had been prepared to fight, too. For the first time, perhaps, he had truly become Frank Morgan's son on that terrible night.

It was terrible because Rebel had died. So had some of the kidnappers. The way things worked out, it appeared to the world at large that wealthy young businessman Conrad Browning was dead, too. That was fine with Conrad. He had assumed another identity in order to track down the kidnappers who had escaped. With the help of new friends he had run the kidnappers to ground and killed them, one by one, until finally he caught up to the leader of the gang, Clay Lasswell, the gunman who had killed Rebel.

By that time, however, Conrad had figured out that Lasswell had been acting on someone else's orders, some enemy who had set up Rebel's kidnapping in the first place. He wanted Lasswell dead, but he also wanted to know who was truly to blame for what had happened.

Fate had conspired against Conrad once again. Lasswell had died, but without revealing the identity of the mastermind behind the kidnapping. For all the blood he had spilled, Conrad's vengeance was still hollow and unfulfilled. His true enemy was still out there somewhere.

That was why Conrad Browning lived again. Rebel was buried in the mission cemetery in the small settlement of Val Verde, east of Lordsburg. She had been raised in the Davis Mountains of West Texas, where her father had a ranch, but the spread had gone under because of rustlers and the family had moved to New Mexico Territory. The Callahans had lived for a time in Val Verde, and Rebel's brothers knew she had liked the place. They had chosen to have her buried there. Tom and Bob had been forced to make the arrangements because at the time everyone believed Conrad to be dead.

Conrad was on his way to visit his wife's grave, and he intended to do so right out in the open. He wanted everybody in Val Verde to know why he was there. Whoever had set up Rebel's kidnapping hadn't been interested in the ransom money; that was just to pay off the owlhoots who had carried out the job. Lasswell's actions in killing Rebel had made it clear that the real objective was to torture

Conrad, to make him suffer the almost unendurable pain of watching his wife die.

Someone had a damned strong grudge against Conrad Browning. That was why he intended to use himself for bait to lure them out into the open.

And once he knew who it was . . .

The killing wasn't over yet. It had just gotten started.

Those thoughts whirled madly through Conrad's brain. Waking, sleeping, it made no difference. The painful memories were always there. He let out a long sigh and rolled onto his side. He would try to sleep now, but he didn't figure it would work out well.

He had just closed his eyes when he heard a horse neigh.

The sound was faint, and Conrad was sure that it hadn't come from inside the barn. That meant a horse was moving around outside somewhere, and where there was a horse, there was usually a rider.

He couldn't think of a single good reason for somebody to be skulking around the MacTavish place on a stormy night like that, but he could think of plenty of bad ones. Leaving the lantern unlit, Conrad reached out in the darkness and closed his hand around the butt of his gun. The Colt's grips fit his palm like they had grown there.

He came up on his knees and crawled quickly over to the little door that allowed bales of hay to be lifted into the loft from outside. It had a simple latch on it. Conrad unfastened it and pushed the door open several inches. The rain was falling straight down now, since the wind had died away, and the barn's eaves kept it from coming in the opening.

Conrad's eyes narrowed as he peered through the wet, murky gloom. He saw several figures moving around near the dugout, but they were just deeper patches of darkness. He couldn't make out any details. Given the fact that he had heard a horse, though, he was fairly sure they were men on horseback. He leaned forward to watch them.

Suddenly, despite the rain, a match flared to life. They had to be shielding it somehow. Conrad saw hands moving in the harsh glare, holding something toward the flame . . .

Sparks spurted. Conrad's hand tightened on the Colt as he realized what he was seeing. One of the men had just lit a fuse. The powder-laced length of cord would burn in spite of the rain.

At the other end of that fuse was a stick of dynamite!

Chapter 4

Conrad didn't waste any time wondering who the men were or what they intended to do. His keen brain understood instantly what was going on. Devil Dave Whitfield, or at least, some of his men, had returned to the MacTavish ranch with the intention of blowing the dugout to kingdom come.

The Colt in Conrad's hand leveled and fired in the blink of an eye, as the man with the dynamite drew back his arm to hurl the explosive at the dugout. The man yelled in pain and stiffened in the saddle.

"Throw it!" one of the other men yelled. "Throw it, you damned fool!"

Instead, the dynamite slipped from the wounded man's hand and fell to the ground at his horse's feet. Conrad hoped the mud would put out the fuse, but it continued spitting sparks as it burned.

The men stampeded, mud flying under the hooves of their horses as they tried to put as much distance as they could between themselves and the dynamite.

The wounded man had the presence of mind to try to get away, too, but he was too late. With a booming crack and a blinding flash, the dynamite went off. The explosion sent man and horse flying through the air.

"In the barn!" a man shouted. "The son of a bitch is in the hayloft!"

Conrad threw himself down as gun flame bloomed in the stormy night. He guessed there were three or four of the raiders left, and they were all doing their damnedest to kill him by blazing away at the hayloft door. He heard slugs thudding into the door and the wall around it. The lead chewed splinters from the wood.

Conrad poked the Colt through the opening and returned the fire. At the same time, shots roared from inside the dugout. The explosion had roused the MacTavishes from sleep, and they were joining the fight.

That put the raiders in a crossfire. A couple of them sagged in their saddles as if they were hit, even as they turned and fired back toward the dugout. After a moment, they realized they were in a bad spot, wheeled their horses and put the spurs to the animals, galloping out of the muddy yard between the dugout and the barn.

They left behind the man and the horse that had been caught in the blast. Neither dark shape on the ground was moving. Conrad figured both of them were dead.

Working easily by feel, because he'd had plenty of practice these past few months, he thumbed fresh cartridges into the Colt to replace the ones he had fired. Then he climbed down from the hayloft and lit the lantern. Draping the oilcloth over his head and his left arm, he carried the lantern in that hand and the revolver in the other as he walked out of the barn.

The dugout door opened. Hamish and James came out of the dwelling, wearing slickers and hooded ponchos. Hamish had the shotgun, James his Remington. They stopped on the other side of the bodies from Conrad, who held the lantern high enough for its yellow glow to spread over the gruesome sight.

The man and the horse were torn up pretty bad. The man's face was unmarked, though, and James said, "That's another of Whitfield's men. I think his name was Dugan, or something like that."

"Dumont," Hamish corrected. "He was there that day in Val Verde, the day your brother . . ."

Hamish's voice choked off, but Conrad knew what he was talking about—the day Charlie MacTavish had died in a gunfight with one of Whitfield's men.

"They were going to blow in the front of the dugout with dynamite," Conrad said. "I was still awake and heard their horses. Once I realized what they were planning, I did what I could to stop them."

Hamish nodded at the bodies. "It looks like ye did a good job of it. I think we winged a couple o' the other bastards, too."

Conrad agreed. He gestured toward the dead man and said, "You should take his body to the law in Val Verde. The authorities can't ignore the fact that

Whitfield's men tried to dynamite your home."

"They can't, eh?" James asked with a disgusted snort. "No offense, Mr. Browning, but that shows how little you know about the law. Whitfield can claim that he didn't know anything about it. Just like he'll claim that he didn't send his hired killers over here earlier to harass us. And the sheriff will believe him, because the Circle D is one of the biggest spreads around here. The law won't side with the likes of us against Whitfield."

Conrad knew the young man was probably right, although things might be different if he threw the weight of his own name behind the MacTavishes. Dave Whitfield might be an important man in these parts, but he didn't carry as much influence in the entire territory as Conrad Browning did.

The problem was that Conrad had his own mission, and he couldn't allow anything else to get in the way of it.

"We appreciate what ye've done for us, Mr. Browning," Hamish said. "This makes twice ye've saved us from disaster. If there's anything we can do for you . . ."

"You've done plenty," Conrad said with a shake of his head. He realized that the rain had stopped spattering down on the oilcloth. He moved it aside and looked up at the sky. Stars peeked through here and there. The clouds were beginning to break up. It looked like the storm was over.

That particular storm, anyway.

James dragged the dead man's body into the barn. "Looks like you'll have company for the rest of the night," he told Conrad with an unfriendly grin. Conrad wasn't sure what he had done to earn the young man's dislike, other than having money. Evidently that was enough where James MacTavish was concerned.

They left the horse where it was. Come morning, they could tie ropes to the carcass and drag it off.

Conrad didn't figure Whitfield's men would try anything else tonight, after the losses they had already suffered, but after he climbed back into the hayloft, he slept fitfully, waking often to open the loft door and have a look around. Knowing that a dead man lay below him in the barn didn't make him sleep any better, either.

The atmosphere at breakfast the next morning was subdued. The MacTavishes knew their troubles weren't over, not by a long shot. With Conrad's help, they had turned back two attacks on their homestead, but Conrad was leaving, and their enemy Dave Whitfield remained. It was just a matter of time until he struck at them again.

When they were finished eating, Hamish said, "Rory, go out and hitch up Mr. Browning's horse to that buggy."

"I can take care of that," Conrad said.

Rory got to his feet. "No, really, I don't mind, Mr.

Browning. I like working with horses, and those two of yours look like fine animals."

"They are," Conrad admitted. The buckskin had carried him hundreds of miles already on his quest for justice, before he'd started this trip to New Mexico Territory in the buggy.

Rory went out to the barn, followed by James. Conrad thought the boy looked a little nervous about the idea of going in there where Whitfield's dead gunman lay under a piece of canvas, but Rory wasn't going to let that stop him from carrying out the chore his father had given him.

As Conrad and Hamish lingered over cups of coffee, Hamish asked, "If ye don't mind me pryin', Mr. Browning, how did your late wife come to be buried in Val Verde?"

"Her family lived there for a while," Conrad explained, "and her brothers thought it would be a good place."

"I would have thought it would be up to ye to decide such a thing."

"I wasn't available at the time," Conrad said with a shrug. "One place is as good as another." That might sound callous, he thought, but it was true. Where a person was buried did nothing to change the fact that he or she was dead.

"Well, I hope that visitin' her grave brings ye some peace," Hamish said. "Beggin' your pardon again, but ye have the look of a haunted man about ye."

That was an apt description. He had been haunted since that awful night in Black Rock Canyon. He hoped that settling the score with the people responsible for Rebel's death would lay those ghosts to rest, but he had come to doubt it. He wasn't sure anything would ever ease the pain.

But he had learned to function in spite of it. He could even smile from time to time, as he did now. "I appreciate your concern, Mr. MacTavish," he said, "but I think you have enough problems of your own to deal with, without worrying about mine."

Hamish sighed. "'Tis true. Whitfield will be upset that he's lost another man."

"I'm the one responsible for this death," Conrad said. "Tell Whitfield to look for me in Val Verde if he wants to take it up with me."

While Margaret cleaned up after breakfast James hurried back inside, an anxious expression on his face. "Riders comin', Pa," he reported.

"Whitfield's men," Hamish guessed heavily.

"Not just them. I think the big skookum he-wolf himself is with 'em this time."

Hamish scraped his chair back and stood up. He took the shotgun down from its pegs on the wall. "Let me do the talkin'," he ordered. "I'd like to get through this without any more killin', and you're a bit of a hothead, James, if I do say so meself."

James looked like he might have argued, but Hamish was already on his way out the door. James followed, loosening the Remington in its holster on his hip as he did so.

Conrad still sat at the table, savoring the last of the strong, black brew in his cup. Margaret came over to him and asked, "Are you going out there, Mr. Browning?"

Conrad drained the coffee cup and sighed. "I am. But before I go, let me say thank you for breakfast, Miss MacTavish. It was mighty good."

Margaret blushed again, as she seemed to at every compliment. "You said it yourself," she told him in a low voice. "This isn't your fight."

"I don't reckon Dave Whitfield will be in much of a mood to listen to explanations right now." Conrad pushed his chair back and stood up. He hadn't put his coat on yet, but he wore the trousers and vest from his dark gray tweed suit, along with a white shirt and a black string tie. He walked over to the open doorway and leaned a shoulder against the jamb as half a dozen men rode into the yard in front of the dugout.

The man in the lead, who rode a big, handsome palomino, was a thick-gutted, barrel-chested hombre. A granite-like slab of jaw dominated his face. He jerked his horse to a halt, and the rough way he handled the reins made Conrad dislike him on sight.

The other five men brought their mounts to a stop behind him. Hamish and James faced them, not backing down. Rory watched from the barn doors.

Conrad knew the boy had taken his Winchester with him. The rifle was probably leaning against the wall just inside the doors, out of sight.

The odds weren't too bad, Conrad thought, instinctively assessing the situation and trying to figure out what would happen if gunplay broke out. They were four against six, and the four of them were spread out a little, while Whitfield and his men were bunched up. That was potentially a tactical mistake on Whitfield's part.

But maybe it wouldn't come to shooting. Hamish spoke up, saying, "What are ye doin' here, Whitfield? Ye know that ye ain't welcome on my spread."

"I came for my man Dumont," Whitfield replied, his voice harsh with anger.

"He's dead."

Whitfield's scowl didn't change. "I figured as much," he snapped. "I hear you've got some sort of hired gun working for you now, MacTavish. Did he kill Dumont, or was it you or one of your boys?"

Without straightening from his casual pose in the doorway, Conrad called, "It was your own man who blew himself up, Whitfield. If anyone's to blame for his death . . . it's the man who sent him over here with dynamite."

Whitfield turned his horse a little so that he could glare murderously at Conrad. "You'd be the hired gun," he snapped.

"No," Conrad said flatly. "I'm just passing

through these parts on my way to Val Verde. I stopped and took a hand because I didn't like the odds against the MacTavishes. That's all."

"What's your name, mister?" Whitfield demanded.

"Conrad Browning."

Whitfield frowned, as if the name was somehow familiar to him but he couldn't place it. "Well, you've made a bad mistake by stickin' your nose in where it ain't welcome, Browning. This bunch you're defending is nothing but a gang of rustlers and murderers."

"You're a damned liar, Whitfield," Hamish burst out. "My son told ye that to your face, and now I'm tellin' you."

One of the men edged his horse forward. "Want me to take care of this trash for you, boss?" he asked.

The man wasn't very impressive-looking. Even on horseback, he wasn't very big. The marks of some childhood disease pocked his dark, narrow face. He wore a cowhide vest and a black Stetson pulled down low. A quirley dangled from the corner of his mouth.

Conrad knew, though, that appearances were deceptive. The way this man carried himself in the saddle with his hand never straying far from the butt of his gun, the muscular thickness of his right wrist, the cold, dark eyes . . . They all added up to the fact that he was a gunslinger. Conrad had grown to know the signs all too well.

"That's all right, Trace," Whitfield snapped as he lifted a hand to motion the gunman back. "I can stomp my own snakes."

"Evidently not," Conrad said. "You come visiting with a handful of hired guns at your back."

Whitfield's already florid face flushed even more with anger. "Because I don't want to wind up with a bullet in my back, like three of my riders did when a hundred head of my cattle disappeared!"

"We didn't steal your cattle, and we sure as hell didn't shoot any o' your men!" Hamish said.

"What happened to them, then?"

"The border's not all that far away," Conrad pointed out. "Bandidos could have crossed over, ambushed your men, stolen those cattle, and run them back across into Mexico without much trouble. That sort of thing happens all the time."

"It never happened around here until this greasy-sack outfit moved in," Whitfield argued.

"Because ye run roughshod over ever'body else in this part o' the country until they're all scared o' ye," Hamish said. "There's a good reason folks call ye Devil Dave."

"By God, I won't stand for that!" Whitfield's hand started toward his gun.

Before it could get there, Conrad's Colt was out and leveled, his draw a flicker of movement hard for the eye to follow. At the same time, the man called Trace slapped leather as well. Everyone froze, with Conrad's gun pointed at Whitfield and Trace's revolver trained on Conrad.

"Put it down, Browning," Trace grated, "or you're a dead man."

"Not before your boss is," Conrad said without taking his eyes off Whitfield. His thumb looped over the Colt's hammer was the only thing holding it back, and he knew Trace could see that.

So could Whitfield. "For God's sake, pouch that iron, Trace. That lunatic will kill me."

Trace hesitated for a second before lowering his gun. "You're the boss, Mr. Whitfield," he said, but Conrad heard the obvious reluctance in the man's voice and saw it in his eyes as well. Trace was the sort of man who didn't like to put his gun back in its holster until he had killed somebody.

He did now, though, and Conrad lowered his gun.

"Ye came for Dumont," Hamish said. "His body's in the barn. Take it, and welcome to it. Why don't ye drag his horse away while you're at it and save us the trouble?"

Whitfield flipped a hand, motioning for his men to take care of retrieving Dumont's body from the barn. "For what it's worth, MacTavish," he said, "I didn't send those men over here last night with that dynamite. That was their idea."

James glanced over at Conrad with a smirk, as if to say, *See? I told you so.*

"What about that business yesterday evenin', just

49

before dusk as the storm was movin' in?" Hamish asked.

Whitfield snorted in contempt. "Your boy caused that ruckus by opening fire with a shotgun. I've still got cows going missing, and I sent my men over to ask you if you'd seen anything unusual lately."

"Sent them over to accuse us of bein' thieves, you mean!"

Whitfield shrugged and said, "Seems to me that you reacted just like guilty men would have."

Conrad still held his gun at his side. He stepped out of the doorway as he said, "We're not getting anywhere here. The MacTavishes have told you that they're not guilty, Whitfield, and in the absence of proof, I think you'd be wise to accept their assurances."

Whitfield sneered at him. "What are you, some sort of lawyer? You talk like one."

"No, I'm not a lawyer. But I've been around plenty of them, and I know something about the law. What you're doing amounts to nothing more than a campaign of terror against these people, and you'd be well-advised to stop it, otherwise the authorities will have to step in."

Trace chuckled. "I'd like to see that."

Whitfield shot him a narrow-eyed glance. "I'm a law-abiding man," he told Conrad, "but I won't be stolen from, and I won't allow my men to be shot from ambush without doing something about it."

"I don't blame you, but you're on the wrong track here."

"We'll see," Whitfield said as a couple of his men came out of the barn, leading a horse with Dumont's body draped over the saddle and lashed into place. The two men would have to ride double on the way back to the Circle D.

Two more of the men tied ropes to the legs of the dead horse and lashed them around their saddle-horns. They began to drag it off, following the men who had taken charge of Dumont's body.

That left Whitfield and Trace sitting there for a moment, glaring at the MacTavishes and Browning. Whitfield turned away first with an angry mutter. Trace lingered a couple of seconds longer, his eyes intent on Conrad.

They had taken each other's measure with those draws, Conrad thought. Each of them now knew that the other was fast. They couldn't be sure *how* fast, though, unless they actually faced each other in a showdown. Conrad could see in Trace's eyes that the little gunman believed that day was coming.

All Conrad could do was bite back a disgusted curse. The disgust was directed against himself. Against all his better judgment, he had just involved himself hip-deep in the troubles of the MacTavishes. He had made enemies out of Whitfield and Trace, and they weren't the sort of men to forget a confrontation like that. Sooner or later, he'd be forced to deal with them. The added complication wasn't what he needed right then.

On the other hand, he realized suddenly, news spread fast, even in sparsely settled country like this. It wouldn't be long before everybody in this part of New Mexico knew that a man named Conrad Browning had ridden in and sided with the MacTavishes in their struggle against Devil Dave Whitfield.

His first goal had been to resurrect Conrad Browning from the dead. He figured he was well on his way to doing that.

Chapter 5

Rory brought out the buggy with the black hitched to it and the buckskin tied on behind, as they had been when Conrad arrived. He had his rifle in one hand, the black's reins in the other. Conrad had guessed right about the boy having the Winchester ready in case of trouble.

"Here you go, Mr. Browning," Rory said as he handed over the reins. "It was a pleasure takin' care of these fine horses for you."

Conrad smiled. "It looks like you did a good job, too." He took a coin from his pocket and handed it to Rory. "Thanks."

"That's not necessary, Mr. Browning," Hamish said. "Scots are a thrifty folk, as ye no doubt know, but that don't mean ye have to pay us for our hospitality."

"It's not much—" Conrad began, but Rory interrupted him.

"Not much, the man says! 'Tis a double eagle, Pa!"

From the excitement in Rory's voice, the family didn't see twenty-dollar gold pieces all that often. Hamish started to protest again, but Margaret, who had emerged from the dugout once Whitfield and his men were gone, took the coin from Rory and said, "This will come in mighty handy the next time we go to Val Verde to buy supplies, Pa, and you know it. We're cash poor right now." She turned to Conrad. "Thank you, Mr. Browning. As much as you've already done for us, I hate to take this, too . . . but I will."

"And you're welcome to it," Conrad told her with a smile. He climbed up into the buggy. "Good luck to you," he said, nodding to the MacTavishes as he flapped the lines against the black's back and got the big horse moving.

Conrad didn't look behind him as the buggy rolled away from the MacTavish ranch. He hoped that the family's troubles were over, but he knew better. Dave Whitfield was used to getting his own way around there, and with that gunman Trace to back him up and goad him on, Whitfield would continue acting like it was still open range days, when the only law that counted was what a man packed in his holster.

The storm the night before had left the ground fairly muddy, with puddles of water standing here and there, but this was a region that didn't see rain all that often, so the thirsty earth quickly sucked up most of the moisture. The sun was out, too, helping to dry the mud. Conrad was able to drive around the worst of the muck as he headed south toward Val Verde.

The name meant "Green Valley," and it was appropriate because the settlement was nestled in a small valley watered by a creek. Cottonwoods lined the banks of the stream, and the grass was thicker along it. In this semi-arid landscape, even a little vegetation was enough to qualify as an oasis.

The settlement had started out as a wide place in the trail, a trading post and way station on the Butterfield stagecoach line. It hadn't been much more than that until the Southern Pacific Railroad came through years later and caused it to grow. It still wasn't a big town, by any stretch of the imagination, but it had developed into a fair-sized community, with a main street that ran for several blocks, paralleling the train tracks.

South of the steel rails were the saloons, gambling dens, and whorehouses, while the respectable folks lived north of the tracks. Also north of the tracks, on the edge of the settlement, was the local mission, and behind the big stone-and-adobe building with its bell tower was the graveyard.

Conrad had been to Val Verde before, several years earlier when he and Frank were passing through this area on the way to the railroad spur that Conrad was building at the time. He recognized the mission's bell tower when he saw it rising in the distance, and he felt a catch in his throat as he thought about the cemetery that it overlooked.

His wife was buried in that cemetery, he thought. The remains of the beautiful, charming, vibrant young woman who had been Rebel Callahan Browning would lie there for all eternity, cold and lifeless.

Conrad didn't allow himself to think too much about that. He was here for a reason, but it wasn't to mourn his wife. He had already done that and would continue to do so, probably for the rest of his life.

He was here to avenge her.

He drove straight to the Val Verde Hotel, which was a block away from the train station. Leaving the buggy tied up at the hitch rail in front of the two-story adobe building, he went inside. The day had grown warm, but the lobby was pleasantly cool because of the thick walls.

Conrad crossed the room to the desk, noting as he did so that two men in suits, probably traveling salesmen, sat reading newspapers by the front window. A middle-aged woman herded along a brood of children out of the dining room. A younger woman in a stylish traveling outfit stood at the desk, talking to the clerk. She turned away as Conrad came up and gave him a smile in passing. He returned it politely, noting that she was attractive, with honey-blond hair piled in an elaborate arrangement of curls under a fashionable bottle-green hat. He felt her looking back and scrutinizing him as she walked away.

The clerk, a round-faced man with thinning brown hair, smiled as well and asked, "What can I do for you, sir?"

"I need a room," Conrad said.

"Of course. For how long?"

Conrad shook his head. "That's hard to say. I expect to be here a few days."

"Business or pleasure?"

"Pardon me?" Conrad asked, raising an eyebrow.

"Is it business or pleasure that brings you to Val Verde?"

"Oh. Business, you'd have to say." It certainly wasn't pleasure—although a person might think he would get some pleasure, or at least a little satisfaction, out of killing the son of a bitch responsible for his wife's death.

Conrad had learned through bitter experience, though, that there was nothing pleasurable or satisfying about it. He had killed more than a dozen men who'd had a hand in what happened to Rebel, and their deaths hadn't eased the hurt inside him at all.

Maybe when it was finally over and done with, he thought. Maybe . . .

"Well, then, I hope it's a successful stay for you," the clerk said, bringing Conrad out of his momentary reverie. "If you'll just sign here . . ." He turned the register book so that it faced Conrad and pushed pen and inkwell forward with the other hand.

Conrad scrawled his name in the book, adding "Carson City, Nevada" after it in the place for his residence. The name on the line above was Angeline Whitfield. That caught his attention, but he didn't show it.

The clerk must have been pretty experienced at reading upside down. His eyes widened as he said, "Conrad Browning?"

Conrad looked up at him coolly. "That's right. You've heard of me?"

"I keep up with the financial news as best I can in this backwater town," the man said. "Of course I've heard of you, Mr. Browning. You're one of the country's leading financiers and industrialists. But I thought . . ."

Conrad smiled as the man's voice trailed away. "That I was dead?" he asked.

"Well . . . yes, sir, that's right. It was reported that you died in a fire in Carson City."

"Those reports were premature," Conrad said. "I'm alive and well, as you can see for yourself."

"But what are you doing in Val Verde? Are you going to build another railroad spur, or—Oh, Lord, I forgot all about—I mean, I'm so sorry . . . I . . ."

"It's all right," Conrad told him. "Yes, I'm here to visit my wife's grave, among other things. I'd appreciate being left in peace to do so."

"Of course, sir! I'll see to it that you're not disturbed. No one will even know you're here."

Conrad didn't believe that for a second. The clerk had the look of a natural-born gossip, and he figured that the man would be scurrying around town within minutes to spread the word that not only was Conrad Browning still alive, but also that he

58

was there in town to pay his respects at his late wife's grave.

That was exactly what Conrad wanted.

"Where's the closest livery stable?" he asked, even though he already knew the answer. He had seen the barn for himself as he drove in.

"It's right down the street," the clerk replied. "Would you like for me to have someone take your horses down there and have them seen to?"

"That would be excellent," Conrad said with a nod. The sort of man he had once been would expect others to handle such menial chores for him. "I have a carpetbag in my buggy, too."

"I'll have it brought up to your room. I'll tend to this right away." The clerk took a key off the rack behind him and held it out. "Room Twelve. It's the best in the house."

"Thank you." Conrad took the key. He started to turn away from the desk, then paused. "The young lady who was here just before me . . ."

"Miss Whitfield, sir." The clerk supplied the information without hesitation. "The daughter of one of the local ranchers. She's come for a visit with him." The man smiled. "A very lovely young woman."

Conrad nodded. "Indeed."

Well, that was interesting, he thought as he climbed the stairs. Devil Dave had a daughter who obviously didn't live with him.

At least, it would have been interesting if it was any of his business—which it wasn't.

The hotel room was nice, at least for Val Verde. It didn't compare to the finest that Boston or San Francisco had to offer, of course. The bed was a sturdy four-poster, and there was a thickly woven Navajo rug on the floor. Conrad freshened up using the basin of water that sat on the dresser. While he was drying his face, a soft knock sounded on the door.

He put his hand on the butt of his gun as he went over and called, "Who is it?" As soon as the words were out of his mouth, he took a quick step to his left and drew the Colt. If it was an ambush and whoever was in the hall planned on pumping a double load of buckshot through the wall or the door, the odds were on Conrad's side that the would-be killer would miss. Of course, there was still a one in three chance that he'd be stepping right into the blast . . .

"Got your bag here, Mr. Browning," a man's voice said.

Conrad twisted the knob and opened the door. An elderly black man with only a few wisps of white hair left on his head stood there with the carpetbag in his right hand. He had Conrad's Winchester in his left hand.

"I brung your rifle, too," the man said. "Didn't figure you'd need it here in town, but didn't seem like you'd want to leave it at the stable with your buggy and horses and saddle, neither."

Conrad nodded and stepped back. He holstered

his gun, noting as he did so that the man hadn't seemed too surprised to see him holding the Colt.

"Just put them on the bed," he said with a casual wave of his left hand toward the four-poster. "Are you the one who took the buggy down to the stable?"

"Yes, sir, I am." The man placed the carpetbag and rifle on the bed as Conrad had indicated. "Name's Linus."

"Well, thank you, Linus." The man wore a suit coat and string tie over a white shirt. Conrad went on, "I take it you work here at the hotel?"

"Yes, sir. General factotum to Mr. Rowlett, who owns the place. That was him down at the desk when you checked in. Factotum means—"

"I know what it means," Conrad said. "A man of many jobs." He smiled. "I sort of fit that description myself."

"Yes, sir, I heard about you. You got mines and banks and railroads to run. Matter of fact, I used to work for you myself."

"You did?" Conrad asked.

"Yes, sir. I was a brakeman on that spur line you built over west of here, until I got too stove up to handle the job. Then I worked as a porter for a while. Finally decided I wanted to settle down in one place, though, which a fella can't hardly do if he works on the rails."

"No, that's true," Conrad admitted with a nod. "Well, it's good to meet you, Linus." He handed

61

the old man a silver dollar. "Thank you for bringing my things from the stable. I assume that if I need anything else . . . ?"

"You just let me know," Linus said.

As he started to turn away, Conrad stopped him. "Actually, there is one thing I'd like to know. You're aware that my wife is buried here in Val Verde?"

With a solemn look on his weathered face, Linus nodded. "Yes, sir. I'm mighty sorry for your loss."

"Do you know if her grave has been well cared for?"

"Oh, yes, sir, it sure has. Father Francisco down at the mission wouldn't have it no other way."

Conrad clapped a hand on the old man's shoulder. "Thank you. I appreciate knowing that."

Linus hesitated, then said, "If you don't mind my askin', sir . . . did you come to visit her?"

"That's exactly why I'm here, Linus," Conrad said. The more people who knew that, the better, and he figured the old man would help spread the word.

He felt certain that whoever had hired Clay Lasswell to carry out the kidnapping would have heard about Lasswell and the rest of the outlaws being killed off one by one. The mastermind would have to wonder about that and even ask himself if it was possible that Conrad could still be alive, despite the reports from Carson City. Conrad's hope was that the man would have someone keeping an eye on Rebel's grave, just in case.

It was even possible that the man was here in Val Verde himself, watching to see if Conrad would turn up at the cemetery. If that turned out to be true, then within days, or even hours, Conrad might find himself face to face with the man who had taken away everything precious in life to him.

"Mister B-Browning?"

Linus's worried voice snapped Conrad out of his thoughts. He looked at the old man and asked more sharply than he intended, "What is it?"

"F-For a minute there, you looked like you was ready to kill somebody, Mr. Browning. You surely did."

Conrad forced a smile onto his face. "Not at all," he lied.

He *was* ready to kill somebody. He was more than ready.

Conrad went downstairs a few minutes after Linus left the hotel room. There was no point in postponing the inevitable.

When he reached the lobby, though, someone called his name. He looked over in surprise and saw Angeline Whitfield approaching him. She had taken off the hat from her traveling outfit but still wore the same dress. And she still looked lovely.

She smiled as she came up to him and offered him her hand. "Mr. Browning, you don't know me," she said, "but I once saw you in Philadelphia.

A friend of mine pointed you out to me. I hope you don't think it too forward of me to introduce myself like this. I'm Angeline Whitfield."

"Miss Whitfield," Conrad said as he took her hand. Her skin was cool and smooth. "It is *Miss* Whitfield?" he asked, even though he knew good and well that was the case.

"Yes, of course," she replied. Her fingers lingered in his.

"As for being too forward, well, times are changing, aren't they?"

"Indeed they are," she said. "In less than five years, it will be a whole new century."

Without being rude about it, Conrad slipped his hand out of hers and asked, "What can I do for you, Miss Whitfield?"

"I'm sure you have no way of knowing this, but my father has a ranch about twenty miles north of here. I just arrived for a visit, and I'm a couple of days early. Father won't send a wagon for me until the day after tomorrow. So I was wondering if I might prevail upon you to escort me to the ranch? I can't make the trip alone, of course. It wouldn't be proper."

"Not to mention it might not be safe," Conrad said. "But I'm not sure it would be proper for me to accompany you, either."

"Why, of course it would, Mr. Browning. You're a gentleman, after all. And once we're there, I think it would be perfectly charming if you spent a few days on the ranch. If your schedule would permit it. I know you must be a very busy man, what with all your business interests."

There had been a time when such blatant flirting by a beautiful young woman would have flattered and pleased Conrad. That time was in the past, though.

"Miss Whitfield, perhaps you haven't heard," he said gently. "I was married."

Her eyebrows arched in surprise. "Married?" she repeated. "No, I had no idea . . . Wait a minute. You said *was?*"

"That's right. My wife . . . passed away several months ago."

Angeline lifted a hand to her mouth. "Oh, my Lord! I'm so sorry, Mr. Browning. I didn't know about your loss. I didn't mean to be so . . . so . . . You must forgive me!"

"Of course. And I wish I could help you. But under the circumstances . . ." Conrad lifted a hand, as if to say that there was nothing he could do.

Although, he thought with the shadow of a grim smile hovering around his mouth, it might have been interesting to see Dave Whitfield's reaction if the man who had befriended the MacTavishes had ridden up to the Circle D with his daughter for a visit.

"I understand," Angeline said, still visibly embarrassed. "I won't trouble you any longer."

"No trouble," Conrad said. "I'm glad to meet you. I hope you enjoy your visit on your father's ranch."

And I hope no more hell breaks loose while you're there, he added to himself, for the MacTavishes' sake.

Conrad tugged on the brim of his hat, excused himself, and left the hotel. His steps turned toward the mission. He steeled himself for what lay before him.

Then he walked up the street to the graveyard where his wife was buried.

Chapter 6

Linus was right. Everything about the mission was neat and well cared for, including the cemetery. A black, wrought-iron fence surrounded it, and several flowerbeds provided some splashes of color. Someone had trimmed the grass. The gravestones appeared to be freshly polished.

Conrad paused outside the stone pillars with a wrought-iron arch between them that formed the gate into the cemetery. He couldn't bring himself to walk between them.

As Conrad stood there, a side door in the big adobe church, which was more than a hundred years old, opened and a priest walked out into the sunshine. He smiled as he approached Conrad.

"God's peace be with you, my son," the priest said. He was a slender man with soft dark eyes and skin the color of old saddle leather. Even though he appeared to be Mexican, he had no trace of an accent. "I saw you standing out here and thought perhaps something was wrong."

"Something is very wrong, Father." Conrad nodded toward the graveyard. "My wife is buried in there. She wasn't even twenty-five years old when she was killed."

A look of solemn sorrow replaced the priest's smile. "I was afraid it was something like that. Usually when I see someone hesitating outside

67

the gate, it's because they have a loved one buried within."

"Does that happen often?"

"More than you would think. More than I like to think about."

"You're Father Francisco?"

"That's right."

"You take good care of the cemetery," Conrad said.

The smile, now tinged with sadness, reappeared on the priest's face. "Just because some of the members of my flock have passed on doesn't mean I can't continue to care for them."

"My wife wasn't one of your parishioners. She hadn't lived here for several years."

Father Francisco shrugged. "Once they pass through these gates, they are in God's hands, and I am God's servant. Through my efforts on their behalf, I serve Him."

"Well, I appreciate it." Conrad took a deep breath. "I guess I'd better go in."

"Would you like for me to come with you?"

Conrad thought about it, but only for a second. Again, the more people who knew who he was and why he was here, the better. So he said, "Thank you, Father. I'd like that."

The two men walked through the gate. Father Francisco asked, "What is your wife's name?"

"Rebel Browning."

"Ah! Such a tragedy! I remember. I conducted

the service." The priest looked over at Conrad with a frown. "But as I recall, it was the poor woman's brothers who made the arrangements, because her husband had been killed as well."

"That's what they believed at the time. I just . . . couldn't make it here."

Father Francisco's lips pursed in obvious disapproval. "You couldn't make it to your own wife's funeral?"

"I was injured," Conrad said. That wasn't a lie. He'd been wounded during the battle with Rebel's kidnappers. In fact, after leaving Carson City on that horrible night, he had passed out from loss of blood and probably would have died if a Paiute Indian named Phillip Bearpaw hadn't found him and taken him to a doctor.

"Well, at least you're here now," Father Francisco said. "I'm sure your wife knew how much you cared for her."

"I hope so," Conrad said.

"What happens after people are gone is much less important than how we treat them while they're still here. That's one of the things I try to make my parishioners understand." The priest stopped and waved a hand at one of the graves. "This is where your wife is buried, Mr. Browning."

Conrad had been through a great deal in his relatively short life. Outlaws had murdered his mother. Some of those same desperadoes had kidnapped and tortured him. Bushwhackers had shot at him from ambush on numerous occasions, and in recent months he had been mixed up in several gunfights. He knew all too well the smell of powdersmoke, the sound of a bullet whining past his ear, the terrible, flesh-ripping impact of a slug hitting his body.

But he had never felt more like turning and running away than he did at that moment. He wasn't sure he could face it.

This was all part of his plan, he reminded himself. Anyway, he owed it to Rebel. She had lost her life because someone had a grudge against him. The least he could do was take a look at her final resting place.

One of the cottonwoods dotted around the cemetery cast sun-dappled shade on the grave. An expensive marble headstone with an angel's wings engraved on it gave Rebel's full name, the dates of her birth and death, and then underneath, an epitaph that read BELOVED DAUGHTER, SISTER, AND WIFE.

For a second, Conrad was annoyed that the acknowledgment of Rebel's marriage came last in that ranking, but he reminded himself that it was her brothers who'd been responsible for the stone. It was reasonable that they would hold Rebel's place in their family higher. She had been a daughter and a sister for a lot longer than she had been a wife, after all.

But it should have said more than that, he thought. Rebel deserved more.

What Rebel had really deserved was a long, happy life, surrounded by the children that she and Conrad would never have. That was forever out of reach.

Conrad's eyes narrowed as he looked at the bouquet of fresh-cut flowers lying on top of the gravestone. He nodded toward them and asked Father Francisco, "Who put those there?"

"The flowers?" The priest shook his head. "I have no idea. I didn't see whoever it was who left them. But it could have been almost anyone. The cemetery is open day and night, you know. Anyone can come in, any time."

"Have you ever noticed anyone showing an interest in this grave?"

Father Francisco frowned in thought. "No. I don't believe . . . Wait a moment. There was someone . . . A woman. I've noticed her here in the cemetery. She could have brought the flowers, I suppose."

"A woman," Conrad repeated. He couldn't think of any woman who would have been visiting the grave. Rebel's mother was dead, and she hadn't had any sisters. "What did she look like?"

"I'm afraid I can't tell you. She wore a shawl around her head, and I never got a look at her face. But I'm sure it was the same woman. I saw her several times in the past couple of months."

Confusion filled Conrad's mind. He had thought that the bastard who'd sent those kidnappers after Rebel might be watching the grave, but he hadn't expected some mysterious woman to be involved.

"Can you tell me *anything* about her?"

"Well . . . I think she was young. At least, she didn't move like an old woman."

"You never talked to her, never asked her what she was doing here?"

Conrad heard the slightly accusatory tone in his voice. He didn't really mean the question that way, but that was how it came out.

"I told you, the cemetery is open day and night. People come to mourn, to talk to their loved ones who are gone, or just for the peace and quiet. All are welcome."

Conrad nodded. "I know. I'm sorry, Father."

"No apologies necessary, my son," Father Francisco said with a smile and a shake of his head. He gestured toward the grave. "Would you like to be alone?"

"I . . . I think so. For a few minutes."

Father Francisco nodded. "I'll be in the church, if you need me."

He walked off, leaving Conrad in front of the grave. Conrad realized abruptly that he still had his hat on. He snatched it off and held it awkwardly in front of him. "Rebel," he began, then paused, unsure what to say. She isn't *really* here, he told himself. Her soul was out there somewhere in the wind, galloping across the heavens, her hair streaming out behind her as she laughed.

Conrad took a deep breath. "I've told you a hundred times how sorry I am for what happened. I could say it a thousand times, and it wouldn't change anything. So I'll just say that I'm going to put things right, Rebel, at least as much as I can. Whoever's to blame for this, I'll see to it that he pays. That's all I can do."

He closed his eyes and stood there a moment longer, then sighed and turned away. He didn't put his hat on but continued to hold it as he went into the church through the side door Father Francisco had used.

He found the priest in the sanctuary and said, "Thank you for your help, Father. If you happen to see that woman again, could you let me know? I'll be staying at the hotel."

"If the woman comes to visit your wife's grave, I'm sure she has her reasons, Mr. Browning, and the same holds true if she's the one who brought the flowers. I'm not sure it's my place to do anything to disturb her mourning."

Conrad reined in the surge of impatience he felt and said, "I don't want to disturb her. I just want to know who she is and why she's visiting Rebel's grave."

"That would be her business, not yours," Father Francisco said, his voice gentle but inflexible.

Conrad drew in a deep breath through his nose.

"All right, Father. You have to do what you think is best." He put a hand in his pocket. "I suppose the church takes care of the widows and orphans around here?"

"We do our best to take care of everyone in need."

Conrad took out a handful of double eagles. "Then I know you'll put this to good use," he said as he held out the coins.

Father Francisco's eyes narrowed. "Mr. Browning . . . are you trying to bribe me?"

"Not at all," Conrad answered honestly. "It's just that since Rebel died, money doesn't mean a whole lot to me except for the good it can do."

"In that case . . . this money can do quite a bit of good, indeed."

The priest took the double eagles. Conrad nodded to him, turned, and walked out the front door of the church, not clapping his hat on his head until he was outside again. He headed for the hotel, pausing to look back at the graveyard one last time.

It was empty, no mysterious woman to be seen anywhere.

But Conrad had a feeling she would be back, and when she was, he intended to be there and get some answers from her.

When Conrad got back to the hotel, he studied the situation for a few minutes, then asked Mr. Rowlett, the proprietor, if he could switch rooms.

"But Room Twelve is the best in the house," Rowlett said.

"I know, but I'd rather be on the front," Conrad told him.

Rowlett frowned. "It'll be noisier. You'll be right over the street."

"That's what I want," Conrad insisted.

"Well, of course, if that's your preference . . ." The hotel man turned to look at the rack of keys. "Let's see . . . I can put you in Room Seven. That overlooks the street."

Conrad nodded. "That'll be fine."

Rowlett gave him the key to Room Seven. He went upstairs to move his gear across the hall. Once he was in the new room, he went to the window and looked out, prepared to go downstairs and ask to move again if he didn't like what he saw.

The view was all right, though. He could see the graveyard behind the church from there.

For the next two days, Conrad spent most of his time at the window of his hotel room, watching the cemetery. He moved the room's single chair over to the window and sat there for hours on end, dozing occasionally but for the most part alert. He left his self-appointed post to go downstairs and take his meals in the hotel dining room, and he slept at night, since he couldn't see what was going on in the graveyard, but other than that he barely took his eyes off the place.

Not too surprisingly, the woman in the shawl didn't show up. Those flowers Conrad had seen on Rebel's headstone had been placed there recently. It might be a week or more before the woman came to visit the grave again. If it took that long, or even longer, Conrad didn't care. He would wait as long as it took.

The presence of Angeline Whitfield in the hotel could have been a distraction, if he had allowed it to be. She ate in the hotel dining room, too. While she waited for the wagon her father was supposed to send to Val Verde, Conrad saw her there at nearly every meal. She smiled politely at him. He could tell that she wanted to come over and talk to him, but she didn't. Knowing that his wife had died recently caused her to be discreet. She hadn't totally lost interest in him, though. He could tell that, as well.

Around the middle of the afternoon on the second day, a flash of bright red hair in the street caught Conrad's eye. He took his attention away from the graveyard long enough to look down and see Margaret MacTavish at the reins of a wagon coming into town. Her little brother Rory sat beside her on the wagon seat, and James MacTavish rode alongside. Hamish wasn't with them, so Conrad supposed that he had stayed out at the ranch.

As Conrad watched, Margaret pulled the wagon to a stop in front of the general store across the street. The MacTavishes had come to Val Verde to pick up supplies.

Conrad frowned as he looked back along the street. Another wagon was entering the edge of town, flanked by several riders. Conrad recognized Dave Whitfield and the gunman called Trace among them.

A grimace tightened Conrad's mouth. He had known that Whitfield was due to arrive today to pick up his daughter, but it was sheer coincidence that the MacTavishes had come to town on the same day, and practically the same time, at that. Coincidence, or pure bad luck. In this case, they might be one and the same.

Conrad glanced at the cemetery. His job was to stay here and wait for the mysterious woman to show up again, he told himself. Surely no real trouble would break out between the MacTavishes and Whitfield's bunch right there in the middle of the settlement.

But he couldn't be sure of that. He recalled how hotheaded James MacTavish was. It would be easy for Trace to goad the young man into a fight, if the gunfighter decided to do that. Conrad didn't know if Trace was the one who had gunned down Charlie MacTavish, but it wouldn't surprise him a bit to learn that was true. Nor would it surprise him if Trace had provoked the fight.

Even if that wasn't the case where Charlie was concerned, it could happen easily with James that day. Conrad knew he couldn't stand by without trying to prevent it.

With a sigh, he stood up, abandoning his post for the moment. He shrugged into his suit jacket and put his hat on. By the time he went downstairs, through the lobby, and out onto the porch, he saw that Margaret and Rory had gone into the store. James was still outside, lounging with a shoulder against one of the posts holding up the awning over the store's porch.

Conrad looked to his left and saw the Whitfield wagon approaching the hotel. Dave Whitfield heeled his horse into a trot and came on ahead of the wagon, followed by Trace.

Whitfield stiffened in the saddle as he spotted Conrad standing there. At the same time, Trace said, "Boss," and jerked his head toward James MacTavish on the porch of the general store. Whitfield hauled back on the reins and brought his horse to a skidding stop in front of the hotel as he moved his other hand toward the butt of the gun on his hip.

"What the hell is this?" he demanded. "A trap?"

"Take it easy, Whitfield," Conrad snapped. "My being here has nothing to do with you."

Whitfield sneered. "You could've fooled me. I see one of those hotheaded MacTavish boys on one side of the street, and their hired gunman on the other. Looks to me like you're just waiting to get us in a crossfire."

"If that's what they plan, boss," Trace said, "they're about to be mighty sorry."

Conrad could tell that the gunman was just aching to slap leather. He shook his head and said, "You've still got it all wrong. I'm not working for the MacTavishes. I haven't even seen them in the past two days, until now. It's just a coincidence that they came to buy supplies at the same time you got here to pick up your daughter."

Whitfield's slab of a jaw hardened even more. "What the hell do you know about my daughter?" he demanded harshly.

Before Conrad could answer, the young woman herself put in an appearance, coming out of the hotel and saying in a bright voice, "Daddy, there you are! I thought I saw you riding into town from my window." She stopped short. A frown appeared on her face. She noticed the dangerous feeling of tension in the air. "What's wrong?"

"Go back inside, honey," Whitfield told her. "It's about to get mighty noisy out here."

Chapter 7

"Dad, what's going on here?" Angeline asked with a worried frown.

"Those damned MacTavishes and their hired gun are tryin' to start a ruckus," Whitfield answered. "Get back inside the hotel now!"

Without taking his eyes off Trace, Conrad said, "That might be a good idea, Miss Whitfield."

"I'm not going anywhere," Angeline insisted. "I don't see any hired gunman, Dad."

Whitfield gestured with his left hand toward Conrad. "This fancy-dressed hombre right here."

Angeline laughed. "Are you joking? This is Conrad Browning. He's no hired gun."

Whitfield's frown deepened. "How do you know him? Has he been botherin' you, honey?"

"Not at all. In fact, he's been a perfect gentleman . . . which is just what you'd expect from one of the wealthiest businessmen in the country."

When he heard that, Whitfield's eyes widened. "What in blazes are you talkin' about, girl?"

"This man is Conrad Browning," Angeline repeated. "He owns railroads and mines and banks. He's not a gunman, and even if he was, he wouldn't have any reason to hire out to a bunch of ragged squatters like the MacTavishes."

Conrad heard the scorn in her voice. It caused his estimation of her to drop a little more, even though he once might have felt the same way himself.

James MacTavish started across the street toward the hotel. "I hear you over there, Whitfield, you damn blowhard!" he called. "If you've got something to say about the MacTavishes, you can damn well say it to our faces!"

"Jack, deal with that dumbass," Whitfield told Trace.

The gunfighter's gaze was still fastened on Conrad and he ignored Whitfield's command. "Conrad Browning, eh?" Trace mused. "I thought the name was familiar when I heard it out at the MacTavish place the other day, and now I remember why. Frank Morgan's son, aren't you?"

"That's right," Conrad said.

"I always thought Morgan was overrated. Now he's just a broken-down old has-been."

A thin smile stretched Conrad's lips. "Maybe you can take that up with him yourself, one of these days. I'd like to see that."

Trace's face darkened with anger. "Are you sayin' I'd be scared to face off with Frank Morgan?"

"No, I'm just saying I'd like to see it."

James had come to a stop about a dozen feet away. "Hey!" he said. "Whitfield, I was talkin' to you."

Across the street, Margaret and Rory came out of the store, their arms full of packages wrapped in brown paper. The bundles in Margaret's arms slipped free and fell at her feet as she caught sight of the confrontation going on in front of the hotel.

"James!" she cried as she started toward her older brother. "James, come away from there!"

James twisted around and slashed an arm at her. "Meggie, get back."

Trace went for his gun.

Conrad knew in that split-second what was going to happen. Trace intended to kill James MacTavish and then claim that he'd thought James was drawing on him, saying that he had mistaken the intent of James's motion. That would be enough to satisfy the law, at least there in New Mexico Territory. James's death would be marked down as an accident, or at worst, a case of self-defense on Trace's part.

Conrad wasn't going to let that happen, but he didn't want a full-scale shootout to erupt, either. Too many innocent people were around who might get in the way of flying lead. Instead he leaped forward, shouting and waving his arms.

That sudden commotion caused Whitfield's horse to shy violently away from Conrad. Trace's horse was right next to it and the two animals collided. Trace's horse bucked and reared, throwing off the gunman's aim just as Trace pulled the trigger. The revolver blasted, but the bullet shot harmlessly into the sky.

By the time the horse's hooves came back down to the dirt of the street, Conrad had his gun out and leveled at the gunfighter. "Drop it, Trace," he said. From the corner of his eye, he saw the rancher moving and added, "Forget it, Whitfield."

Leaving his gun in its holster, Whitfield scowled and said, "See what I mean, Angel? I don't care how much money this varmint has, he's still a gunman."

"I see that," Angeline said coldly as she looked at Conrad.

Luckily, he didn't really give a damn what she thought of him.

"This is twice you've interfered with me, Browning," Trace snarled. "There isn't gonna be a third time."

"You haven't dropped that gun," Conrad reminded him.

"And I'm not going to. You can just go ahead and shoot me, if that's what you want." When Conrad didn't pull the trigger, Trace snorted in contempt and jammed his Colt back in its holster.

"Are your things packed, Angeline?" Whitfield asked his daughter.

"Yes, they are," she told him.

Whitfield turned to look at the driver of the wagon, who had brought the vehicle to a stop about ten feet away. "Brody, go up and get Miss Angeline's things. Load them on the wagon and take her back to the ranch. The rest of the boys will go with you."

"Sure, boss." The cowboy hurried to obey the orders.

"What about you, Daddy?" Angeline asked. "Aren't you coming back to the Circle D with me?"

"I'll be along later," Whitfield told her. "Jack and I are going to stay here in town for a while."

Conrad understood what Whitfield was doing. The rancher didn't want it to look like he and his pet gun-wolf were turning tail and running. Maybe Whitfield really had business here in Val Verde, but Conrad doubted it.

"I wish you'd come with us," Angeline said.

"Just do as I told you." Whitfield's voice was sharp, and Conrad saw the sudden flare of hurt in Angeline's eyes.

She firmed her jaw and lifted her chin, though, and said, "Of course, Father. I'll just get a few of my personal things that Brody doesn't need to be messing with."

She stalked back into the hotel.

Since Jack Trace had holstered his gun, Conrad did likewise, but he kept an eye on Trace as he walked over to James and Margaret. Margaret had hold of her brother's arm and was urging him to come with her, back to the general store.

"We already have everything we need, James," she said. "Mr. Hamilton had our usual order all packaged up ready for us. If you'll go settle up with him, we can be on our way back to the ranch."

"You know there's not gonna be any settling up," James said, his voice bitter. "All I can do is ask Hamilton to add the supplies to our bill."

"Ah, but you've forgotten about this," Margaret said as she slipped a twenty-dollar gold piece from the pocket of her dress. Conrad knew it was the double eagle he had given Rory a few days earlier. "We can pay him for what we're getting today, and some on account."

James grunted. "Yeah, I reckon you're right." He glared at Conrad. "You didn't have to interfere again, Browning. I would've been all right."

"You'd have been dead is what you would have been," Conrad said. His voice was flat and hard. "Trace would have killed you without any trouble."

James jerked his arm loose from Margaret's grip and took a step toward Conrad. "What makes you think that?"

Conrad stood his ground and said, "Because it's his job to kill reckless hotheads like you."

For a second, he thought James was going to take a swing at him. But Margaret grabbed James's arm again, this time with both hands, and pulled him back. "That's enough," she said. "Come on, James."

He looked at her. "You shouldn't boss me around. I'm older than you, you know."

"Then act like it."

James didn't have an answer for that. He glared at everybody, then allowed Margaret to tug him back toward the general store.

From behind Conrad, Dave Whitfield asked,

"Are you really a rich man, Browning, like my daughter claims?"

Conrad turned and shrugged. "Some people would say so."

"Then why the hell are you gettin' mixed up with trash like the MacTavishes? You could probably buy and sell the whole lot of 'em a dozen times over."

"No," Conrad said with a shake of his head. "I could buy and sell *you* a dozen times over, Whitfield . . . not that I'd want to."

With that, Conrad started back toward the hotel, ignoring the angry glower on Whitfield's face.

He had just stepped onto the porch when he noticed something that froze him in his tracks. He saw a woman walking past the church, a woman in a long dress, wearing a shawl wrapped around her head and shoulders so that he couldn't see her face or even tell what color her hair was. He stood there watching her, waiting to see what she was going to do.

When she reached the corner of the building, she turned onto the little path that ran alongside it to the graveyard.

Conrad's breath caught in his throat. His heart seemed to shudder to a halt in his chest and lie there like a lump, no longer beating. He heard a roaring in his ears.

That's her, he thought. Even though she wasn't carrying any flowers for Rebel's grave this time, he felt certain that was the woman who had visited the cemetery before and left the bouquet.

"Browning." Trace's voice was an insistent drone behind him. "Browning, this isn't over. There'll be another time, mark my words, and it's gonna be different then."

"Whatever you say, Trace," Conrad responded without looking around. He started walking toward the church and the graveyard.

"Hey!" Trace called. "Hey, don't you walk away from me, you bastard! You hear me, Browning?"

Conrad heard him. He just didn't care. He walked faster.

"You son of a—" Trace's curse stopped short, and then Conrad suddenly heard hoofbeats pounding behind him, practically on top of him.

Instinct made him wheel around in time to see Trace about to ride him down. Rage contorted the gunman's face. Conrad twisted aside, barely avoiding the charging horse. He reached up and grabbed Trace's cowhide vest as the horse lunged past him.

With a grunt of effort, Conrad heaved on the vest. Trace let out a startled yell as Conrad pulled him from the saddle. He crashed to the ground. Luckily for him, his feet had slipped out of the stirrups. Otherwise, the horse would now be dragging him along the street.

Trace rolled over in the little cloud of dust caused by his hard landing. He reached for his gun as he started to surge to his feet. The Colt was only halfway out of its holster, though, when Conrad's fist smashed into Trace's jaw and laid him out flat on the dirt again. The gun slipped from the holster and landed in the dust. Conrad kicked it out of Trace's reach.

The fight had taken less than a minute. When Conrad turned toward the graveyard, he saw that the woman was still there, just reaching the gate and evidently paying no attention to the commotion going on down the street. He started toward her again.

He had taken only a couple of steps when Trace yelled, "You son of a bitch!" and tackled him from behind. Conrad's knees buckled under the impact. His legs went out from under him. Trace landed on top of him, laced his fingers together, and clubbed his hands down on the back of Conrad's neck.

The blow drove Conrad's face into the dirt. For a second or two, a black curtain seemed to drop over his brain. Red streamers shot through the darkness.

Then consciousness returned, driving away the stupor that had threatened to overwhelm him. He brought his right elbow back sharply, jabbing it into Trace's midsection. Trace gasped in pain. Some of the weight left Conrad's back. He bucked up off the ground, throwing Trace to the side.

Trace didn't stay down long. He scrambled to his feet again as Conrad glanced toward the cemetery.

The woman had gone inside. She walked slowly toward Rebel's grave.

Conrad heard Trace panting right behind him and twisted around as the gunman threw a punch at his head. The blow grazed Conrad's ear. It was painful but didn't do any real damage. Trace wasn't very big, but he fought with a crazed intensity that made him dangerous. He threw a hard punch for a smaller man. Conrad blocked a couple of them, then shot home a powerful right jab into the middle of Trace's face.

The punch rocked Trace back but didn't put him down. He came at Conrad again. Trace threw so many punches that Conrad couldn't block all of them. A couple of the blows made it through and stung badly. One landed on the corner of Conrad's mouth, the other just above his left eye.

He couldn't spend all day waltzing around like this with Trace. The answers to everything he needed to know might be waiting there in the cemetery at this very moment.

With a furious roar, Conrad lowered his head and bulled forward, ducking under the gunman's flailing punches. His arms went around Trace's waist. He kept moving forward as Trace's feet came off the ground. Conrad didn't let up on the bear hug as he drove Trace backward. He ignored the few blows that Trace landed on his back.

Conrad knew there was a water trough behind the gunman. He dumped Trace into it, throwing him down with enough force so that he hit the water hard. As Trace came up sputtering, Conrad planted a hand in the middle of his face and shoved him back down. Trace began to struggle frantically, but he was getting weaker.

A shot blasted. "Let him up!" Dave Whitfield shouted. "Let him up, Browning, or by God, I'll kill you!"

Panting and snarling, Conrad looked back over his shoulder and saw the rancher lowering the six-gun he had just used to fire into the air. The barrel swung in line with him. Conrad knew Whitfield meant the threat. Instead of holding Trace under the water, Conrad took hold of his shirt and hauled him up and out. He dropped Trace beside the trough. Trace lay there only half-conscious, gasping for air and moving his mouth like a fish out of water.

"Next time he gets in my way, I'll kill him," he told Whitfield. Behind the rancher, the Circle D hands watched in open-mouthed awe. Angeline stood on the porch, her face pale and drawn. Across the street, the three MacTavishes looked on as well, with worry etched on their faces.

Conrad saw all that, but only in passing as he turned once more toward the cemetery. He didn't see the woman in the shawl. His heart sank as he realized that the cemetery appeared to be empty.

He broke into a stumbling run toward the grave-yard anyway. Maybe she was behind a tree, or kneeling behind a headstone so that he couldn't see her. Maybe she had gone into the church.

Father Francisco emerged from the big adobe building as Conrad approached. With a look of disapproval on his thin face, the priest said, "I saw you brawling just now in the street, Mr. Browning—"

"Did she come inside?" Conrad broke in.

"Who?"

"The woman in the shawl!"

Father Francisco shook his head. "I haven't seen her. Was she here?"

Conrad hurried on to the cemetery gate, pausing just inside it. He looked around. He could see the entire graveyard from there. There was no place the woman could be hiding from him. He let out a groan of despair.

"She was here," he told Father Francisco, "but she's gone now."

And with her, he thought, possibly everything he needed to know.

Chapter 8

Margaret MacTavish came out of the store to meet Conrad as he trudged back toward the hotel.

"Are you all right, Mr. Browning?" she asked. "You weren't hurt in that fight?"

"I'm fine," Conrad told her. *Just disappointed,* he thought, but he didn't say that. He didn't want to have to explain everything to Margaret.

"You really don't need to keep on standing up to Mr. Whitfield for us. He's a bad man to have for an enemy."

"So am I," Conrad said. More than a dozen men could attest to that.

He glanced toward the hotel. A couple of Whitfield's men were loading Angeline's bags into the wagon. Angeline herself had climbed onto the seat next to the driver. Her eyes flicked toward Conrad, then darted away. Her chin lifted in a haughty manner. He knew she intended the gesture to show him just how much contempt she felt for him.

Conrad turned back to Margaret and said quietly, "Keep your eyes open while you're on your way back to the ranch. I don't think Whitfield's liable to start any more trouble while he has his daughter with him, but you never know."

Margaret nodded. "Thank you, Mr. Browning.

Stop by the next time you ride in our direction. You know you'll always be welcome."

The way she blushed when she said that made Conrad wonder if she was just being polite by issuing the invitation, or if she really wanted to see him again. He nodded and said, "All right. Thanks." That didn't commit him to anything.

A still soaking wet Jack Trace sat on the edge of the hotel porch as Conrad approached. His head drooped forward. His dark hair hung over his eyes. He looked up at Conrad through the lank strands. Conrad had never seen more murderous hate in any man's gaze.

Whitfield stood beside Trace. He had picked up the gunfighter's Colt and still held it. "I'll give this back to you when we get out of town," he said. "There's been enough trouble for one day."

"Not enough," Trace rasped as he looked at Conrad. "Not near enough."

Conrad walked past them without seeming to pay any attention to them, although he was actually watching them from the corner of his eye in case either man made a play. Whitfield seemed to have his anger under control now. There was too great a chance that Angeline might be hurt if he let things get out of hand.

A bitter taste filled Conrad's mouth as he went into the hotel. Why had the mystery woman chosen that particular moment to visit Rebel's grave? If it had been any other time, Conrad could have confronted her and maybe gotten some answers.

But no, it had to be at the same time trouble threatened to break out between the MacTavishes and Whitfield and his men. Once again, despite his best intentions, circumstances had forced Conrad to involve himself in somebody else's problems.

If he was going to avenge Rebel, he told himself, he was going to have to learn to walk away from all other trouble.

The drawback was that Rebel wouldn't want him to walk away. She believed in helping people. She would have been disappointed in him, Conrad realized, if he ignored the dangers threatening the MacTavishes.

"Damn it, Rebel," Conrad muttered under his breath. He glanced over and saw Rowlett watching him from behind the desk. The hotelkeeper wore a puzzled look on his face. To him, it appeared that Conrad was talking to himself.

Maybe that was it, he thought. Maybe he'd gone loco. Maybe he had imagined the mystery woman in the shawl.

But Father Francisco had seen her, too, Conrad reminded himself. If he was losing his mind, then so was the priest.

"Can I, uh, do anything for you, Mr. Browning?" Rowlett asked as Conrad paused wearily at the foot of the stairs.

"I don't think so," Conrad replied with a shake of

his head. "Not unless you know something about a woman in a shawl who visits the cemetery."

Rowlett shook his head. "Sorry, Mr. Browning. I don't know what you're talking about."

"I'm not sure I do, either," Conrad said. He gripped the banister and wearily climbed the stairs to his room.

A short time later, after resuming his post at the window, he saw the MacTavishes leaving town, their wagon rolling north with Margaret at the reins, Rory beside her with his rifle across his knees, and James riding alongside. About ten minutes after that, accompanied by the ranch hands serving as outriders, the Whitfield wagon left, carrying Angeline and her bags to the Circle D. Dave Whitfield and Jack Trace remained in town. Conrad hoped that Whitfield could keep the gunman under control and wouldn't let him go after the MacTavishes.

As for himself, it was his habit to keep his eyes open and watch out for ambushes, but he didn't really think he had to worry about Trace bushwhacking him. Trace was the sort to come at an enemy head-on, so that he could prove he was faster. His arrogance demanded that.

By nightfall, Conrad hadn't seen the woman in the shawl again. His lips had swelled where Trace hit him, and the contusion over his eye was bruised and sore, giving him a headache. With a sigh, he left his place at the window and went downstairs to have supper, even though he didn't feel much like eating.

While he was sitting at the table, trying to ignore the pain from his swollen mouth, Father Francisco hurried into the dining room. The priest glanced around. Conrad thought he looked uncomfortable, as if he didn't like being away from the church.

Father Francisco's eyes stopped on Conrad, who felt his heart lurch suddenly. If the priest was looking for him, there had to be a good reason. Conrad hoped it had something to do with the woman at the cemetery.

Father Francisco came across the room and stopped beside the table where Conrad sat. "I found this in the church a short time ago," he said as he held out an envelope.

Conrad's eyes widened—which caused a fresh jolt of pain to shoot through the bruised place on his forehead—as he saw his name written on the envelope. The letters were in what appeared to be a woman's handwriting.

The envelope wasn't sealed. He opened it and took out the paper inside, unfolding it and spreading it out on the table next to his plate. The message was simple and unsigned.

I saw you today. If you want the truth,
come to the cemetery.

Conrad looked up at Father Francisco. "You didn't see who left this?"

"No. I don't mean to pry in your affairs, Mr. Browning, but I couldn't help but read the note when you spread it out like that. I didn't see anyone in the cemetery when I came up here."

Conrad came to his feet. "That doesn't matter." He slipped the paper back in the envelope and stuffed it into his pocket. "I have to go down there."

Father Francisco put out a hand. "I'm not sure that's a good idea," he said. "You don't know who sent this note, or why."

"Like you said, Father," Conrad smiled, "the cemetery's always open. I don't think you can stop me."

The priest's lips tightened for a second. Then he shrugged. "You're right, of course. But I'm coming with you."

"Now *that* might not be a good idea."

"*You* can't stop *me,* Mr. Browning."

"No," Conrad admitted as he picked up his hat. "I don't suppose I can."

The two men left the hotel. Conrad didn't give a second thought to the food he hadn't finished. He didn't really have much of an appetite these days, anyway. He just ate to keep going.

Bright light and tinny piano music came from a saloon down the street, and the general store was still open. Other than that, Val Verde was quiet and peaceful, pretty much shut down for the night. Conrad looked toward the church. He couldn't see much of the cemetery. Darkness hid it.

In a soft, nervous voice, Father Francisco said, "You know this could be a trap, don't you?"

"I know," Conrad said. "That's why I didn't think you should come with me, Father."

"Anyone who would use hallowed ground for such a purpose . . ." The priest's voice trailed off, as if he couldn't conceive of such a thing.

"If there's one thing I've learned, it's that some people will do . . . *anything.*"

Like murder a beautiful young woman who never harmed anyone in her life.

They reached the gate, and suddenly, without any warning, Father Francisco stepped ahead of Conrad and called, "Hello? Is anyone—"

Conrad opened his mouth to warn the priest to be careful, but he was too late. Gun flame stabbed through the shadows as a shot blasted. Father Francisco grunted in pain and rocked back under the impact of a slug.

Conrad didn't know how bad the priest was hit. Lunging forward, he hit Father Francisco with his left shoulder and knocked him to the ground to get him out of the line of fire. Conrad's right hand palmed out the Colt on his hip and brought it up. He triggered twice, aiming at the spot where he had seen the muzzle flash.

Whoever was out there in the darkness returned

the fire. The slugs ripped through the air near Conrad's head. "Stay down, Father!" Conrad called as he angled to his right, toward one of the cottonwoods. "Get behind a headstone and stay there!"

He didn't believe for a second that Father Francisco was the bushwhacker's intended target. That first shot had been aimed at him, and Father Francisco was just unlucky enough to have stepped into the way of the bullet at exactly the wrong time. He hoped the priest wasn't hurt too badly.

Conrad pressed his back against the trunk of the cottonwood. A bullet rustled through the tree's branches. The trunk wasn't thick enough to shield him completely from the bushwhacker's fire, so he couldn't stay there. Crouching low, he came out from behind the cottonwood and fired twice in the direction of the hidden gunman. At the same time, he launched himself in a dive that carried him behind one of the nearby gravestones.

A bullet chipped granite from the stone and showered dust on him. He regretted that the attempt on his life was inflicting damage on a marker commemorating someone who had passed on, but it couldn't be helped.

Conrad heard a man's voice rasp, "Get around behind him!" So there were at least two of them, he thought grimly. The voice didn't sound like that of either Dave Whitfield or Jack Trace. What other enemies did he have in Val Verde?

The man responsible for Rebel's kidnapping, maybe?

The woman in the shawl had been bait. That bitter realization filled Conrad's mind. His enemy had figured out that he was still alive and had used the woman to set a trap for him. Whoever it was had known that Conrad wouldn't be able to ignore the mysterious woman who left flowers on Rebel's grave. He would have to know who she was . . . and so he would walk right into an ambush to find out. The woman had probably been hired for the job and hadn't even known Rebel.

The best way to find out the truth was to capture one of the ambushers and make him talk. Conrad lay there behind the gravestone, listening intently. After a moment, he heard a whisper of sound to his left. The man coming at him from that direction had brushed against one of the headstones.

Conrad rolled as muzzle flame once again gouted redly in the night, but he rolled toward the would-be killer, rather than away from him. He came up on his hands and knees, staying low as he drove forward. Another shot blasted, right above him as he crashed into a pair of legs.

The bushwhacker yelled in surprise and alarm as Conrad knocked him down. Conrad lashed out with the gun in his hand, trying to hit the man in the head and knock him out. Instead, the man flailed around with his gun, and the barrel struck Conrad across the throat. For a second, his windpipe was paralyzed, and no air could get through. He was left gagging and gasping.

"Hogan! Hogan, he jumped me!"

Conrad had no idea who Hogan was. The name meant nothing to him. But before he had time to try to figure it out, a woman screamed somewhere close by.

"Careful, damn it! She's gettin' away!"

That was the same man who'd given the order to circle around Conrad. Hogan, Conrad thought as he was finally able to drag some air back into his lungs.

"Stop her! She's got a gun!"

The man Conrad had tackled hit him in the belly, then shoved him away. Conrad rolled onto his side. He heard the man scrambling up and running among the tombstones. More shots rang out. A man yelled in pain.

"Let's get out of here!" That was Hogan again. "The plan's ruined!"

Conrad pushed himself to his feet and fired toward the sound of the shouts. A gun cracked to his right, but the shot didn't seem to be aimed at him. The woman? Hogan had said that she'd gotten her hands on a gun.

Conrad stumbled over to a tree, leaned on the trunk. He heard a swift, sudden rataplan of hoof-beats in the darkness. The bushwhackers had had horses hidden behind the cemetery and they were lighting a shuck out of there. Their ambush had been unsuccessful. He had put up more of a fight than they expected, he supposed.

Trying not to breathe too heavily in case any of the gunmen were still lurking in the shadows, Conrad waited a moment longer to let the pounding of blood in his head subside. His throat ached, but he was able to get air through his windpipe again without any trouble. He straightened and called, "Miss? Miss, are you here?"

From what he had overheard, the woman had been a prisoner. They had been forcing her to help them, not paying her. If he could find her, Conrad thought, she would probably be willing to help him. He wanted her to tell him everything she knew about the men who had set this trap.

She didn't respond, though. Some yells came from the direction of the hotel and the saloon, where men had heard the shooting and were coming to see what the ruckus was about. But the graveyard itself was as quiet as . . . well, a grave, Conrad thought.

Except for a sudden groan of pain. *Father Francisco.* Conrad hadn't forgotten about the priest, but there hadn't been a chance until then to check on him.

Conrad turned and hurried through the cemetery toward the gate. He hoped the priest had been able to get behind cover and hadn't been hit by any of the other bullets flying around.

"Father, where are you?"

"O-Over here . . ."

Conrad followed the weak voice and found Father Francisco sitting up with his back against the back of a gravestone. He knelt beside the priest and asked, "How bad are you hit?"

"In the arm . . . it hurts like the devil . . ." Father Francisco gave a hollow laugh. "So to speak."

Conrad felt relieved. An arm wound could be very painful, but chances were that it wasn't life threatening as long as the bullet hadn't nicked a vein.

"How bad are you bleeding?"

"A lot . . . seems like a lot . . . to me, anyway."

Conrad holstered his gun and slipped his arm around the priest. "Let's get you into the church so a doctor can take a look at that wound." He saw people from the settlement approaching the cemetery gate as he lifted Father Francisco to his feet. "We'll have plenty of help in a just a min—"

"Conrad?"

The woman's voice came from behind him. A shock went through Conrad as he recognized it. Surprise made him turn, taking the wounded priest with him.

She stepped out of the shadows, stopping a few feet away. The shawl was still wrapped around her head, but she lifted her hands and eased it down so that it slipped to her shoulders and revealed her face. He couldn't see her well in the dim light, but he knew the face anyway. Once he had known it very well indeed.

"Pamela?" he said. "Pamela, is it really you?"

"It is, Conrad," she said. "I . . . I thought you were dead. I thought I'd never see you again."

Father Francisco said, "You know this woman . . . Mr. Browning?"

"Yes, I know her," he told the priest. "At one time I was engaged to marry her."

Chapter 9

Shocked down to his bones by Pamela Tarleton's reappearance in his life, Conrad still had a wounded man to take care of. He turned and called to the townspeople approaching the cemetery gate, "Someone fetch the doctor! Father Francisco has been shot!"

That raised even more of a commotion. A couple of men ran off down the street, hopefully to summon the local sawbones. The rest rushed into the graveyard and clustered around Conrad and the priest.

Conrad glanced over his shoulder at Pamela. He was a little surprised to see that she was still standing there. He thought she might have vanished like a will-o'-the-wisp; like a phantom who had never really been there, just a figment of his imagination.

Several men offered to help Father Francisco. A couple of them stepped forward and slung their arms around him. Another man put his hand on the butt of his gun. He glared ominously at Conrad as he asked, "Did you shoot him, mister?"

Before Conrad could answer, Father Francisco spoke up. "No, no, not at all. Mr. Browning had nothing to do with my injury."

That wasn't strictly true, Conrad thought. The priest wouldn't have been shot if he hadn't been with Conrad, answering the summons contained in that note.

"He helped me," Father Francisco went on. "In fact, he drove away the men who wounded me, at the risk of his own life."

Conrad noticed that the priest didn't say anything about Pamela or the note. He saw the look that Father Francisco gave both of them, though, and he knew that sooner or later he would have to explain the relationship between them. The bullet hole in the priest's arm bought him that much consideration, at the very least.

As the men helped Father Francisco down the street, Conrad hung back. He turned to Pamela and asked, "Are you all right? None of those shots hit you?"

"I'm fine," she said. She reached out tentatively, as if she were about to put her hand on his arm, then stopped the gesture. "What about you?"

"The bushwhackers missed me," he said. In fact, he realized that none of the bullets had come really close to him. Father Francisco's accidental interference with their plan must have upset their aim. Even a hardcase with blood on his hands might get upset at having wounded a priest.

"Conrad, I . . . I read in the newspaper that you had died in a fire in Carson City. I heard about your wife, too. I'm so sorry."

Conrad's jaw tightened. Sympathy was probably the last thing he would have expected from Pamela

Tarleton. She had hated Rebel, because Rebel had taken him away from her. There had been more to it than that though. Pamela's financier father had tried to ruin him.

Clark Tarleton had almost succeeded in sabotaging the railroad spur so he could take over building it and become one of the most powerful men in the territory. He had been willing to resort to murder to get what he wanted and had wound up in jail, thanks to Frank Morgan.

Conrad suddenly recalled what had happened to Tarleton while he was awaiting trial. Someone had knifed him in his cell, killing him. As far as Conrad knew, no one had ever solved the slaying.

He knew he ought to respond to Pamela's condolences. He ought to tell her that he had heard about her father and was sorry, too. But he couldn't. Not after the things Clark Tarleton had done, the crimes he had committed. Conrad wasn't sorry the man had died.

Instead, he took Pamela's arm and said, "Let's go up to the hotel. I want to hear all about what happened here and how you got mixed up with those bushwhackers."

"It's not a pretty story, Conrad," she warned him.

"I'm not expecting a pretty story," he told her. "Just the truth."

Conrad led her into the hotel dining room. They sat down at one of the tables, and he asked a waitress to bring them coffee. Then he sat back and took his first good look at Pamela Tarleton in several years.

Time had been kind to her, despite the trying circumstances of her life. Her brown hair was as thick and lustrous as ever. It fell in waves around her face and shoulders. Her green eyes possessed the same compelling power they'd always had. She was still beautiful. Ever since he'd first met her, Conrad had thought that Pamela Tarleton was one of the most beautiful women he'd ever seen.

"You've . . . changed, Conrad," she said. "I mean . . . of course you have, you're older now, but . . . it's more than that."

"My wife was murdered, and I was badly wounded. No man could come through that horror unchanged."

"No, certainly not. I suppose that's it." Pamela's mouth tightened. "I lost someone, too, you know."

"I'm sorry," Conrad forced himself to say, even though it was a lie. "I heard about your father."

She gave a little shrug. "He wouldn't have been where he was if he hadn't decided to break the law. It took me a long time to come to terms with that fact and accept it, but I have." With a little shake of her head, she added, "Unfortunately, not everyone has."

"What are you talking about?"

"The man who's responsible for everything that's happened to you . . . and to your wife. My uncle. Anthony Tarleton."

Conrad leaned back in his chair. There it was, just like that. The answer he'd been searching for. The identity of the man who had ripped his heart out.

"Your father's brother?" he said.

Pamela nodded. "That's right."

"I don't recall you or your father ever mentioning him."

Pamela laughed, but there was no humor in the sound. It was cold and hollow.

"That's because Uncle Anthony was the black sheep of the family, as they say. He was Father's younger brother, and he was always gone when I was growing up, off somewhere looking for adventure and trying to make a fortune for himself. Father always said that if Uncle Anthony had worked as hard at the family business as he did at avoiding responsibility, he would have been a huge success."

Conrad frowned. "He doesn't sound like the sort of man who'd go to such lengths to avenge his brother."

"That's where you're wrong," Pamela said. "Even though they didn't see each other very often, there was still a bond between them. When Father . . . was killed . . . Uncle Anthony inherited a share of his holdings. That's how he was able to afford to hire Clay Lasswell."

Conrad's jaw clenched at the mention of the man who fired the shot that killed Rebel. "His goal was to punish me for what happened to your father?"

"That's right. He planned for you to die eventually, of course, but he wanted you to suffer first. But then, the newspapers all reported that you had died in the fire that destroyed your house in Carson City." Pamela hesitated. "The stories implied that you . . . you might have killed yourself. That didn't sound like the Conrad Browning I knew, so I didn't know what to believe."

Conrad gave a hollow laugh of his own. "Yes, back then I was much too fond of myself to have ever ended my own life, wasn't I?"

Pamela didn't answer that. She went on, "Please understand, Conrad, I wasn't anywhere around Uncle Anthony when that was going on. I didn't know he was involved. All I knew was what I read in the papers. It was later that I found out he . . . he had hired those men to kidnap your wife and gave Lasswell specific orders to kill her in front of you when you came to pay the ransom."

The lump in Conrad's throat kept him from speaking for a moment. It was just as well that the waitress arrived then with their cups of coffee. Conrad sipped the strong, black brew, and was able to go on. "How did you find out about all this?"

"Uncle Anthony came to see me in Boston. He . . . he said he needed my help. By then he had heard that some of the men Lasswell hired had been killed. He thought it was too much of a coincidence, especially after Lasswell himself

110

died. He decided you must still be alive after all, and he . . . he . . ."

"Wanted to set a trap for me," Conrad finished. "With you as the bait."

Pamela looked down at the table. Her hands tightened on the coffee cup until Conrad thought she might shatter it.

"He asked me to help him find out the truth about you," she said. "I'll be honest with you, Conrad. I spent a lot of time hating you after you broke off our engagement and then Father died. I blamed you and *your* father for that. Eventually I came to realize that it wasn't really your fault. At least, not that part of it. I still hated you for marrying that woman instead of me, though."

"So you agreed to throw in with him," Conrad said flatly.

"I agreed to help him find out if you were alive, like I said. I suppose . . . in the back of my mind . . . I knew even then that he planned to hurt you. But he still hadn't told me that he was responsible for what happened to your wife. I found out about that after we came here to Val Verde. He had me visit her grave. He thought that if you were alive, sooner or later you would come here, and you would be curious about the mysterious woman who left flowers on your wife's grave."

So he had figured it correctly all the way around, Conrad thought. He didn't take any pleasure from knowing that his deductions were correct.

"Those men in the graveyard made it sound like you were a prisoner," he said. "Then you shot at them. But now you're telling me you were working with your uncle of your own free will."

"Only at first," Pamela said. "When I saw Hogan and those other men, I recognized them for what they are: hired killers. I demanded that Uncle Anthony tell me what his real plans were. He didn't try to hide the truth from me any longer. He said that his men were going to kill you. He didn't want to take a chance on you getting away again." She shrugged. "That's when I told him I wasn't going to help him anymore. But he didn't give me any choice. For the past couple of weeks, I *have* been his prisoner, Conrad. His men watched me constantly. I had to go to the cemetery and keep up the charade. Uncle Anthony said that if I didn't cooperate, he . . . he would kill me. I believed him. He's insane with hatred, Conrad."

"But you double-crossed him tonight," Conrad pointed out.

"I had to. When I saw them start shooting at you, I couldn't take it anymore. I couldn't be a party to murder. I managed to get behind the man who was guarding me and hit him with a piece of stone that had crumbled off one of the grave markers. I got his gun and . . . and started shooting." She shuddered. "I didn't want to hurt anybody, but I wasn't going to stand by and let them murder you, either."

They had carried on the conversation in quiet

voices, so that no one at the other tables in the dining room could overhear. Pamela glanced up, over Conrad's shoulder, and said, "I think someone is looking for you."

Conrad turned and saw a couple of the men who had come to the graveyard to find out what all the shooting was about. They spotted Conrad and Pamela and started toward the table.

"You're Mr. Browning, ain't you?" one of the men asked.

Conrad nodded. "That's right."

"The doc asked us to tell you that Father Francisco is gonna be all right. The bullet knocked a chunk of meat out of his arm but didn't bust the bone. The worst of it was the blood he lost. But he'll recover, the doc says, and the padre wanted to make sure you knew that."

Conrad stood up and held out his hand. "Thank you for letting me know," he said as he shook hands with both men. "I was worried about him."

"Now, if you don't mind my askin', Mr. Browning . . . what in blazes was that shootout all about?"

"That's a personal matter," Conrad said.

The man moved aside his coat lapel, revealing a badge pinned to his vest. "Well, not really," he said. "My name's Saul Winston. I'm the marshal of Val Verde. This is my deputy, Pete Carey."

Conrad looked more closely at the man. Marshal Winston was only medium-sized, with a ragged, salt-and-pepper mustache, but he had a bulldog-like tenacity in his eyes and the set of his jaw.

Despite that, Conrad wasn't going to tell him the truth. Not all of it, anyway. He half-turned and indicated Pamela with a motion of his hand.

"I went down to the cemetery to speak with this lady," he said. "Father Francisco was with me. Several men started shooting at us. I have no idea why." That was the only actual lie. "Father Francisco was hit. I tried to drive off the men who shot him."

Marshal Winston frowned as he took off his hat and nodded politely to Pamela. "Ma'am, I hate to bother you, but do you know who shot at the padre?"

"I'm sorry, Marshal, I don't," she said. "I think the men must have been robbers. I never got a good look at them."

"Why were you, uh, meetin' Mr. Browning in a graveyard?"

Conrad felt a surge of anger. He was about to say something to the lawman again about prying in personal matters, but Pamela said, "Mr. Browning and I are old friends. In fact, at one time we were engaged to be married. I simply wanted to say hello to him and pay my respects to his late wife, who's buried in that cemetery."

Winston looked uncomfortable. "Yeah, I seem to remember hearin' about that. I'm sorry for your loss, Mr. Browning."

Conrad gave the man a curt nod in response.

"No offense, ma'am," Winston went on, "but it seems a mite odd to me that you'd be meetin' Mr. Browning at his wife's grave, especially at night."

"Father Francisco was there," Pamela said, her voice sharper now. "There was nothing improper about it, Marshal."

"No, ma'am, I didn't mean to suggest that there was." Winston turned back to Conrad. "You didn't get a good look at the varmints, either?"

"I didn't see any of them at all," Conrad said. "All I saw were muzzle flashes."

"Well, I'm mighty sorry this happened. Val Verde's a peaceful place most of the time. Of course, there was a ruckus here this afternoon, too . . ." The lawman scratched his beard-stubbled jaw and regarded Conrad intently. "Come to think of it, you were mixed up in *that,* too, weren't you, Mr. Browning?"

"Just defending myself, Marshal. I don't recall seeing you there when Dave Whitfield and his pet gunman were trying to run roughshod over the MacTavishes."

Anger glittered in Winston's eyes. Conrad knew he shouldn't have made the comment. He had probably just made an enemy out of the lawman. He didn't particularly care, though. He had learned to handle his own problems, without depending on the law. The past few months had taught him that much.

"Are you plannin' on stayin' in Val Verde long?" Winston asked, his voice cool.

"I don't know. I suppose that depends on what else happens."

"Don't take it inhospitable-like, but if trouble's got a habit of followin' you around, maybe it'd be best if you moved on elsewhere."

A tight smile tugged at Conrad's mouth. That was exactly the sort of thing that lawmen usually said to his father, Frank Morgan, the notorious Drifter.

He supposed the apple really didn't fall too far from the tree.

"Thank you for letting me know about Father Francisco, Marshal."

"Yeah, you're welcome, I reckon." Winston clapped his hat on. There was nothing left to say to Conrad, so he jerked his head at his deputy and said, "Come on, Pete."

When the two star packers were gone, Conrad sat down across from Pamela. She leaned forward and said, "I've caused you a great deal of trouble, haven't I?"

Conrad shook his head. "You just played a small part in it, and most of that was against your will. The person who really caused the trouble is your uncle."

"And it's not over, Conrad. You don't think Uncle Anthony will give up just because of what happened tonight, do you? He'll still be coming after you."

"Good," Conrad said. "Because I still have a score to settle with him, too."

Chapter 10

Conrad asked Pamela where she had been staying. "There's another hotel here in town," she explained. "Not nearly as nice as this one, but Uncle Anthony didn't want to call any attention to us." An embarrassed flush spread across her face. "He allowed the proprietor to think that he and I were . . . well, that I was his mistress."

"One more mark against him," Conrad snapped. "You can't go back there, of course. We'll get you a room here. What about Hogan and the rest of the gunmen?"

"They're staying there, too."

"How many are there?"

"All I ever saw were Hogan and two other men. I can't say for certain there aren't more somewhere else."

More gunmen could be camped somewhere outside of the settlement, Conrad supposed. But that didn't really matter. If they weren't with Anthony Tarleton all the time, he probably didn't need to worry about them.

Pamela reached across the table and clasped his hand. It was an unself-conscious gesture, totally spontaneous. "Conrad, what are you going to do?"

"First of all, I'll make sure that you're safe, that you don't have to take part in any more of your

117

uncle's sick, twisted games. Then I'm going after him."

Pamela began shaking her head before Conrad even finished his answer. "You can't do that. They'll kill you. You should let the law handle it."

"You mean Marshal Winston and his deputy?" Conrad laughed. "You saw them, Pamela. They might be able to handle some drunken cowboys blowing off steam on a Saturday night, but they're not any match for hired killers like Hogan."

"And *you* are?" Pamela shook her head again. "I don't mean to insult you, I truly don't, and I know that you've changed since we last met . . . but you're still Conrad Browning. You're a businessman, not a gunfighter."

She didn't know about Kid Morgan, Conrad thought. But then, not many people *did* know about the connection between him and the gunman known as Kid Morgan or just The Kid.

"I can take care of myself," he said. He put the same sort of arrogance into the declaration that the Conrad Browning who'd been engaged to Pamela would have displayed. "Don't worry about me."

"But I do worry about you, Conrad," she insisted as her fingers tightened on his hand. "You've already been hurt enough. I . . . I don't want to see anything else happen to you."

He was touched by her concern. She might not look any different, but it seemed that she had

118

grown up over the past few years. Tragedy had changed her, just as it had him.

"Well," he said, "I won't do anything tonight. And we'll discuss the situation again before I make any sort of move. All right?"

"Perhaps you should send for your father," Pamela suggested.

Conrad shook his head. He knew that Frank would be glad to help him. He had said as much when Conrad last saw him in San Francisco, in the office of their lawyer Claudius Turnbuckle.

But the days of Conrad running to Frank Morgan for help were over and done with. Frank knew that and respected it. The fact that Conrad didn't need him as much just strengthened the bond between father and son.

"We'll talk again in the morning," he said as he got to his feet. He held Pamela's chair for her as she stood. They left the dining room and went into the lobby. Rowlett was in his usual spot behind the desk.

"How are you, Mr. Browning?" the hotel man asked. "I heard there was more trouble."

"Nothing I couldn't handle, Mr. Rowlett." Conrad nodded toward Pamela. "Miss Tarleton needs a room. I hope you can accommodate her."

"Of course." Rowlett chuckled. "The hotel does a good business, but we're rarely full up. Not in a town like Val Verde." He moved the registration book toward Pamela. "If you'd just sign in, miss."

"I'll be taking care of the bill," Conrad said as Pamela took the pen from the inkwell.

She looked sharply at him. "That's not necessary."

"I insist." Conrad gave Rowlett a stern look as the man's eyebrows rose in surprise. "Miss Tarleton and I are old friends."

"Yes, sir, of course. None of my business, Mr. Browning. That's a lesson you learn mighty quick in the hotel business."

Conrad felt a prickle of irritation at Rowlett's smug attitude and the assumption the hotelkeeper had obviously made. Going on about it would just be protesting too much, though, and would probably only strengthen Rowlett's suspicions.

Let the man think whatever he damned well pleased, Conrad decided. He was long past the point himself where he gave a damn what anyone thought about him.

"Just give Miss Tarleton her key," Conrad said in a stony voice once Pamela had signed in.

"You'll, uh, want her room near yours, I reckon . . ."

Resisting the impulse to reach across the desk, grab the man by the collar, and shake some respect into him, Conrad said, "That doesn't matter."

In fact, he did want Pamela's room near his, but only for the sake of her safety. Now that she had escaped from her uncle, Anthony Tarleton might guess that she was at the hotel with Conrad. He could send men to kidnap her and take her back to him.

Tarleton wouldn't get away with kidnapping any more women. Conrad made that vow to himself.

To make sure it didn't happen, he intended to strike first, no matter what he had told Pamela.

Rowlett handed over a key. "Room Eleven. It's a couple of doors down from Mr. Browning's."

"That'll be fine," Conrad said. He took Pamela's arm and led her toward the stairs.

As they climbed to the second floor, he went on, "I'm sorry you had to abandon all your things at the other place. We'll go to the store and get you everything you need tomorrow."

"Conrad," she said with a soft laugh, "you're sweet, but surely you don't really think that a general store in a town like Val Verde will have *everything* that a lady needs."

She hadn't changed completely. She still had a touch of superiority about her. Conrad hadn't really expected otherwise.

"We'll do the best we can," he promised. "Until you can get to a bigger town."

He took the key from her as they approached the door of her room. There was no reason to worry about an ambush here, he told himself. Anthony Tarleton couldn't be sure where Pamela was, and he couldn't possibly have found out already which room was hers.

Still, Conrad made sure that his right hand wasn't far from the butt of his gun as he unlocked and opened the door.

The room was empty. Conrad lit the lamp. He turned back to Pamela and said, "Tell me what your uncle looks like."

"Why?" she asked with a puzzled frown.

"So that I'll recognize him if I happen to see him," Conrad said. He didn't add that he fully intended to see Anthony Tarleton just as soon as possible. "He may still be here in town."

"That's true," Pamela admitted. "He's a big man, a powerful man. He's worked all over the world. He has brown hair, starting to go gray, and a mustache. I'm afraid that's all I can tell you about him."

"What about Hogan?"

"Medium-sized. Balding. He'd be a rather handsome man if not for a bad scar down the left side of his face."

"What about the other two gunmen?"

"One is a Mexican called Vicente. The other is a man named Loomis. You'll know him right away if you see him. He's an albino." Pamela shuddered slightly. "I hate to look at him. He reminds me of some creature you'd find under a rock."

Conrad nodded. He would know his enemies now if he saw them. Which he intended to do, soon.

"I'm in Room Seven, if you need me," he told Pamela. "Don't hesitate to call on me."

She smiled at him. "You've been remarkably considerate, Conrad, considering the history between us."

"So have you," he said. Even though her father had been a criminal, his death must have been painful for her. It wasn't unreasonable for her to think that he and Frank had been partially responsible for what happened—although Conrad himself didn't feel that way and never would. Clark Tarleton had made his own bed.

Pamela moved closer to him. Her head tilted back slightly so she could look into his eyes. She said, "Conrad, I know this isn't the time or place—"

He didn't let her go any further. "No, it's not," he said. He saw the brief flare of hurt in her eyes. It couldn't be helped. In an odd way, he was glad to see her again. She was a link to his past, and yet he would never be able to think of her without thinking of Rebel as well.

And thinking too much about Rebel was just too damned painful.

Pamela swallowed hard. "I guess this is good night, then."

"Yes," Conrad agreed. "Good night. I'll see you in the morning. Don't worry about anything."

She summoned up a smile. "I won't."

Conrad had left the door open. He turned and put his hat on as he left the room. He eased the door closed behind him, glad that he didn't have to look at Pamela anymore. Beautiful though she might be, she was a painful reminder of his past and everything he had lost.

Maybe things would be different tomorrow, he thought.

By tomorrow morning—by the time he saw her again—he would have settled things, *El Señor Dios* willing.

And her uncle would be dead, just like her father. The only difference was that Anthony Tarleton was going to die by Conrad Browning's hand.

Or rather, by the hand of Kid Morgan.

As soon as he was inside his room, Conrad unbuckled the plain black gunbelt, took off his boots, and began stripping off the sober gray tweed business suit he wore. When he was down to the bottom half of a pair of long underwear, he opened his bag and took out denim trousers and a fringed buckskin shirt. He unwrapped the shirt from around a brown gunbelt and buscadero holster.

Conrad pulled on the trousers and strapped the gunbelt around his hips. He took the Colt Peacemaker from the black holster and settled it in the one he wore now. The buckskin shirt went over his head. He took a hat from the bag. It had been flattened to fit in the bag, but it took him only a moment to punch it back into shape and put it on. The brown felt hat had a broad brim and a flat crown. The last thing he took from the bag was a red-checked bandanna that he tied around his neck. Then he stepped back into the high-topped black boots he'd been wearing before. As he turned toward the door, he caught a glimpse of himself in the mirror over the dresser.

With the broad brim of the hat pulled down to shield his face, no one would recognize him from a distance. Conrad Browning had returned to life for a while, but now he was dead again.

Long live Kid Morgan.

The Kid took the hotel's rear stairs so he wouldn't have to deal with Rowlett's curiosity. He slipped into the alley out back and walked toward Val Verde's main street. Even his walk was a little different, a bold stride that proclaimed he would back down from no man.

Pamela had said there was another hotel in the settlement. Conrad hadn't noticed it while he was there—but The Kid intended to find it.

He walked along the street, checking the buildings he passed. He held out a hand to stop the first man he encountered and asked in a gruff voice, "Is there a hotel around here?"

The man swayed a little. The smell of whiskey came from him as he answered, "Yeah, the Val Verde Hotel. Right up the street."

"No, another one," The Kid said. "I'm not partial to anything that fancy."

The man turned and indicated a building in the next block. "Go down to Sloan's, then." He chuckled. "Nothin' fancy about that place, but Sloan'll rent you a room if he's got any empty ones."

"Obliged," The Kid said with a curt nod.

The townie called after him, "From what I hear, if you stay at Sloan's, you'll have company. Lots of little, crawlin' company."

The Kid's jaw tightened. The idea of Pamela being forced to stay in a place like that rubbed him the wrong way. She must have been miserable.

He walked on and found the place he was looking for, a ramshackle frame building that looked like it would be drafty. The sort of place where sand would get in and grate constantly underfoot. A crudely lettered sign read SLOAN'S—ROOMS FOR RENT—BEER.

It was half saloon, half hotel from the looks of it. Lights still burned on the lower floor, but the upper story was dark.

The Kid circled the building, looking for a rear door. He found one, but it was locked. He grasped the knob, put his shoulder against the panel, and shoved hard as he twisted the knob. He could have kicked it open, but that would have made too much noise. Instead he kept up the pressure, and after a minute, the door gave with a small, splintering sound. With luck, no one up front had heard it.

The Kid eased inside and found himself in a dark hallway. He drew his gun and moved toward the front of the building. The floor was gritty with sand, just as he expected.

He reached an arched doorway with a dimly lit room beyond it. Staying back where the glow wouldn't reach him, he studied the room and saw that it was a dusty, shabby hotel lobby. To the right, another door led into the saloon part of the establishment. The Kid heard the clink of glasses and bottles and a few voices, all of them male.

He edged forward and risked a glance into the lobby. A sleepy-looking clerk dozed behind the desk. No one else was in the lobby.

The stairs were on the other side of the desk. The Kid couldn't reach them without going past the clerk. He reached into his pocket and pulled out a double eagle. Crouching, he reached around the edge of the door and, with a flick of his wrist, rolled the coin along the floor.

The gold piece rolled right under the stool where the clerk sat and came to a clinking, clattering stop against the first step in the staircase. The sound roused the clerk from his half-slumber. He looked around, blinking in puzzlement. Then his gaze lit on the coin. Like a flash, he was off the stool, hurrying over to pick up the double eagle.

A couple of long, swift strides brought The Kid right up behind him. The Colt's barrel dug into the man's back as The Kid's left hand reached around and clamped over his mouth. Leaning close, The Kid breathed into his ear, "Don't make any commotion, or I'll blow your backbone in two."

The clerk stiffened, but he didn't fight. "We're taking the stairs," The Kid went on. "Not a sound, you understand?"

The clerk jerked his head in a nod.

"Up you go," The Kid said.

They climbed the stairs in near-silence. When they reached the landing at the top, The Kid took his hand away from the clerk's mouth. "Don't yell," he warned. "This gun's got a hair-trigger."

It didn't, but the clerk didn't have to know that.

"There are four men staying here with a woman," The Kid went on. "The leader's a big man, with graying brown hair and a mustache. One of the other men is an albino. You know the bunch I'm talking about?"

It was possible that this wasn't the hotel Pamela had meant, The Kid thought. But the clerk nodded. He licked lips that had gone dry with fear and husked, "They're here, all right, mister. But I just rented 'em the rooms. If you got a grudge against 'em, I ain't got nothin' to do with it."

"Just tell me which rooms they're in."

The clerk pointed with a shaking finger. "Them two right down there at the end of the hall, across from each other. The woman on the right, the fellas on the left."

"Are they in there now?"

"Hell if I know, mister. I don't keep up with folks' comin's and goin's."

"All right. I reckon that's all I need from you."

The clerk started to relax. "Don't you worry, mister, I know how to mind my own business—"

The Kid brought the gun up and chopped down

with it. The barrel thudded against the clerk's skull. The man's knees buckled. The Kid caught him and lowered him silently to the threadbare carpet runner. He hadn't hit the clerk hard enough to put him out for very long. But for a few minutes The Kid didn't have to worry about the hombre raising a ruckus.

He knew that Pamela's room was empty, since she was up at the Val Verde Hotel. With any luck, Anthony Tarleton and his hired gunmen would be in the other room, trying to figure out what to do now that their ambush had failed. The Kid cat-footed up to the door of that room and took his hat off so that he could place his ear against the panel. He listened for voices but didn't hear anything. A lamp was burning in there, though. He could see the glow through the cracks around the poorly fitted door.

The knob was locked, he discovered when he wrapped the fingers of his left hand around it and tried to turn it silently. That left only one way in. The Kid backed off as much as he could in the narrow corridor, lifted his right leg, and lunged forward, driving his boot heel against the door beside the knob. The jamb splintered. The door flew open. The Kid went into the room low, ready to fire as he tracked the Colt from side to side.

The creaking of a floorboard behind him was the only warning he had before the roar of a shotgun crashed through the hallway.

Chapter 11

That split-second of warning was enough. The Kid was already twisting aside as the scattergun belched fire and lead from across the hall, from the door of the room where Pamela had been held prisoner. He felt the sting as several of the balls scraped his leg and side, but the double load of buckshot hadn't had room to spread out very much.

Since the man with the shotgun had fired both barrels, that meant the weapon was useless to him until he reloaded. The Kid didn't intend to give him that much time.

He spun so hard that he lost his balance and went down on one knee. His left hand slapped against the floor to catch himself. His right brought the Colt up and he squeezed the trigger. The muzzle flame lit up the dim hall. In the glaring flash, The Kid saw a stocky figure in *charro* jacket and sombrero throwing aside the empty shotgun and clawing at a holstered revolver. The Mexican didn't make it. The Kid's bullet punched into his midsection. He doubled over and staggered back a couple of steps before collapsing.

The Kid surged up and sprang across the corridor. He had already seen for himself when he first charged into the room on the left that it was empty. The bitter realization that he had walked into yet another trap filled his mind for a second.

Frank Morgan wouldn't have made a mistake like that. The Kid had plenty of gun-speed and guts. What he lacked was experience, and he was going to need luck to live long enough to gain that wisdom.

He would worry about that later, he told himself. He saw that the Mexican had one hand pressed to the wound that welled blood through his fingers, but the other hand was still trying to fumble that revolver free of its holster.

The Kid bent and jerked the gun away. He tossed it on the bed, then knelt beside the Mexican. Pressing the Colt's barrel hard under the wounded man's chin, he leaned over and said, "Listen to me, Vicente. You've got a bullet in your gut. You're a dead man. Question is, will you die now . . . or five or six hours from now after you've gone through hell?"

Vicente blinked tear-filled eyes up at him. "You . . . you would spare me that pain . . . Señor?"

"Tell me where to find Anthony Tarleton," The Kid said.

"He and Hogan . . . and Loomis . . . rode out," Vicente gasped. "They left me here . . . in case you came looking for them. The señorita . . . *aiiieee . . .*" The spasm in his gut left the Mexican breathless with agony for a moment. Then he was able to resume, "The señorita . . . told you . . . where to find us . . . just as . . . just as . . ."

"Just as Tarleton expected," The Kid finished. "Where were they going?"

Sweat beaded on Vicente's face. He shook his head. "I don't know . . . No one told me . . ."

The Kid heard loud voices downstairs. No one had come to check on the gunshots yet. It was the sort of place where people minded their own business. He knew that their curiosity would get the better of them in a minute or two, and then footsteps would sound on the stairs.

"How many men does Tarleton have? Just Hogan and Loomis?"

"No, Señor . . . Twelve more . . . camped outside of town."

So the odds were more than a dozen to one. The Kid didn't care. He would take on hundreds—thousands, if he had to—in order to avenge Rebel.

"Sorry you had to die, Vicente," he said. "That's what you get for throwing in with a man like Tarleton."

"A man like . . ." The Mexican began to laugh.

Then he brought up the bloody hand that he had pressed to the wound in his belly. The Kid's eyes caught a flash of light on cold steel. He realized that Vicente had slipped a knife from his belt, below the bullet hole. The Kid threw himself backward as the blade threatened to rip open his own belly.

The Colt in his hand roared and bucked again as the knife missed him by a whisker. Vicente's head snapped back. There was a small black hole in his forehead, and a much larger one where the slug had blown out the back of his skull after boring through his brain. Blood and gray matter smeared the floor behind him.

Vincent had made it to hell quickly, all right, but he hadn't managed to take The Kid with him.

The Kid stood up. He didn't glance at the body again as he went into the room where Tarleton and the other men had been staying. He stalked over to the window and thrust the sash up. The clerk hadn't gotten a look at him, and Vicente wasn't going to be doing any talking. Even if Marshal Saul Winston bothered to investigate Vicente's death, he wouldn't find out much.

The Kid holstered his gun and threw a leg over the windowsill. He climbed out, hung by his hands, and then dropped the six feet or so to the ground.

He was in an alley behind Sloan's, so he followed it back up the street toward the Val Verde Hotel. He had to cross the street to reach the hotel. As he paused at the corner of a building, he saw the marshal and his deputy hurrying toward Sloan's. Winston had probably heard the shotgun go off and was going to see what the ruckus was about.

The lawman would be too late to do anything except fetch the undertaker for Vicente.

Disappointment gnawed at The Kid's gut. He wished he'd been able to get the Mexican to talk. It was possible, though, that Vicente really didn't know where Tarleton and the others had gone. The Kid would have to find the spot where the rest of the gunmen had been camped and pick up the trail there.

When Winston and Carey were out of sight, The Kid walked across the street to the hotel. He used the back stairs again to reach his room. As he paused in the corridor, he glanced at the door of Pamela's room. He wanted to make sure she was all right, but he couldn't very well knock on her door looking like this. A faint smile curved his lips as he thought about what her reaction might be to the sight of Kid Morgan.

Five minutes later, with The Kid's outfit back in the carpetbag, wearing an expensive dressing gown, Conrad Browning rapped softly on Pamela's door. He heard her sleepy murmur from within the room. "Who is it?"

"Conrad," he said. "Are you all right, Pamela?"

"Of course." She sounded more wide awake now. "Why wouldn't I be?"

"No reason. I just wanted to check on you before I turned in."

He heard a step on the other side of the door. The key rattled in the lock, and then the door opened a couple of inches. Pamela looked out at him, her green eyes still drowsy. "I'm fine, Conrad," she said. "It's sweet of you to be so thoughtful."

The door eased open a little more. Conrad saw an appealing stretch of bare shoulder and arm. He suddenly found himself wondering if she was wearing anything.

He forced that thought out of his head and gave her a curt nod. "Well, I'll say good night, then. Again."

"Good night, Conrad," Pamela said. She was clearly puzzled by this late night visit and his attitude, but she didn't say anything else. The door clicked shut behind Conrad as he turned toward his room.

It had been a violent, eventful day. He was tired.

And yet, as he often did, he lay in bed for a long time, staring up at the ceiling of the darkened room, before sleep finally came to him.

After a restless night with too many of the familiar nightmares, he woke up in the morning, dressed, and went along the hall to Pamela's room. She answered his knock immediately. Even wearing the dress she'd had on the day before, she looked better than any woman had a right to this early in the morning, Conrad thought. In fact, the only woman he had ever known who looked better first thing in the morning was—

He caught his breath, forced himself not to think about that, and smiled. "How are you?" he asked.

"Fine. I slept better than I have in weeks, thanks to you." As if realizing how that might sound, she went on hastily, "I mean—"

"I know what you mean," Conrad said. "Are you ready for some breakfast?"

"Oh, yes. And then what are we going to do?"

She came out into the hall and closed the door behind her. Conrad took her arm and led her toward the stairs. He said, "We're going to the general store, as I mentioned last night, and once we've taken care of that, we'll go to the train station and see about getting you a ticket on the next eastbound train."

Pamela stopped and frowned at him. "You mean I'm leaving?"

"There's no reason for you to stay here, now that you're free of your uncle and his gunmen," Conrad pointed out.

"But . . . you're here."

He shook his head. "Not for long."

"You're going to confront Uncle Anthony?"

Conrad realized he had said too much. Pamela wasn't stupid. Her eyes widened with understanding when he didn't reply.

"You've already gone after him, haven't you?" She clutched his arm. "Conrad, did . . . did you kill him?"

"I didn't see your uncle. I found the hotel where you'd been staying, but he and his men were already gone."

He didn't see any point in telling her about the shootout with Vicente. With any luck, he could get her out of Val Verde before she even heard about that. He hoped there would be an eastbound train coming through today.

"But you're going to try to find him, aren't you?"

she asked grimly. "You won't rest until you track him down."

"He's responsible for Rebel's death," Conrad said. "You don't think I can just forget about that, do you? Not to mention the fact that he held you prisoner and threatened to kill you, too."

Pamela dismissed that with a wave of her hand. "Uncle Anthony may have threatened me, but he never would have really hurt me. At least, I don't believe he would have."

"What about those gunmen working for him? If something had happened to him, how do you think *they* would have treated you?"

Her face paled as she considered that possibility. "You're right," she admitted. Her fingers tightened on his arm. "Still, you're no match for those men. I don't mean to offend you, Conrad, dear, but you're simply not."

Conrad, dear . . . It had been a long time since she had called him that. The term must have slipped out from habit, since any romance between them was long since over.

"If you're bound and determined to see this through," she continued, "you should at least get your father's help. Send for Frank Morgan and stay here until he arrives, Conrad."

He shook his head. "I'll handle this as I see fit," he said, not bothering to keep the harsh tone out of his voice.

"You always were an infuriatingly stubborn

137

man," Pamela said. Her voice was cool now. "Very well. At least if you insist on getting yourself killed, *I* won't have any part in it. I'm grateful to you for that, anyway."

With that new air of tension between them, they went on downstairs and into the dining room. Conrad ordered breakfast for both of them.

They didn't talk much during the meal. Conrad was lingering over his coffee while Pamela finished her food, when pounding hoofbeats in the street outside caught his attention. He looked up, glancing through the front window in time to see a wagon race in front of the hotel, careening along barely under control.

Unless Conrad was mistaken, Rory MacTavish was at the reins, slashing the team with the lines and urging them on.

Conrad came quickly to his feet. Pamela saw the look of alarm on his face.

"What is it?" she asked. "What's wrong?"

"I don't know," he replied, "but Rory MacTavish just drove by in the family's wagon, whipping the horses for all they're worth."

"That doesn't have anything to do with you," Pamela pointed out.

"I know. But they treated me well."

"Only because *you* helped *them*."

Conrad started for the dining room door. Behind him, Pamela called his name, but he ignored her. He knew logically that she was right, that whatever trouble had befallen the MacTavishes now, it was none of his affair. He had responsibilities of his own, such as tracking down Anthony Tarleton.

But once again, he couldn't help but think that Rebel would want him to help them if he could.

He strode quickly through the lobby and out of the hotel. The wagon had come a stop down the street, in front of one of the houses. The youngster's bright red hair was unmistakable. Rory had hopped down from the seat and was at the back of the wagon, watching anxiously as several men lifted someone from the wagon bed. As Conrad hurried closer, he saw that the man being taken from the vehicle was Hamish MacTavish.

A bloody bandage was wrapped around Hamish's midsection. Conrad saw a sign hanging on a post in the front yard announcing that the house was where Dr. Edward Churchill practiced medicine. The townsmen who had responded to Rory's frantic calls for help carried Hamish up onto the porch, where a middle-aged man with gray hair waited.

"Take him inside and put him on the bed in the front room," the man instructed. The townies disappeared into the house with their burden.

Rory would have followed, but Conrad had caught up to him. He stopped the boy with a hand on the shoulder. Rory jerked around to face him, wide-eyed with fear and shock.

"Rory," Conrad said. He put enough urgency in his voice to break through the emotions that held Rory in their grip. "Rory, what happened?"

"Pa's been shot!"

"I could see that." Conrad took hold of Rory's other shoulder. "Who did it?"

"I don't know! They . . . they attacked the place in the middle of the night! Shootin' and yellin' . . . they set the barn on fire . . . Pa and James ran out to try to stop them, but Pa got hit!"

"What about James? Was he hurt?"

Rory shook his head. "Not then. I don't know about now."

That made no sense to Conrad, but he figured he could sort it out as he went along. "How about Margaret?"

"Meggie's gone!"

Conrad resisted the impulse to shake the boy. Rory was so scared and upset, it was a wonder he was making any sense at all. Still, Conrad had to find out exactly what had happened before he could start figuring out what to do about it.

"Listen to me, Rory. Listen to me. You have to tell me what happened. Take a deep breath, and start at the beginning."

Tears trickled down Rory's cheeks. He gulped and then took a deep breath, as Conrad had told him to do. "It was the middle of the night, like I said," he began. "When the shootin' started, we looked out and saw that the barn was on fire. Pa told me to stay inside with Meggie. He and James ran outside and started shootin' at the men. Pa was hit, and James dragged him behind the smoke-house. That was the closest cover."

Conrad nodded encouragingly. Rory was telling a coherent story now, and he wanted the boy to continue.

Rory took another deep breath. "Some of the men charged the dugout. I couldn't stop 'em, and neither could James. They got inside, and I thought for sure they were gonna kill me. But one of them just walloped me and knocked me out." He gestured toward an ugly bruise on his face. "I heard Meggie screamin' . . . and when I came to, she was gone. James said they dragged her out and took her with them."

Horror filled Conrad. Another innocent young woman carried off by killers. It made him sick to think about it.

"James tried to stop 'em, but there were too many of them," Rory continued. "He had to duck back behind the smokehouse to keep them from filling him full of lead. As it was, he got creased a couple of times."

"You said the men came into the dugout. Did you get a good look at any of them?"

Rory hesitated. "Not really," he said. "We hadn't lit any lamps, so it was dark in there. And I think they had bandannas over their faces." His voice took on a fierce tone. "But they were Devil Dave's men. They had to be. Nobody else around here would've done such a terrible thing."

As far as Conrad knew, Rory was right about that. Whitfield was the only real enemy the MacTavish family had. Whitfield and Jack Trace had been forced to back down here in Val Verde the day before. That would have eaten at them, especially the arrogant gunman, Trace. Conrad could easily imagine Trace talking Whitfield into the raid on the MacTavish ranch.

"What happened after that?"

"We . . . we had to take care of Pa. We carried him back in the dugout, and we stopped the bleedin' as best we could and bandaged him up. Then James said . . ." Rory swallowed. "James said he was goin' after Meggie and for me to bring Pa to town and get him to the doc. That's what I did."

"James went after the men who raided your place? By himself?"

"Yeah. There was nobody else to help us."

The words didn't carry any tone of accusation, but Conrad felt a twinge of guilt, anyway. He wished he could have been there to lend a hand to the MacTavishes.

But he'd had plenty of trouble on his own plate the night before.

"You said you didn't get a good look at the men. How did James know where to go? Or did he wait and follow their trail this morning?"

Rory shook his head. "No, he left before sun-up.

He was goin' straight to the Circle D. He said he knew that's where he would find Meggie."

If that was true, then Whitfield and his men, including Trace, were probably waiting for James MacTavish. James might be dead by now, shot to pieces by Trace and the rest of Whitfield's gun-wolves.

But maybe, just maybe, there was a chance James was still alive.

"You go on inside now," Conrad told the boy. "I'm sure the doctor will take care of your father to the best of his ability."

"You look like you're gonna do something, Mr. Browning."

"I am," Conrad said. "I'm going out to Whitfield's ranch and do whatever I can to help your brother. If your sister is there, we'll get her back. You have my word on that, Rory."

Chapter 12

After getting directions to the Circle D from Rory, Conrad headed back to the hotel. He saw Pamela waiting on the porch for him.

"What's happened?" she asked him as he went up the steps.

"Hamish MacTavish has been shot," he replied, "and his daughter Margaret was kidnapped."

"Dear Lord! I'm sorry to hear that." She frowned at him. "You're not going after her, are you?"

Conrad nodded. "I am."

Pamela put a hand on his arm. "Conrad, you should leave this to the law. It's not your place to go chasing after a bunch of—" She stopped short as a look of horror appeared on her face. "Oh, my God. It's almost like . . ."

Her voice trailed off as if she couldn't bring herself to go on.

"That's right," Conrad said with a grim nod. "Margaret MacTavish doesn't deserve what's happening to her any more than Rebel did."

Pamela tightened her grip on his arm. "But you're not married to this MacTavish girl. I understand why you feel sorry for her, but it's not your responsibility to go off and get killed trying to help her!"

Conrad pulled away from her. "I'm not going to get killed."

"Can you guarantee that?"

"There are no guarantees in life, Pamela. You know that."

"All too well," she said with a bitter edge in her voice. "I once thought my happiness was guaranteed, but look how *that* turned out."

Conrad turned away. There was nothing he could do to change the past. He said, "I'm sorry I can't see about putting you on an eastbound train. I'm sure you can handle that for yourself."

"Of course," Pamela said coldly. "I'm used to doing things for myself now. I had to learn when I lost my father *and* my fiancé."

Conrad refused to give in to the guilt she was trying to make him feel. He strode into the hotel and headed up the stairs.

When he went back down a minute later, he was carrying the carpetbag in which he had the clothes he wore as Kid Morgan. He didn't see Pamela in the lobby or the dining room and was grateful for that. He didn't want to waste any more time in useless argument with her.

He left Val Verde a short time later in the buggy. The hostler at the livery stable had tied the buckskin behind the vehicle, as Conrad requested. He didn't know if he would need the saddle horse, or his other clothes, but he would be ready if he did.

Dave Whitfield's spread was east of the MacTavish place. Conrad veered in that direction when he passed a spire of rock that split about halfway up, the first landmark Rory had told him. He followed the directions the boy had given him and after a couple of hours, he knew he ought to be getting close to the Circle D.

It had been hours since James MacTavish had ridden over there. Conrad had a bad feeling that whatever was going to happen—had already happened.

Because of that pessimism, he was a little surprised a short time later when he heard gunshots popping in the distance. He slapped the reins against the buggy horse's rump, urging him on to greater speed. If there was a chance James MacTavish was still alive, there was no time to waste.

Conrad knew he was on Circle D range by now. He came to a narrow creek that twisted through some rolling hills. According to Rory, if he followed it, it would lead him to the ranch headquarters.

The gunfire grew louder over the next ten minutes. Conrad sent the buggy up a rise. It sounded like some of the shots were coming from just over the crest. As he topped the rise, he was already reining in, hauling the big black to a halt. He reached down and plucked the Winchester from the floorboards as he caught sight of a cloud of powdersmoke hanging over a cluster of boulders. Someone in there was firing at a number of buildings spread out along the creek about two hundred yards down the hill.

Conrad had no doubt the hidden rifleman was James MacTavish. He also knew that James was in more trouble than he realized.

A group of riders had just burst from some trees along the rise to the right and were about to close in on James from that direction.

Conrad leaped from the buggy and ran to a nearby pine tree. He leaned against the trunk and brought the rifle to his shoulder. As the horse-backers opened fire on the boulders, Conrad began squeezing off shots in their direction.

He aimed in front of the galloping riders. As his bullets began to kick up dust, the men instinctively yanked on their horses' reins in surprise. One of the animals got its legs tangled and went down, spilling its rider. The man's companions had to swerve wildly around him to prevent their mounts from trampling him.

As the riders became aware that the man in the boulders wasn't alone, some of them turned their guns toward Conrad. He ducked behind the tree as bullets chewed pine bark from the trunk, which wasn't really wide enough to protect him.

Luckily, James MacTavish—or whoever was in the boulders—took advantage of the opportunity to throw some lead toward the men on horseback. As that blunted their charge even more, Conrad dashed behind the rocks.

Sure enough, James was the man who was holed up there. He glanced at Conrad and exclaimed,

"What the hell! You again?" Then he cranked the lever of his Winchester and continued firing at the riders, who were trying to circle around the boulders to get a better shot at him and Conrad.

Conrad crouched behind one of the rocks and joined James in peppering Whitfield's men. He assumed they were from the Circle D. Under the circumstances, he couldn't think of anybody else who'd be trying to kill James.

The riders broke off their attack and wheeled their horses, heading back into the trees. Two men in the boulders were considerably harder to root out. The gunmen had been taking advantage of the fact that James wasn't able to fire in two directions at once. Now Conrad could cover his back.

"Looks like they're gonna give us a little breathin' room," James commented as he lowered his rifle. He took a handful of cartridges from his pocket and started thumbing them into the Winchester's loading gate. He went on, "Maybe you'll have time to tell me what in blazes you're doin' here, Browning."

"Saving your sorry hide, from the looks of it," Conrad replied. "That was a damn-fool stunt, taking on Whitfield and all of his men by yourself. Don't you think your family deserves better than to have you commit suicide that way?"

James bared his teeth in a grimace. "I'm still alive and fightin', ain't I?"

"Yes, but you might not be by now if I hadn't shown up when I did to give you a hand."

"You don't know that," James snapped. He frowned. "If you're out here, you must've seen Rory in town. Is . . . is my pa still alive?"

"He was when they carried him into Dr. Churchill's house," Conrad said. "But that was a couple of hours ago."

James sighed. "He was hit bad. I didn't know if he'd even make it to town."

Conrad nodded toward the bloody bandages tied around James's upper left arm and right thigh. "Rory told me you were wounded, too."

"These are nothin' but scratches," James said with a disgusted snort. "They didn't stop me from ridin' over here and havin' a showdown with Dave Whitfield."

Dryly, Conrad pointed out, "I see that you're holed up in these rocks, and you don't have your sister with you."

"The bastards claim they don't have her. They say they don't know anything about that raid on our ranch last night." James spat. "The lyin' sons o' bitches."

No shots were coming from the ranch buildings at the moment. Conrad risked a look. He didn't see anyone moving around down there.

"While we've got a chance, why don't you tell me what happened this morning?" he suggested. "To be honest, I figured I'd find you dead when I got here. I thought you'd go riding in with guns blazing and get yourself shot to pieces."

James snorted. "I reckon that's what would've happened . . . if I was the idiot you make me out to be. I knew these rocks have a good view of Whitfield's place. I hid up here, waited until one of his hired killers was walkin' outside, and plugged the no-good bastard."

"You murdered a man from ambush?" Conrad asked.

"Hell, no. I just winged him." There was a note of pride in James's voice as he added, "I'm a damn good shot."

"What did that accomplish?"

"It got their attention, didn't it? When some other hombres ran out to see what the shootin' was about, I made 'em dance by puttin' bullets around their feet. They ducked back into cover mighty quick-like. Every time one of them stuck his head out after that, I parted his hair for him. They could see I meant business. Once the fella I'd wounded had crawled back inside the barn, I hollered down to Whitfield and told him to let Meggie go, or I'd keep them bottled up there and pick them off one by one."

"And Whitfield claimed he didn't have Margaret." Conrad's words were a statement, not a question.

"That's right. What kind of damn fool does he take me for? Who else could have carried her off?"

That was a good question, but Conrad was starting to wonder if there might not be an answer to it.

"When those men raided your ranch last night, did you get a good look at any of them?"

He had asked the same question of Rory, and gotten the same answer. James frowned and said, "Not really. I was too busy duckin' bullets and tryin' to kill some of the bastards."

"Then you didn't recognize any of them as being Whitfield's men."

"Well . . . no. But who the hell else could it have been?"

Conrad didn't try to answer that just yet. Instead, he said, "So Whitfield claimed he and his men didn't attack your ranch and didn't kidnap your sister?"

"That's what I just said, ain't it?" James responded irritably.

"Did he offer to let you come down there and take a look around, so you could see for yourself that Margaret's not there?"

"As a matter of fact, he did. But I knew it was a trick, so I told him to go to hell. They would have blown me to pieces the second I stepped out into the open."

Unfortunately, that might have been true, since James had shot down one of Whitfield's men from ambush. Conrad closed his eyes for a second and tried not to sigh in exasperation. James's mule-headed refusal to admit that he might have jumped to the wrong conclusion had done more harm than good.

Plus, it had been stupid of him in the first place to come charging over here alone when Whitfield had a whole crew of tough cowboys and hired gunmen. Taking them by surprise had given James a momentary advantage and kept him alive that long, but it wasn't going to last. Probably at that very moment, more of Whitfield's men were trying to circle around and get the drop on him.

And he had plunked himself right down in that same boat, Conrad realized. He and James were trapped there.

A fresh volley of shots from the ranch headquarters reinforced that point. Bullets hummed and sang in the air around the boulders. Some of them ricocheted, adding high-pitched whines to the racket. All Conrad and James could do was keep their heads down and hope that none of the slugs found them.

As Conrad crouched there, he realized that this barrage might have another goal besides just possibly killing them. Whitfield could be trying to distract them so that some of his men could sneak up on the rocks and capture them.

No sooner had that thought gone through Conrad's mind than the guns abruptly fell silent. He began, "Look out, James, they're going to rush—"

Boots pounded against the ground even as Conrad started to voice the warning. With a grunt of effort, a man bounded on top of one of the boulders and launched himself in a flying tackle at James. They crashed together. Both men went down.

Conrad heard harsh breath right behind him. He tried to twist around to meet the threat, but he made it only halfway before a heavy body collided with his and smashed him back against the rock. Pain shot through his ribs. The impact drove the breath from his lungs and left him gasping for air.

He realized he had dropped his gun. He brought his fist up and felt it hit hard against bone, probably his assailant's jaw. The punch rocked the man back a step and knocked his hat off. Conrad got a good look at his face and recognized him as one of the men who had been with Whitfield in Val Verde the day before.

Although still shaken and breathless, Conrad brought his left fist around in a hard, crossing blow that jerked his opponent's head the other way. He hooked a right into the man's belly, doubling him over. The man was in perfect position for a left uppercut, but Conrad didn't get the chance to throw it.

Another man tackled him from behind. He fell forward. His legs tangled with those of the first man. All three of them sprawled on the ground. Conrad was on the bottom, the weight of both his enemies crushing him.

Some of that weight disappeared as James MacTavish roared a curse. Conrad figured that James had disposed of the man who'd jumped him and was lending a hand to his reluctant ally. Using his hands and knees, Conrad heaved himself to the side, and threw off the man who had tackled him.

He turned the move into a roll that carried him into the open. As he looked up, he saw half a dozen men surrounding him and James. They had no chance against numbers like that. The smart thing would be to surrender and hope that Whitfield's men wouldn't kill them. That was his best chance of surviving in order to continue his quest for vengeance against Anthony Tarleton.

Unfortunately, in the heat of battle Conrad wasn't thinking that much about being smart. He was filled with anger—anger at Whitfield and the MacTavishes for their damned feud, at the men who were closing in to pound and stomp him into submission, at himself for getting mixed up in this mess to start with.

That fury burst out of him as he surged up off the ground with a yell and waded into his enemies, swinging punches right and left.

The feel of his fists smashing into their faces sent a savage exultation through him. At the exclusive university he had attended back east, he had listened to languid professors who had never been in a fight in their lives debate the fundamental nature of mankind. Back then, Conrad had been just as arch and pretentious as they were.

But he had learned. He knew why the barbarians had enjoyed the ultimate triumph in every clash down through the ages—what civilized man simply could not comprehend; that in order to survive, sometimes you have to smash your enemy before he can smash you. The barbarians knew that. The knowledge was in their bone and muscle and blood.

And Conrad knew that, too—or rather, Kid Morgan did. Every time blood spurted from an opponent's nose as The Kid's knuckles flattened it, every time a man grunted in pain as The Kid's fist sunk wrist-deep in his belly, every time fists and feet smashed into him and he ignored the pain because he simply wouldn't let himself fall, wouldn't allow himself to lose . . . those moments were like rousing from a long sleep and being truly awake and alive for the first time in ages. Maybe ever.

Aching and battered, blood dripping from his mouth and nose, swaying with exhaustion, Conrad found himself still on his feet, with four men sprawled on the ground around him, stunned and only semi-conscious. James MacTavish was still upright, too, having accounted for two more men. He stared at Conrad and said, "My God, man, where'd you learn to fight like that?"

Conrad knew he had always known how to fight

like that. It had just taken tragedy, hatred, and out-rage to wake him up to the fact.

He didn't have the time to explain that to James. Instead, he started looking around for his gun, saying, "More of Whitfield's men will be here any minute—"

The metallic sound of a gun being cocked stopped him. A voice drawled, "No, Browning, we're already here."

Conrad looked up and saw Jack Trace standing about twenty feet away, along with half a dozen more of Whitfield's hired guns. All of them had their revolvers drawn and leveled at Conrad and James.

"I didn't expect to see you," Trace went on, "but I've got to admit, I'm glad you're here. Whitfield told us to bring MacTavish back alive, but he didn't say a damned thing about you, Browning . . . and there's nothing I'd like better than an excuse to put a bullet in you, you son of a bitch."

Chapter 13

Conrad smiled as he looked at the gunman. "If you shoot me now, Trace," he mocked, "we'll never know which one of us is faster, will we?"

Trace's face darkened with anger. "I know, damn you! No fancy pants Easterner can outdraw me!"

One of the other men said, "Take it easy, Trace. Maybe we better take both of 'em down to the ranch house and let the boss decide what to do with them."

Trace's head jerked toward the man, and for a second Conrad thought Trace was going to swing the gun around and pull the trigger. The man who had spoken up thought that, too, because his face went pale under his tan.

But Trace controlled his killing rage and snapped, "Fine. Take 'em down. Just don't ever cross me again."

The man muttered something Conrad couldn't catch. Maybe an apology, maybe a promise that he wouldn't interfere with Trace's wishes in the future.

The men surrounded Conrad and James and gathered up their guns. Then they prodded the two unarmed men down the hill from the rocks toward the ranch house.

"Where's my sister?" James demanded.

"You mean that pretty little redhead?" Trace

asked from behind the prisoners. He chuckled. "I don't have any idea, but I know where I'd like for her to be. Right there in my bunk, with all that red hair spread out on my pillow."

James grated a curse and started to turn around. Conrad stopped him with a hard grip on his arm.

"That's just what he wants you to do," Conrad warned. "Whitfield told him to take you alive, but that won't stop Trace from blowing your knee apart."

Trace laughed again. "You're a smart man, Browning. Too smart for your own good, I reckon."

Conrad didn't say anything. He didn't want to antagonize Trace—but at the same time, he wasn't going to forget any of the marks against the gunman.

As they neared the ranch house, the front door opened and Dave Whitfield stepped out onto the porch, trailed by several of his men. All of them held rifles. From the set of the rancher's slab-like jaw, Conrad knew that Whitfield's rage was barely contained.

"MacTavish!" Whitfield barked as soon as the prisoners came to a stop in front of the porch. "As soon as I heard the first shot, I knew it was one of you damn squatters causin' trouble again!"

"We're not squatters!" James snapped. It seemed a little foolish to Conrad to be arguing over words right now, but James went on, "We own our spread

158

free and clear. Pa saved for years to buy the land from the government."

"I've used that range for years."

Conrad spoke up, saying, "The open range days are over, Whitfield. You're intelligent enough to know that."

Whitfield glowered at him. "Just 'cause some fella in Santa Fe or Washington says something, it don't mean that's the way it ought to be!"

"I couldn't agree with you more. Unfortunately, the law doesn't see things that way. Nor does it condone kidnapping."

"Damn it!" Whitfield roared. "If you're talkin' about Meggie MacTavish, I don't have her! I never did!"

"You lie!" James yelled.

Whitfield's big, callused hands tightened on the rifle he held. For a second, Conrad thought that James had pushed the cattleman too far. Whitfield looked like he was about to use the gun.

Then, with a visible effort, Whitfield controlled his anger and said, "Listen to me, MacTavish. Get this through your thick, dumb skull. *I didn't kidnap your sister. I don't know where she is.*"

"What about your men?" Conrad asked. "You claimed you didn't send them over to the MacTavish spread with dynamite the other night. Couldn't some of them have raided the place and carried off the girl without telling you about it?"

"Not damn likely!" Whitfield said.

"But not impossible."

Whitfield glared at Conrad for a moment, then turned to one of the men on the porch with him. "Ramsey, you control the crew. Any of them unaccounted for?"

The man called Ramsey, who had the weathered face and drooping white mustache of a long-time cowboy, shook his head. "Nope. I know where each and ever' one of 'em is, boss, and they didn't kidnap no gal, last night nor any other night!"

"That's just the ranch crew your man's talking about, Whitfield," Conrad pointed out. "What about the hired guns?" He knew that on the Circle D, those were likely two separate and distinct groups. "They'd be the ones more likely to have carried out such a raid."

Whitfield looked at Trace. "What about it, Jack?"

James snorted contemptuously before Trace could answer. "Why should we believe anything a killer like him says?"

Trace ignored James and said, "We were right here on the ranch all night, Mr. Whitfield." With a sneer, he added, "Normally, I wouldn't mind lyin' to trash like MacTavish, but in this case, it's the God's honest truth."

Whitfield looked at James and said, "There you go. I believe my men. Now I've got half a dozen injured men because you flew off the handle, MacTavish. What are you gonna do about that?"

"What am I gonna do?" James repeated. "I'm

160

gonna tell you all to go to hell! You're lyin', and one way or another, I'll prove it!"

Conrad's patience finally ran out. "James, shut up!" He stepped forward, ignoring the startled glare that James gave him. "Listen to me, Whitfield. If your men are telling the truth, then you shouldn't object to helping us prove that they didn't kidnap Margaret MacTavish and shoot Hamish."

"Hamish is hurt?" Whitfield asked with a frown.

"That's right. He was wounded during the attack on his ranch."

"How bad?"

Conrad shook his head. "I don't know. Rory took him to Val Verde in a wagon, and some of the men from town carried him into the doctor's house. That's the last I saw of him. That's how I found out what had happened at the MacTavish place, and when Rory told me that James had ridden over here, I figured I'd better see if he was all right."

Trace drawled, "You got a bad habit of stickin' your nose in where it ain't wanted, Browning."

"I didn't ask him to help me," James snapped.

Conrad bit back a curse at James's galling attitude. Instead, he asked, "How many men attacked your place last night?"

James frowned and shrugged. "I don't know. It was dark. Eight or ten, I'd say. Maybe a dozen."

Conrad looked at Whitfield again. "That many riders will have left tracks. I suggest we ride over

161

there and have a look around. Maybe we can follow them and find the men who took Margaret."

Whitfield lowered his rifle and rubbed his jaw. He appeared to be considering Conrad's suggestion.

Trace said, "Careful, boss. This damn Easterner could be tryin' to trick you."

"I don't see how it could be much of a trick," Whitfield said, "considerin' that there's only two of them and more than twenty of us. Of course, I wouldn't take all the crew along. Just you and maybe four or five of your men. That's still plenty to handle these two."

"What if Browning's tryin' to lead you into a trap?"

"Who's left to spring it?" the rancher asked. "Hamish MacTavish is hurt. We got this boy, and the other one's just a kid."

"What about the other little ranchers around here?"

Whitfield shook his head. "I haven't had any trouble with any of those greasy-sack outfits. They're all too scared to go against me." He gestured toward James. "Those damn Scottishers were the only ones with gumption enough to rustle my stock."

"We never rustled any of your stock!" James yelled.

Quietly, Conrad said, "We're wasting time arguing. We can settle the matter of Margaret's kidnapping, by picking up the trail of the men who took her."

"You're right," Whitfield said with an abrupt nod. "Pick five of your men, Jack, and get your horses saddled. We're ridin' to the MacTavish place."

Trace began, "I still think it's a—", but he stopped when he saw the hard look that Whitfield gave him. Devil Dave was used to having his orders obeyed without question, Conrad thought.

While Trace went off to see about getting his men ready to ride, Conrad said to Browning, "My rig is at the top of the hill. My saddle horse is tied on behind it."

Whitfield nodded. "I'll have a man bring it down. What about you, MacTavish? Where's your horse?"

James gestured sullenly toward the rise. "Up there in the trees, too, probably not far from where Browning left his buggy."

"All right, I'll see to it." Whitfield started to turn away, then paused. "For what it's worth, I hope we find your sister and that she's all right. I don't make war on women."

"Bullets don't distinguish between the sexes," Conrad said. "Neither does dynamite."

Whitfield scowled. Maybe he knew he had allowed his feud with the MacTavishes to get out of hand. Maybe he would do something about it in the future. Conrad would believe that when he saw it, though. Old-time cattlemen like Whitfield were sometimes too set in their ways to ever change.

A few minutes later, one of Whitfield's punchers drove Conrad's buggy down the hill to the ranch headquarters. Another Circle D cowboy led James's horse. Conrad got the saddle from the buggy and put it on the buckskin. He wished he could change into the Kid Morgan garb, since it was considerably more comfortable for riding, but he didn't want to make it too obvious that Conrad Browning and The Kid were one and the same. No one around here even knew that The Kid was in these parts.

He managed to slip the trousers, shirt, hat, and gunbelt into his saddlebags, though, and threw them over the buckskin's back, lashing them in place. The Winchester went in the saddle boot. Reluctantly, he left the Sharps behind.

One of Whitfield's men saddled the rancher's horse and led it out. Whitfield had gone back into the house for a few minutes. He came out with saddlebags draped over his shoulder.

"We may be on the trail for several days before we catch up to the varmints," he said. "I told my cook to put some supplies on a pack horse for us."

"Good idea," Conrad said. Whitfield gave him a sour look that said he didn't care if Conrad agreed with him or not.

Trace and five more of the hard-faced gun-wolves rode out of the barn. Conrad didn't like the idea of being accompanied by the hired killers. He didn't trust Trace or any of the other men. He barely trusted Dave Whitfield. As long as Whitfield was paying their wages, though, Conrad thought the rancher could keep Trace and the others in line.

They left the ranch and headed for the MacTavish place. It was nearing midday, and the sun was high and hot overhead. Conrad took off his coat.

It took more than an hour to reach their destination. Conrad spotted the charred rubble of the burned-down barn before he saw the dugout that served as the family's home.

"Better slow down," he called to Whitfield, who had been setting a fairly fast pace. "We don't know which way the kidnappers went. We don't want to trample right over their tracks."

Jack Trace sneered at him. "What are you, some kind of scout?"

"I know a little about tracking," Conrad said, without explaining that what he knew, he had learned from his father. If Frank Morgan had been there, Conrad would have felt more confident about being able to pick up the trail of the men who had abducted Meggie MacTavish.

But Frank wasn't there, and that was the way Conrad wanted it. He would handle this problem on his own.

"Browning's right," Whitfield said as he reined his horse back to a walk. "Keep your eyes open."

He looked over at James. "Did you see which way they went when they left your ranch?"

"East," James snapped. "Straight toward your ranch."

"Have you seen their tracks goin' in that direction?" Whitfield demanded. "The only hoofprints *I've seen are* the ones you left when you went gallopin' off half-cocked to the Circle D."

"Whitfield's right, James," Conrad added. "We haven't come across the tracks of a large group of riders like the bunch that attacked your ranch."

"Well, then, who else could've done it?" James asked with exasperation plain to hear in his voice.

Conrad still didn't try to answer that, although he had his suspicions. The theory that had begun to form in his head, though, didn't make sense. He was missing some connection.

Whitfield suddenly grunted and pulled his horse to a stop. "Look there," he said, leveling an arm and pointing.

The rest of the group followed his lead and reined in as well. Conrad leaned forward in the saddle and studied the ground. He could see the marks left behind by numerous riders who had come along there. The tracks curved off to the southwest.

"Would you look at that," Whitfield said as he glanced at James. "A bunch of men on horseback headed east from your ranch, then started circlin' back to the southwest less than a mile later. Hell, boy, if you'd just opened your ears, you could've *heard* 'em swingin' around this way."

James's face flushed angrily. "I was too busy tryin' to stop my pa from bleedin' where he'd been shot!"

"But not by me or any of my men," Whitfield said. "You were dead wrong. You came over to my spread and started shootin', woundin' my men and just generally raisin' hell, and you had the whole thing wrong."

"I don't know that," James insisted.

Whitfield flung a hand toward the tracks. "There's your damn proof, right there!"

James shook his head stubbornly. "All that proves is that they turned southwest. We don't know if they kept going that way."

"There's an easy way to find out," Conrad said.

"Yeah." Whitfield heeled his horse into motion again. "Come on."

The trail continued to lead southwest, circling completely around the MacTavish ranch. The landscape became flatter and more arid. Conrad knew they wouldn't have to ride much farther south to reach the Mexican border, although the way the trail curved, they would still be on American soil the rest of the day.

Some low but rugged-looking mountains appeared on the horizon. During a break to rest the horses, Whitfield nodded toward them and said, "Looks like the varmints are headin' for the

Hatchets. Have you about got it through your head, MacTavish, that me and my men ain't responsible for what happened?"

James didn't answer for a long moment. Finally, he said, "Maybe. Maybe not. If you really took Meggie, you're goin' to pretty long lengths to convince me you didn't."

Whitfield threw his hands in the air. "You're the stubbornest fool I ever run across!" He pointed at James. "I don't take kindly to bein' called a liar, and that's what you called me, right to my face. You're gonna see that I was tellin' the truth, and when you do, you're gonna apologize . . . or you and me are gonna have even more trouble than we'd had so far."

"Your men have murdered my brother and maybe my father and tried to blow up our home," James replied. "How much more trouble do you intend to cause, Whitfield?"

Muttering curses, Whitfield just shook his head and turned away. He and James might have called a truce—but Conrad wasn't sure there would ever be any real peace between them.

The men pushed on a short time later. By the time the sun had lowered toward the western horizon, the Hatchet Mountains didn't look much closer. Conrad and his companions had to make camp and wait until morning to push on, or else risk losing the trail in the dark.

He nudged the buckskin up alongside Whitfield's

mount and said, "Don't you think you can give James and me our guns back now?"

Whitfield regarded him with narrow eyes. "You, maybe," the rancher said after a moment. "I don't reckon you're the sort to go off half-cocked. But I'm not puttin' a gun back in that boy's hands just yet."

Conrad shrugged. He was willing to accept a partial victory as long as it meant that he would have his Colt again. Anyway, there was something else on his mind.

"Does it seem to you that we didn't have much trouble picking up and following this trail?" he asked Whitfield.

"You mean it's almost like they *want* us to follow them?"

"Exactly."

Whitfield nodded. "The thought crossed my mind. But it's pretty hard to cover up a trail out here."

"Not really. We've passed several rocky stretches where they could have veered off and not left any tracks for a while, if they wanted to."

Whitfield's eyes narrowed even more. "What are you gettin' at, Browning? You think we're ridin' into a trap?"

"Could be."

"Why would anybody think that grabbin' Meggie MacTavish would make me follow 'em? I ain't exactly a friend of the family, and everybody in these parts knows that."

"Maybe it's not you they baited the trap for," Conrad said. "Maybe it just happened to work out that way."

"What the hell does *that* mean?"

Before Conrad had to decide whether to answer or not, Jack Trace spurred up to the front of the group, too, flanking Whitfield on the right. "I've got news for you, boss," the gunman said. "While we've been followin' these tracks . . . somebody's been followin' us."

Chapter 14

Whitfield reined in sharply and hipped around in the saddle. "What the hell are you talkin' about?" he demanded.

Conrad twisted to look back, too, but he didn't see anything behind them except a semi-arid wilderness.

"It's just one man, as far as I can tell," Trace said. "He's stayin' pretty far back, too. But he's there. I've seen him a couple of times this afternoon."

"Remember what we were just talking about, Whitfield," Conrad said.

"One man don't make a trap," the rancher snapped.

"What's this about a trap?" Trace asked. His right hand drifted toward his gun. "If you've double-crossed us, Browning . . ."

"Take it easy," Conrad said. "I haven't double-crossed anybody. Whitfield and I were just talking about how it seems like this trail has been pretty easy to follow."

Trace's eyes slitted with suspicion. "Yeah, you're right about that. I reckon it *could* be a trap. Not much of one, though, if there's only one hombre following us."

"We don't know what's up ahead," Conrad pointed out.

James said, "I don't care. My sister's up there

somewhere, and I'm not stoppin' until I have her back, safe and sound."

Conrad hoped that was the way it turned out. He had worried ever since they picked up the trail that they might find Meggie MacTavish's body lying used and broken in some gully. So far, that hadn't happened.

He felt a twinge every time James blustered about saving Meggie. He had been full of the same confidence and resolve, back there in Carson City when Rebel was kidnapped.

Just because that situation had ended in tragedy, it didn't mean this one had to, Conrad reminded himself.

"Why don't the rest of you push on toward the mountains and find a place to camp?" he suggested. "I'll split off from the group, circle back around, and see if I can jump whoever is following us. If I can get my hands on him, that might give us some answers."

"How do we know you won't just go runnin' back to Val Verde?" Trace asked.

"I didn't *have* to come with you, remember? I didn't have to get mixed up in this mess at all. I'm here to help save Margaret, that's all."

"Unless you're workin' with whoever's back there and the two of you are gonna ambush us once we make camp."

Whitfield rasped his fingers over his beard-stubbled jaw and said, "Jack's got a point there, Browning."

"No, he doesn't," Conrad said. "I don't know who's back there any more than you do. It's certainly not anyone I'm in cahoots with, because I don't have any friends or partners in this part of the country."

"Yeah, I reckon that makes sense . . . and your idea's a good one. I'd like to know who's trailin' us, too. But I'd feel better about it if Jack went with you."

An ugly grin spread across Trace's face. "I reckon I could do that."

Conrad was about to object when Whitfield moved his horse closer and reached into his saddlebag to pull out a Colt Peacemaker. Conrad recognized it as his gun.

"Don't get any ideas, Jack," Whitfield cautioned as he held out the revolver to Conrad, butt first. "You've been a good hand for me, but I don't cotton to murder."

"Furthest thing from my mind, Dave," Trace said coolly.

Conrad checked the loads in the Colt and then pouched the iron. He met Trace's look with a cold, level stare of his own.

"I'm ready when you are."

"Lead the way, dude," Trace said, grinning again. "Since you know what you're doin' and all."

Conrad wheeled the buckskin and started back along the trail they had been following. He swung off to the right, recalling that he had seen an arroyo in that direction as they passed it a short time earlier. He didn't look back to see if Trace was coming with him, but he could hear the hoofbeats of the gunman's horse.

When Conrad reached the arroyo, he followed it until he came to a place where the bank had caved in, allowing him to ride down into the defile. Trace followed right behind him. As the two men rode along the sandy floor of the arroyo, Trace moved up alongside Conrad and said, "I'm curious about something, Browning."

"Everybody's curious about something, I suppose," Conrad replied without looking over at Trace.

The gunman chuckled. "Take it easy. You don't have anything to worry about. I'm not gonna shoot you in the back or even try to get you to throw down with me."

"Because out here, there's no one to *see* it," Conrad guessed.

"Damn right. When I outdraw you and kill you, I want plenty of folks around watching, so they'll know I'm faster than you and tell all their friends they were there when Jack Trace killed the son of Frank Morgan."

"Be more impressive if you killed Frank Morgan."

"Hell, I know that. But I'll get to that. You'll do for now. What I want to know is, how'd you get to be as fast as you are? Some of it you must've inherited from your old man, but I've got a hunch you been practicin', Browning. Tryin' to impress your pa?"

"Whatever is between my father and myself is none of your business, Trace. I'd advise you to keep your questions to yourself."

"Sure, sure." Trace chuckled. "Anyway, I reckon I got my answer."

Conrad wanted to smash the smugness out of the gunman, but that could wait. Rescuing Meggie MacTavish came first, and then dealing out some long-delayed justice to Anthony Tarleton. Trace's goading was just an annoyance compared to those two things.

A potentially dangerous annoyance, to be sure.

"Answer something for me," Conrad said.

"Sure. We're pards now. We don't have any secrets from each other."

Conrad let that comment go. He asked, "Are you the one who killed Charlie MacTavish?"

Trace shrugged. "He came in talkin' big about how the boss was lyin' when he said the MacTavishes were rustlers. I told him that if he believed in what he was sayin', he wouldn't mind backin' it up with some lead. He slapped leather."

"He never had a chance against you, did he?"

"Not one damn chance in the world," Trace said.

Conrad nodded. It was just as he had thought. Even though legally the shooting was a case of self-defense because Charlie MacTavish had reached for his gun first, to Conrad it was cold-blooded murder. And sooner or later, Trace would have to answer for it.

He'd just have to wait his turn.

When they had followed the arroyo for about half a mile, Conrad reined in where the bank sloped enough so a man could climb it without much trouble.

"Let's take a look," he said as he swung down from the saddle. "We ought to be able see whoever it is following the others when he rides past this spot."

Trace dismounted as well. Both men took their hats off and climbed up the side of the arroyo. They edged their heads above the rim and peered out across the mostly flat landscape.

At first Conrad didn't see anything out of the ordinary. Then movement caught his eye. He honed in on it and saw a rider moving from right to left, paralleling the arroyo about five hundred yards away.

"There he is," Trace breathed. "Wish I had a good pair of field glasses."

"Yeah, so do I." Conrad's eyes were quite keen, but at that distance, even he couldn't make out any details about the rider.

They slid back down the bank, mounted up, and rode on, looking for some place they could get out of the arroyo. Conrad's frustration mounted as they didn't find one. They should have turned around and gone back to the place where they had entered the defile, he thought.

They rounded a bend and saw another spot where the bank had eroded and collapsed. It was a rough climb for the horses, but Conrad and Trace dismounted and were able to lead the animals up the uneven slope. As they came up onto the plain again, they quickly climbed into their saddles and set out after the man who was following Whitfield and the others.

Trace slid his Winchester from its saddle boot. Conrad glanced over at him and said, "What the hell do you think you're doing? We're not supposed to ambush him. We want to capture him so we can find out who he is and why he's been following us."

"Yeah, well, what if he puts up a fight?" Trace asked. "I ain't in the habit of lettin' anybody shoot at me without shootin' back."

"We won't let it come to that."

"How do you intend to stop it?"

Conrad thought for a second, then said, "Let's split up. We'll flank him and come in from two directions at once. He'll see that he can't get rid of both of us and surrender."

"You hope."

"Well, if it doesn't work, we'll deal with that then," Conrad snapped.

"Whatever you say," Trace agreed grudgingly. "Any bullets start to fly, though, and all bets are off."

Conrad didn't like the situation any more than Trace did, but for different reasons. Still, there was nothing he could do except go along with the gunman and hope they could capture the mysterious follower without anyone getting hurt.

He angled the buckskin to the right, while Trace went to the left. The rider was about a quarter of a mile ahead of them. The sun had just dipped below the western horizon, so the light was starting to fade. Night fell quickly out there. Conrad knew they couldn't afford to waste any time, and called on the buckskin for more speed.

The horse had already put a lot of miles behind him that day. He needed rest, just like Conrad did. But the buckskin responded gallantly, stretching out into a gallop, giving it everything he had.

Conrad glanced to the left, where Trace had split off a couple of hundred yards and also pushed his mount into a run. The two of them closed in on the follower. If the man had looked back, he would have seen them, but instead he kept his gaze fixed on the group of riders he'd been trailing all afternoon.

That was good. It was more likely they'd be able to take him alive if he didn't notice them until it was too late. Conrad urged the buckskin on.

In the fading light, he still couldn't see the man very well. As the distance between them narrowed, Conrad veered left to get behind the rider. Finally, when only twenty yards separated them, the man heard hoofbeats and he glanced back. Conrad saw him jerk in the saddle as he realized that the hunter had become the hunted.

Conrad thought the man might pull a gun and put up a fight, but instead, he leaned forward in the saddle and tried to get more speed out of his mount. Conrad looked at Trace and saw that the gunman had his Winchester out again. He waved for Trace to stay back and dug his heels into the buckskin's flanks. The horse responded, spurting ahead to match the increased pace of their quarry.

The rider kept looking back. Conrad could tell that he was getting frantic. The man's horse didn't have the same speed and stamina as the buckskin, and steadily, Conrad closed the gap.

He could see now that the man was dressed in a rough work shirt and trousers, as well as a hat with a broad, drooping brim. As far as Conrad could tell, the man wasn't wearing a gunbelt. He didn't see a rifle butt sticking up from a saddle sheath, either.

What sort of fool would come out here in the middle of nowhere unarmed? Maybe the man had a revolver in his saddlebags.

Conrad was right behind him, only a few feet away. He debated whether to tackle the man and knock him out of the saddle, or just try to grab the reins and bring the horse to a stop. That would be less dangerous. Tackling the man would risk breaking both their necks.

Before Conrad could do either one, fate took a

hand. The man's horse stumbled and went down, spilling the rider from the saddle and landing hard. Dust billowed into the air and obscured Conrad's vision for a second. He couldn't see what had happened to the man. The horse might have rolled over him and crushed him.

Conrad hauled back on the buckskin's reins. As the big, rangy horse skidded to a stop, Conrad swung down, his boots hitting the ground while the buckskin was still moving. He turned toward the fallen horse and rider and drew his gun. Between the dust and the fading light, he still couldn't see much, but he wasn't taking any chances. If the rider hadn't been knocked out by the fall, he might come up with a gun in his hand.

Conrad waited, legs slightly spread and gun in hand, for the dust to blow away. As it did so, the fallen man's form became visible. He was sprawled facedown on the ground a few yards away. Nearby, the horse struggled upright, blowing and snorting as it did so. The animal didn't appear to be badly hurt, although it might be too lame to ride for a day or two.

Something struck Conrad as odd, and as he moved forward and the dust cleared even more, he figured out what it was. The man's hat had fallen off, spilling long, dark hair around his head. It wasn't common to find a man with hair that long these days. And there was something else that didn't seem quite right.

With a shock, Conrad realized what seemed wrong to him. The fallen rider wasn't shaped like a man. Despite the rough work clothes, Conrad could tell that much. The slender waist and swelling hips belonged to a woman. That explained the long hair, too.

Conrad stalked over to the body on the ground, reached down to grasp the woman's shoulder, and rolled her onto her back. As he did, her arm came up suddenly, and he found himself staring into the barrel of a small pistol about six inches from his nose.

Even more shocking, he found himself staring into eyes that he knew were deep green, even though their color was hard to make out in the dim light.

Because those eyes belonged to Pamela Tarleton.

Chapter 15

For a long moment, Conrad was too surprised to do anything except stand there and stare at Pamela. She seemed equally surprised to see him. Her eyes were wide with shock as she looked up at him.

Finally, she said, "Conrad?"

He noticed that the pistol in her hand was cocked, and her finger was taut on the trigger. It wouldn't take much pressure to make the gun go off.

He said, "Pamela, if you don't mind, I really wish you'd point that somewhere else."

"Oh!" she cried out as if just realizing how close she had come to shooting him. She lowered the gun. She didn't object when Conrad took it from her and eased the hammer back down.

"What in blazes? Is that a *woman?*"

Jack Trace's voice reminded Conrad that the gunman had been closing in on Pamela, too. As he straightened, he glanced over his shoulder and said, "It's all right, Trace. She's not dangerous."

Trace grunted. "You could've fooled me. Looked like she had a gun stuck in your face."

Conrad holstered his Colt and then reached down to help Pamela to her feet. She took his hand. When she was standing, she asked, "What are you doing back here, Conrad? I thought you were up ahead with those other men."

"I was . . . until we realized that someone was following us." He frowned at her. "Which brings up an even better question. What are you doing out here, Pamela?" He gestured at her outfit. "Dressed like that, following us . . . I thought you were catching a train back east."

Her head gave a defiant toss that was all too familiar to him as she answered, "You *told* me to catch a train back east. I never agreed to that. As for what I'm doing here . . ." Her voice softened slightly. "I wanted to be with you, of course."

"That's madness. We're on the trail of the men who raided the MacTavish ranch and kidnapped Margaret MacTavish. This is no place for . . . for . . ."

"For a spoiled Eastern girl?" Pamela shook her head. "I told you, Conrad, I've changed. I've learned how to look after myself. And I thought . . ." She shrugged. "I thought you might need my help."

That idea was so ludicrous, Conrad's first impulse was to laugh. But that would insult her, he realized, so he suppressed the urge. Instead, he said, "I think we can handle this, Pamela. Whitfield brought half a dozen men with him, including Trace here."

"But why is Whitfield helping you?" Pamela asked. "I thought he hated the MacTavishes."

Trace spoke up, saying, "He does. But he don't like bein' blamed for something he didn't do. He wants to prove to Browning that he didn't have anything to do with kidnappin' the MacTavish girl."

"Trace is right," Conrad nodded. "So you see, Pamela, we're fine. You shouldn't have followed us."

She smiled. "It's too late to worry about that now, isn't it?"

"What do you mean?" Conrad asked with a sinking feeling.

"I mean that we're a long way from Val Verde, and night is falling. You can't very well expect me to turn around and ride back to town by myself, can you?"

Conrad knew she was right about that. Now that he was aware the person who'd been following them was Pamela, he felt responsible for her. He would have to look out for her. That meant either turning around and taking her back to Val Verde himself, abandoning the hunt for Meggie MacTavish . . .

Or taking her with them on the trail of a gang of bloodthirsty killers.

Luckily, the decision could be postponed, at least until morning. "You'll camp with us tonight," he said. "We'll figure out what to do tomorrow."

"All right. Let me get my horse."

"That horse doesn't need to be ridden after that fall. See, he's limping a little."

With a smile, Trace said, "The lady can ride with me, Browning."

Conrad felt a flash of anger at the leer on Trace's face. He snapped, "No, she'll ride with me. You lead her horse."

Trace shrugged. "Suit yourself."

Conrad swung up into the saddle, then reached down to grasp Pamela's hand and help her climb onto the buckskin's back behind him. She slipped her arms around his waist and hung on tightly as he heeled the horse into motion.

Their positions made Conrad acutely aware of how Pamela's breasts were pressed against his back. Even though there were a couple of layers of clothing between them, he couldn't help but think about the firm, warm mounds of flesh. His jaw tightened. He had too much to do to allow himself to be distracted by a woman, no matter how lovely and sensuous she was. And yet, he was still a man, too.

Whitfield, James MacTavish, and the other men had stopped, Conrad saw a few minutes later as they approached the spot Whitfield had selected for their camp. It backed up to a low, rocky bluff with a small pool of water at its base. Probably in years past, Indians had camped there regularly, but all the Indians were on reservations now, so Conrad knew they didn't have to worry about that.

"What the Sam Hill!" Whitfield exclaimed when Conrad, Pamela, and Trace rode up. "That's your lady friend from town, ain't it, Browning?"

"That's right," Conrad acknowledged. He dismounted. As he reached up and put his hands under Pamela's arms to help her, he went on, "This is Miss Tarleton."

Even in the bad light, Conrad could tell that the gunmen Whitfield had brought with him were eyeing Pamela with lust and greed in their expressions. He intended to stay very close to her that night. He didn't trust those hombres. Not where beautiful women were concerned—or any other way.

"Well, what's she doin' out here?" Whitfield wanted to know.

"I can speak for myself, you know," Pamela said. "You're Mr. Whitfield, aren't you?"

Habit prompted Whitfield to reach up and remove his hat when Pamela spoke to him. "That's right, miss," he said. "Dave Whitfield."

"Mr. Browning and I are old friends," Pamela told him. "I knew he was going to look for Miss MacTavish, so I decided to come along and see if I could help him. I hadn't counted on him joining forces with you men, but that doesn't really change things, does it?"

Whitfield looked confused, but he said, "Uh, no, I reckon it don't. Why would you think Browning would need your help?"

Pamela looked over at Conrad. "To be honest, Mr. Whitfield, I didn't think Conrad needed to be alone in this situation. I'm sure it brings up too many painful memories for him."

Conrad gritted his teeth. He wished Pamela would just quiet down.

That had never been her strong suit, though.

"Painful memories of what?" Whitfield asked.

"Of the time several months ago when his wife was kidnapped and murdered."

Whitfield looked at Conrad, who stood there with his face stony and expressionless. "Don't reckon I'd heard about that," the rancher said.

"That's because it has nothing to do with this," Conrad said. "It's in the past, over and done with."

That was a lie, of course. As long as Anthony Tarleton was alive, it wasn't finished. Not by a long shot.

But Conrad had a feeling everything was coming together. Clearly, Whitfield and his men hadn't raided the MacTavish ranch and carried off Meggie, and as far as Conrad could see, only one other group had the slightest reason to have done so.

That was Anthony Tarleton, Hogan, Loomis, and the rest of Tarleton's hired killers.

It all made sense, assuming that Tarleton had found out somehow about Conrad's connection with the MacTavishes. After the ambush at the cemetery failed and Pamela escaped, Tarleton and all the others except Vicente had left Val Verde. They could have ridden out to the MacTavish spread, wounded Hamish, and kidnapped Meggie, knowing that Conrad would likely follow them if he survived the ambush by Vicente. It was yet one more trap set by Anthony Tarleton, with Meggie as the bait this time instead of Pamela.

Ever since the theory had begun to form in Conrad's head, he had been putting it together piece by piece, and now he was convinced he was right. It explained everything—why the MacTavish ranch had been raided by someone other than Whitfield in the first place, why the kidnappers had made their trail so easy to follow, why their goal from the start seemed to be to carry off Meggie, not to wipe out the rest of the MacTavishes.

That was just one more sick, twisted way for Anthony Tarleton to punish him, to put him through hell by kidnapping a young woman who was bound to remind him of what had happened to Rebel.

"I'm sorry to hear about it, anyway," Whitfield said, breaking into Conrad's thoughts. "We may not see eye to eye on most things, Browning, but I wouldn't wish somethin' like that on my worst enemy."

Conrad nodded curtly. "I appreciate that," he said, "but right now let's concentrate on the present. We'll have to figure out what to do about Miss Tarleton."

"I'm coming with you, of course," Pamela said without hesitation.

Whitfield frowned. "That don't hardly sound safe to me. There's liable to be plenty of gunplay when we catch up to those varmints who carried off the MacTavish girl. I wouldn't want my daughter mixed up in something like that. Shoot, I didn't even leave her out at the ranch while we're gone. I told my foreman Ramsey to put her in the buckboard and take her back to town, so she can stay in the hotel until I get back."

"Perhaps you're too protective of her, Mr. Whitfield," Pamela argued. "How is she going to know how to take care of herself if something happens to you?"

Whitfield shook his head. "I don't plan on anything happenin' to me."

"Neither did my father," Pamela said with a glance toward Conrad. "But he died a few years ago, and I was left mostly on my own. I had to learn quickly that the world can be a cruel, frightening place."

Whitfield cleared his throat and shifted his feet, obviously uncertain how to respond to that. Conrad said, "We'll talk about it in the morning. There's nothing we can do tonight, anyway."

"Nothing except enjoy the lady's company," Trace drawled.

Conrad started to turn angrily toward the gunman, but he stopped himself. He wasn't engaged to Pamela anymore. He hadn't been for years. He didn't have to defend her honor any more than he would have for any other woman. Instead, he asked her, "Did you bring any supplies?"

"A few."

Whitfield said, "We've got plenty of food. Don't worry about that. You're welcome to share with us, Miss Tarleton."

"Thank you," she told him, smiling again. "It's nice to know that *someone* here is a gentleman, anyway."

Conrad ignored that. He started unsaddling the weary buckskin. One of the men had built a small fire, and the smell of coffee beginning to boil filled the twilight air. Thinking back on things that Frank had told him, Conrad knew that there had been a time—not all that long ago, really—when it would have been too dangerous to have a campfire out there. It would have attracted the attention of the Indians. With that threat removed, the only real danger that remained was from bands of Mexican bandits who crossed the border from time to time. The likelihood of running into a bunch like that was small.

As full darkness settled down over the landscape, one of the men rustled up some supper. The meal was simple—bacon, biscuits, and some canned peaches—but Pamela displayed a hearty appetite as she ate along with the men and washed the food down with strong, black coffee. She really *has* changed, Conrad thought. When he'd been engaged to her, she would have found fault with the finest restaurant. Now she ate on the trail and hunkered next to a campfire, without complaint.

When everyone had finished eating, Whitfield assigned guard shifts for the night. Conrad and James were willing to take their turn, but Whitfield split up the duties among his own men.

Conrad spread his bedroll near the bluff and told Pamela, "You take the blankets, unless you brought some of your own."

She shook her head. "I'm afraid I didn't think about that. I'm sorry. I don't want to take your bed, Conrad." She hesitated, then went on, "I suppose we could—"

He shook his head before she could continue. "No. We can't," he said flatly.

"Suit yourself," she said with a shrug. He could tell that she was a little annoyed with him. He supposed she had taken his reaction as a rejection—which, of course, it was.

He waited until she had rolled up in the blankets—with her back turned pointedly toward him—before he stretched out on the ground nearby with his saddle for a pillow. Even though it hadn't been dark long, a chill had already begun to creep into the air. It would be a cold night, and since he'd be spending it on the hard ground, Conrad didn't expect to sleep very well. Considering that his sleep was often haunted by nightmares under the best of conditions, he assumed the same thing would be true there.

The long hours spent in the saddle had taken a toll on him, though. He dropped off to sleep faster than usual. His slumber was deep and dreamless, at least as far as he remembered. The sound sleep actually wasn't what he wanted. He'd planned to doze lightly, so that he'd wake up right away in case of any trouble.

As it was, it took Pamela's frightened scream to jolt him awake, and as he came up off the ground, he was groggy at first, not knowing what was going on or what had happened.

Then he heard another soft cry and the sounds of a struggle nearby. He turned toward the bluff. The fire had burned down to embers, and the moon was only a thin sliver in the sky, casting faint illumination.

But there were millions of stars in the heavens, and they were so bright in the clear, thin, desert air that Conrad could make out the shapes wrestling on the tangled blankets where Pamela had been sleeping.

"Son of a—" Conrad bit off the curse and leaped toward the struggling figures. He reached down, his fingers brushing the coarse fabric of a man's shirt. He grabbed hold and hauled the man away from Pamela, who scooted back against the bluff and screamed again.

By then, the whole camp was in an uproar as Whitfield, his men and James MacTavish cursed and yelled questions. The man Conrad had grabbed twisted around and threw a punch at him. Conrad sensed as much as saw the blow coming and ducked under it. He slammed a fist into the man's stomach. The man's breath smelled of whiskey as it gusted into Conrad's face.

Conrad hit him again, this time a looping left that sent the man flying backward to land on the hard, sandy ground. When he'd first realized what was going on, Conrad expected the man wrestling with Pamela to turn out to be Jack Trace, but he'd been able to tell by the man's thick body that it wasn't the slender gunman. One of Whitfield's other hired killers, then. Conrad didn't care who it was. As the man tried to get up, Conrad waded in again, swinging a left and then a right that slammed home and stretched the man out.

A match flared to life. Clutching a six-gun in his other hand, Whitfield demanded, "What the hell's goin' on here?"

Pamela sat up against the bluff and leveled a shaking finger at the man Conrad had knocked down. "That . . . that man crawled into my blankets and tried to . . . to . . ."

One of the other men stirred up the fire so that the flames started dancing again. Whitfield dropped the match he'd been holding and strode forward to dig his booted toe in the ribs of the man on the ground.

"Is that true, Bourland?" the rancher demanded. "Did you try to molest Miss Tarleton?"

The man sat up and shook his head in an obvious attempt to clear away the cobwebs left behind by the beating Conrad had handed him. "Hell, no," he rasped after a moment.

"I found you tangled up in her blankets," Conrad said.

"Well, yeah, but she invited me to crawl in with her and mess with her."

"That's a lie!" Pamela cried. "I'd never do such a thing."

Conrad glanced at her. She looked horrified. It was certainly true that the bearded, heavy-featured gunman called Bourland wasn't the type of man you'd expect Pamela Tarleton to even talk to, let alone anything more intimate. She'd been angry with him when she turned in, though, Conrad reminded himself.

No. It was impossible. Pamela had said that Bourland attacked her, and Conrad believed her.

"I think you should give this man his time, Whitfield," he said. "He can head back to Val Verde in the morning, or go wherever else he wants to."

Whitfield rubbed his jaw. "Yeah. Hate to lose a gun when we don't know for sure what we're ridin' into, but I can't abide a man who mistreats a woman."

Bourland came to his feet. "I'm tellin' you, I only did what that . . . that bitch asked me to do!"

Pamela gasped.

Whitfield's eyes narrowed. "I ain't waitin' until mornin'," he said. "Gather up your gear and get outta here now, mister. You ain't welcome in this camp."

Bourland glared around at all of them, but he didn't find any sympathy in any of their faces, not even Jack Trace's. Conrad figured that much, at least, was an act. Trace didn't care what happened to Pamela. If he'd believed he could get away with it, he'd have been crawling into her blankets himself.

Bourland turned and took a step toward Pamela. "Tell 'em!" he roared. "Tell 'em it was your idea!"

She pressed the back of her hand to her mouth, muffling the scream that welled up her throat.

Conrad stepped forward and grabbed Bourland's shoulder. He jerked the man around, saying, "Stay away from her, you—"

He didn't finish what he was going to say. Bourland jerked free, stepped back, and reached for the gun on his hip, his hand stabbing toward the Colt.

Chapter 16

Conrad reacted instinctively. He hadn't been a gun-fighter for very long, but long enough to learn that when a man slapped leather intending to kill him, he had only shaved instants of time to react.

His Colt leaped into his hand and roared just as Bourland's gun cleared the holster and started to pivot up toward him.

The bullet, aimed by instinct as well, smashed into Bourland's chest and drove him back a step. He collapsed against the bluff, falling next to Pamela, who cried out again and cringed away from him.

Bourland struggled to get up. He hadn't dropped his gun. As he started to raise it again, Conrad kicked it out of his hand and sent the weapon spinning off into the darkness. Bourland gasped, "Damn you! I'm tellin' . . . the truth . . . she . . ."

He made a gagging sound as blood welled blackly from his mouth. His head fell back against the bluff. His shoulders slumped, and his arms hung limp at his sides.

"Well, hell!" Whitfield rasped into the silence that followed.

Tension gripped the camp. Conrad glanced around, saw that Trace and the other four gunmen had him and Pamela and James surrounded. Bourland had been their friend, or at least, they had ridden together. If they decided to avenge him, Conrad wouldn't have much of a chance. Not only that, but Pamela and James would be in danger as well if lead started flying around.

"I didn't want to kill him, Whitfield," Conrad said. "He didn't give me much choice."

The rancher sighed heavily. "No, I reckon not." He looked at Conrad with narrowed eyes. "That's several times you've shown how slick on the draw you are, Browning. I thought you was supposed to be just some rich Eastern dude."

Trace said, "There's more to Browning than that, boss. He really is his father's son, I reckon, and Frank Morgan's a killer."

Whitfield jerked his head toward Bourland's body. "So's Browning." He took a deep breath and then looked around at his men. "All right. Bourland brought this on himself, the damned fool. It's over. Somebody wrap him up in a blanket, and come mornin', we'll bury him."

One of the men gestured toward Conrad. "You're gonna let this son of a bitch get away with killin' him, boss?"

"I told you, Bourland called the tune. You boys know good and well that when you reach for a gun, there's always a chance the other feller'll be faster." Whitfield turned to Pamela. "Are you all right, miss?"

"I . . . I suppose I am." She started to get up. Conrad used his left hand to take her arm and help her. His right hand still gripped the Colt. Pamela brushed herself off and went on, "I'm sorry about what happened. I . . . I hope I didn't do anything to give that man the wrong idea."

"No, ma'am, I'm sure you didn't. We'll get him away from you, and you can try to get back to sleep."

A couple of the men wrapped Bourland's body in a blanket, as Whitfield had instructed, and carried him to the other side of the camp, going far enough so that they were out of the light of the fire. Since the potential for more gunplay seemed to have faded, Conrad holstered his Colt and knelt next to Pamela as she stretched out again.

"I'm sorry you had to go through that," he told her. "I should have been keeping a better eye on you."

"You're *not* my protector, Conrad. Don't get me wrong, I appreciate what you did, but things aren't like they used to be between us." She paused. "You've made it clear that you don't want them to be that way again."

Conrad grimaced in the darkness. Why couldn't she see that he *couldn't* go back? Too much time had passed. Too many tragedies had taken place. They weren't the same people they had been when he came to New Mexico Territory to build that railroad spur.

And yet . . . wouldn't it be nice to have someone again? Someone with whom he could give and take some comfort? Someone to help stave off the inevitable darkness that was life . . . ?

Conrad stiffened as he caught those thoughts going through his brain. The fact that he had allowed himself to be tempted, even for a second, sickened him. That was the height of disloyalty to his dead wife.

Dead wife, a mocking voice in the back of his head reminded him. Rebel was dead, and nothing would ever change that. Unless he was going to blow his own brains out, he had to go on. He had to find some path so that he could make his way through the rest of his own life. He had dedicated himself to avenging Rebel's murder, but someday—someday soon, he hoped—that task would be accomplished.

What then? Conrad asked himself. What then?

As usual, he had no answers. Adrift in his thoughts, he finally dozed again, only a few feet from the woman he had once loved.

By morning, things weren't any clearer in Conrad's mind, at least as far as his feelings for Pamela Tarleton were concerned. He had come to a decision about one matter, though.

"You're coming with us," he told her as they sat by the fire and drank coffee.

Pamela's eyebrows arched in surprise. "I thought you were determined to send me back to Val Verde, and from there back east."

"I would if there was a way to do it that wouldn't put you in danger. But we're too far away to send you back alone, and I can't turn back until we've rescued Meggie MacTavish."

He didn't mention the idea of sending her back with one of Whitfield's men. All of them might be needed to deal with Meggie's kidnappers. Besides, he wouldn't trust any of them alone with her. He knew that James wouldn't abandon the pursuit until they found Meggie.

Pamela smiled faintly. "Taking me along is going to be dangerous, too, you know."

"Of course it is," Conrad said, a little annoyed with her for stating the obvious. "But at least this way, I can keep an eye on you and try to see to it that you stay out of trouble."

"Be still my heart," she gibed.

Conrad drained the last of his coffee and stood up. He went to check on the horses. As he did so, the two men who had carried Bourland's body a short distance from camp and dug a grave for it came back, their grim chore completed.

A short time later, everyone was ready to ride. They had an extra horse now, which would come in handy when they found Meggie and took her away from the men who'd kidnapped her. She wouldn't have to ride double with one of her rescuers, since Pamela's horse was no longer limping.

Conrad knew the possibility still existed that Meggie was already dead. He wasn't going to give up hope, though, until he saw her body for himself.

And that was an unusual situation for him these days, he realized. Clinging to even a shred of hope in times of trouble was something he hadn't done very often since Rebel died.

The nine of them pushed on toward the Hatchet Mountains as the sun rose higher in the sky. The peaks were gray and purple in the distance where they thrust up from the scrub-covered plains. Conrad didn't know how rugged the mountains were since he had never been there before. He was willing to bet that they held plenty of hiding places.

Places where Anthony Tarleton and his hired killers could lie in ambush and wait for him to follow them, if his theory was right, Conrad thought.

The day quickly grew hotter as the sun climbed higher. He looked over at Pamela and saw the weariness and strain on her face. She had ridden for hours the day before as she followed them, and Conrad knew she was probably very sore and tired. Her jawline was firm and determined, though. She had never been a woman who gave up easily when she wanted something, he recalled.

"You still have that gun you pointed at me yesterday?" he asked her.

"Of course I do. I'm not giving it up, either."

"I wouldn't think of asking you to. Can you handle a rifle? We have an extra Winchester now."

He didn't add that the rifle had belonged to Bourland. Pamela didn't need him to remind her of the dead man.

She shrugged in answer to his question. "I've never fired a rifle, but how hard can it be? I know which end the bullet comes out of."

He didn't bother explaining that a Winchester was pretty heavy, especially for someone who wasn't accustomed to using one. With any luck, Pamela wouldn't ever find out, because she'd never need to use one of the weapons.

They drew steadily closer to the mountains. The Hatchets didn't rise gradually. They thrust up sharply from the flats, with only a few small foothills. Conrad kept his eye on them, hoping to see a flash of reflected sunlight off metal. Something to tell them that they were on the right trail other than the tracks they'd been following for the past two days. The thought that they might be trailing somebody who had nothing to do with Meggie's kidnapping worried him. However, that was unlikely, especially if his theory about Anthony Tarleton was correct. But it couldn't be ruled out.

Around mid-morning, Dave Whitfield said to Conrad, "Somethin's started to worry me . . . Once those fellas we're followin' get into the mountains, they'll be able to look back out here and see us on these flats."

Conrad nodded. "That's true. But if we're right

about them leaving such a clear trail on purpose, they'll expect to see someone following them."

Whitfield grimaced and drew the back of his hand across his mouth. "You intend to ride right into whatever trap they're settin' for us, don't you, Browning?"

"You know of a better way to find out what they really want?"

Whitfield inclined his head toward Pamela, who had fallen back a short distance. "Gonna be mighty dangerous for your lady friend."

"She chose to come after us," Conrad said, keeping his voice deliberately cool. He didn't want Whitfield or any of the others to see just how worried he really was about Pamela's safety. "And she's not my lady friend."

"Maybe not *now,*" Whitfield said with a grin. "I ain't so sure about what she's got in mind for the future, though."

"It doesn't matter—" Conrad began.

"The hell it don't. Once a gal makes up her mind about somethin', there ain't a whole hell of a lot us menfolks can do about it. I was married for nigh on to twenty-five years before my wife passed on, Lord rest her soul, and I learned that much."

A faint smile tugged at Conrad's mouth. He supposed that Whitfield had a point. He and Rebel had been married for only a few years, but already in that time, Conrad had learned that he was wasting his time trying to change her mind about anything she considered important. Why, he remembered once when she—

He stopped short in his thoughts as he realized he was about to chuckle at the memory of something Rebel had done. It didn't matter what it was, or how amusing it had been at the time, she was gone and he had no right to be thinking of her with anything except grief and utter devastation.

The problem was, grief and utter devastation got mighty weary after a while. Surely, it wouldn't hurt anything to remember some of the good times and smile a little at the memories.

Before Conrad had a chance to ponder on that, Jack Trace urged his horse alongside Whitfield's and said, "Smoke up yonder, boss."

"I see it," Whitfield said.

So did Conrad. It was only a thin thread of bluish-gray rising into the sky from somewhere not far into the mountains. It came from a campfire or possibly a chimney, Conrad thought. Chances were, it also marked the destination of the men they had been following.

"If we keep goin', we'll likely be ridin' right into their gunsights," Trace warned. "You want to get killed over some squatter gal, Dave?"

Trace's voice was loud enough for James to hear the callous description of his sister. He started to urge his horse forward, anger on his face, but Conrad motioned him back. With obvious reluctance and simmering resentment, James complied.

Whitfield glared at the gunman. "Damn it, I told Browning I'd help him find the MacTavish girl, to prove I didn't have anything to do with what happened. We ain't found her yet." His eyes narrowed as he stared at Trace. "But if you want to turn around and go back, Jack, I ain't gonna stop you. Same goes for the rest of the boys."

Trace didn't answer for a couple of seconds, then he shrugged and said, "You're payin' our wages. I reckon you're still callin' the tune."

Whitfield jerked his head in a nod. "Damn right I am. Come on."

As the group rode on, Pamela said, "Do you think they're setting a trap for us, Conrad?"

"It's likely," he said. "That's why you're not going with us."

"What?" she asked in surprise. "I've come this far. You can't mean to send me back now."

He shook his head. "No, that's not practical, or I would. But as soon as we get to the mountains, we're going to find a safe place for you to stay while the rest of us check out that smoke."

"You're going to leave me by myself?" She sounded like the prospect frightened her.

"You'll have your pistol," he told her, "and we'll leave you that rifle and plenty of supplies. If anything happens and . . . we don't come back, you'll be able to reach Val Verde in a couple of days. Just take note of where the sun comes up and ride toward it. Once you hit the railroad, you can follow it straight to the settlement."

"By myself?" Her voice shook a little.

He resisted the impulse to tell her that she should have thought of that before she set off after him. Instead, he said as reassuringly as he could, "You'll be fine."

"If you say so," she said. She didn't sound like she believed it for a second.

The mountains took on a greenish tinge due to the scrub pines and clumps of hardy grass on the slopes. The Hatchets were low enough so that none of the peaks were above the treeline. They weren't the same sort of craggy, gray mountains that were found farther north in the Rockies. They still had a bleak look about them, however, despite the vegetation. They might have almost been mountains on the moon, Conrad mused. He felt that far from everything he had ever known.

They reached the mountains in the early afternoon. The smoke was still visible, rising from a point above them. Conrad spotted a cluster of pines at the base of a hill and pointed them out.

"There might be a spring over there," he said. "We can water the horses and leave Miss Tarleton there if there is."

"Sounds like a good idea," Whitfield agreed with a nod. "Let's check it out."

What they found was a little oasis in the middle of this dry, rugged landscape. A spring bubbled out of some rocks, forming a pool about ten feet across. Several pines ringed it, and the grass was thicker and greener on its banks than anywhere Conrad had seen since leaving Val Verde.

"This will be a good place for you," he told Pamela as the riders dismounted and began to water their horses.

"I don't suppose it would do any good to say that I'd rather go with you."

He shook his head. "Not a bit. You've got food, water, and shelter here. If none of us have come back to get you by morning, you head for Val Verde, you hear me?"

"I'm going to have to spend the night here by myself?"

"Possibly. I don't know yet, because I don't know what we'll find further up the mountain."

Pamela sighed. "All right. I know you're just doing what you think is best, Conrad. I hope you're right."

"So do I," he said, and meant it.

After all the horses had been watered and had rested for a while, Whitfield said, "I reckon we might as well mount up and get on up the mountain. Find out what's waitin' for us."

"Trouble," Trace said. "That's what's waitin' for us."

Whitfield grunted. "More'n likely." He grabbed the saddlehorn, put his foot in the stirrup, and swung up. The rest of the men followed suit.

Whitfield gestured toward the smoke and said to Conrad, "This is your party, Browning. Why don't you and MacTavish lead the way?"

Conrad knew what the rancher meant. If there was an ambush waiting up there, Whitfield intended for him and James to take the first bullets.

He was willing to run that risk. He glanced back at Pamela, who stood beside the pool looking forlorn, and then heeled his horse into motion. James was right behind him.

A couple of narrow valleys twisted through the hills at the base of the mountains, rising steadily at the same time. The riders followed them and came out on one of the lower shoulders of the tallest mountain in the small chain.

"That's Big Hatchet Mountain," Whitfield said with a nod toward the peak. "I hunted bighorn sheep on it once, but that was more'n ten years ago. The Apaches did some huntin' on that trip, too. I damn near lost my hair. I, for one, ain't sorry to see them red savages put on reservations."

"That's because you weren't forced off your land like they were," Conrad pointed out.

"Their land? You're sayin' this was their land?" Whitfield snorted and shook his head. "Only because they stole it from some other bunch o' red savages who lived here before them, and *that* bunch stole it from whoever had it before them. I reckon you got to go all the way back to the

Garden of Eden to find some land that wasn't stole from somebody else at one time or another."

What Whitfield said made sense, Conrad supposed. He didn't really care at the moment, though. His only concern was locating Margaret MacTavish and finding out if he was right about the identities of the men who had taken her from her home.

When they were within a few hundred yards of the place where the smoke appeared to originate, Conrad said, "We'll dismount and go ahead on foot from here."

Whitfield and his men complied, although Trace grumbled a little about having to walk. Conrad understood. Even though these men were hired guns rather than cowboys, they shared the common rangeland belief that an hombre shouldn't walk anywhere he can ride.

A ridge jutted up ahead of them, and as they came closer, it was obvious that the smoke came from the other side of it. Conrad motioned for the other men to stop. He said quietly, "The rest of you stay here. James and I will go up to the top of the ridge and take a look."

"Hell with that," Whitfield said. "I'm comin' with you."

"So am I," Trace added.

Conrad thought about arguing with them, then decided that it wasn't worth the trouble. Both Whitfield and Trace had much more experience on the frontier than he did. They wouldn't give away their presence.

Anyway, if he was right, the kidnappers were already waiting for them.

The other four men stayed where they were and held the horses while Conrad, James, Whitfield, and Trace approached the crest of the ridge on foot, as quietly as possible. A few stunted bushes grew on top of the ridge. The men used them for cover as they took off their hats and edged up far enough to peer over the crest.

They looked down the far side of the slope for a long moment, then Whitfield breathed, "Well, what do you know about that!"

Chapter 17

The brushy ridge dropped steeply into a circular depression about five hundred yards across. The ground at the bottom of it was fairly flat and grassy. Stands of stubby pines grew here and there, and other areas were choked by briars, cactus, and scrubby mesquite trees.

It wasn't a very pretty place, but at one time somebody had thought it would make a decent place to live. A large log cabin that looked at least twenty years old sat in a clearing in the pines. The smoke Conrad and the other men had been following rose from a stone chimney at one end of the structure.

A pole corral with a number of horses in it lay behind the cabin. Conrad didn't see anyone moving around.

"They've got her in there, the bastards," James said through gritted teeth. "I know it."

"More'n likely you're right, boy," Whitfield agreed, keeping his rumbling voice as quiet as he could. "I don't see a good way of gettin' in there. I reckon we could lay siege to the place, but who knows how long it'd take to get 'em out that way."

"Too long," Conrad said. "If they have Meggie, they could threaten to kill her if we didn't let them go."

He frowned as he studied the terrain. After a

moment, he went on, "It looks to me like a man could get pretty close to the cabin and still stay in the trees. If he could work his way around behind the cabin, then climb on the roof and throw a blanket over that chimney . . ."

"Smoke 'em out, eh?" Whitfield nodded. "Might work. Fella who tried it would be runnin' a mighty big risk of bein' shot before he ever got there, though."

"I'll do it," James said without hesitation.

Conrad shook his head. "That will be my job. And we'll wait until dusk. That way it'll be harder for their guards to see."

"Dusk is hours away," James argued. "We don't know what's goin' on in there. They could be doin' . . . anything . . . to Meggie."

Trace laughed. "Don't worry about that, MacTavish. Anything they were gonna do to your sister, they've already done . . . probably more than once."

James's face reddened angrily. Whitfield snapped, "Damn it, Jack, there ain't no call to talk like that."

"Just tellin' the truth," Trace said with a shrug.

"Let it go, James," Conrad said. "I know that's easier said than done—"

"Damn right it is," James said. "What if that was your sister in there, Browning?"

Conrad didn't have a sister—at least, not that he knew of for sure, although Frank had dropped hints that there was a girl back in Texas who might be his half-sister—but he had gone through the ordeal of Rebel being kidnapped. He said, "I know how you feel. It'll still be better to wait until the light starts to go."

"Yeah, you're right," Whitfield said. "Why don't we leave a man here to keep an eye on the cabin, and the rest of us can go back to where we left the others?"

That seemed like a reasonable suggestion to Conrad, as long as it wasn't James MacTavish they left behind. He didn't trust the young man not to do something foolish. Trace solved that problem by saying, "I'll stay, boss."

"All right. You let us know if anything changes down there."

Trace nodded. "I will."

Conrad felt worry stir uneasily inside him. He didn't trust Trace, but as far as he could see, the gunman had no reason to betray them now.

He moved back down the ridge with Whitfield and James. Two things filled his mind—concern for Meggie MacTavish, and the knowledge that he might soon be face to face with the man truly responsible for Rebel's death.

When they rejoined the other men, Whitfield explained the situation to them. They nodded, taking the news expressionlessly. They were professional fighting men, so the prospect of one more battle didn't faze any of them. They didn't have any emotional ties to Meggie. This was just another job to them.

Conrad and Whitfield hunkered on their heels to work out the rest of the plan. Everyone except Conrad would take up positions on top of the ridge so that they would have good shots at the cabin in the depression. Conrad said, "Chances are, when the smoke forces them out, one of the men will have Meggie and will try to use her as a hostage. Since I'll be the closest, I'll take him. I'll jump him from the top of the cabin and get her away from him. As soon as I've done that, you open up on the rest of them."

"Gun 'em down, just like that?"

"They tried to kill Hamish MacTavish. They may have succeeded, for all we know. And they kidnapped an innocent young woman. I'd say they deserve whatever happens to them."

Whitfield shrugged. "Don't reckon I can argue with that. One thing worries me, though. We figured they planned on bushwhackin' us. How come they didn't? How come they're just sittin' down there like they're waitin' for us to come callin'?"

Those questions nagged at Conrad, too, but he didn't have any answers for them. "I don't know," he said. "Maybe we'll find out once we've taken the girl away from them."

"*If* she's down there," Whitfield said, voicing another of Conrad's worries.

"She's there," he said. "Where else can she be?"

Where else, indeed.

Conrad knew from experience how difficult waiting could be. That afternoon was a good example. It seemed to drag by as they waited for the sun to dip below Big Hatchet Mountain. Conrad went up the ridge a couple of times to check with Trace and see if there had been any activity around the cabin. Each time the gunman shook his head and said, "Nobody's as much as even poked a head out. Are you sure they're down there, Browning?"

"They have to be," Conrad said. "Their horses are there."

Trace shrugged. "I reckon."

Late in the afternoon, James MacTavish approached Whitfield and said, "You've got to give me my gun back now. You can't expect me not to help rescue my own sister."

"You're convinced that I didn't have anything to do with her bein' carried off?" the rancher demanded.

"Yeah. I don't think even you would've gone to this much trouble to fool me."

Whitfield snorted. "Damn right I wouldn't. I got better things to do . . . like keepin' my beef from bein' widelooped by a bunch of no-good squatters."

James's anger flared up again. "Haven't *you* figured out by now that we're not rustlers?"

"Then what happened to that stock of mine that's disappeared?"

Conrad spoke up, saying, "Any number of things could have happened. Mexican bandits could have come across the border and stolen them, like I told you before." He moved his head in a barely perceptible nod toward the hired gun-wolves who waited nearby. "Or maybe you've got some men on your payroll who are working more for themselves than they are for you."

Whitfield glowered at him. "That's a mighty sorry accusation to be makin', considerin' that you're gonna be fightin' side by side with those boys before too much longer."

"One thing doesn't rule out the other," Conrad said.

"No, I reckon not," Whitfield admitted. His mouth worked as he thought, which made his heavy jaw shift from side to side. "I suppose it ain't impossible . . ."

"But it doesn't have anything to do with the job that's facing us now," Conrad went on. "When we get back to Val Verde, you really ought to sit down with Hamish MacTavish and hash out the problems the two of you have with each other. You'd be better off in the long run if you were friends, rather than enemies."

"How would you know? You don't strike me as a man who has many friends, mister."

That was true, Conrad thought. Phillip Bearpaw might qualify, but there was no telling when, or even if, he would ever see the Paiute Indian again. He and Frank Morgan were friends now, over and above the blood tie between them, but Frank was a man who went his own way. Conrad had inherited that same trait. Even in his younger days, he had never opened up and let anyone get that close to him. He had always been something of a loner . . .

Until he met Rebel. Things had changed then.

And with her death, they had changed again. He might spend time with families like the MacTavishes, might ride for a while with men such as Devil Dave Whitfield . . . but in the end, if he lived, he would move on by himself. That was the way he wanted it. A solitary man.

A loner, now and forever.

The sun finally made its long, slow way down the western sky and slid behind the mountains. As shadows gathered, the men started toward the top of the ridge, taking their horses along with them this time. When they left, they might have trouble on their back trail, so there wouldn't be any time to waste.

James had his long-barreled Remington revolver back, along with his Winchester. Although an air of tension still existed between him and Whitfield, Conrad believed that the two of them had called a truce. He hoped it would last once they got back to Val Verde—assuming, of course, that they made it back to the settlement safely.

He stole ahead of the others, since he'd have to get in position first. He had a rolled-up blanket tucked under his left arm. When he got on top of the cabin, he would use it to block the chimney and cause the smoke to back up into the structure.

As he approached the spot where they had left Trace earlier in the afternoon, he called the gun man's name softly. It was never a good idea to risk spooking a man who made his living with a gun.

Trace didn't respond. Conrad called his name again. Still nothing. Conrad stiffened with alarm for a second, then drew his gun and went on to the top of the ridge.

Trace was nowhere in sight.

Conrad bit back a curse. He had no idea where Trace could have gone. There hadn't been any shots, so it was unlikely that the kidnappers had stumbled on him. Of course, it was possible they might have taken him prisoner without having to resort to gunplay, Conrad supposed.

Regardless of what had happened, he didn't have time to search for Trace right then. He had to get down there and put the plan he'd worked out with Whitfield into action.

Carrying the blanket, he slipped over the crest and started down the slope, half-crawling and half-sliding. He used the brush for cover. If anyone was watching from inside the cabin, they might be able to catch a glimpse of him, but in the fading light, a watcher might not be able to distinguish him from an animal.

When he reached the bottom of the ridge, he stayed in the brush and began working his way around the circular depression. Briars and thorns clawed at him, but he ignored the discomfort and kept his attention on the cabin. He wondered if anyone was even in there, smoke had been rising from the chimney all day, so someone had to be inside feeding the fire.

When he was behind the cabin, he crawled out of the brush, came up in a crouch, and darted behind the nearest tree. Moving from tree to tree, he approached the building. The shadows were thicker since the sun was setting.

Conrad paused behind a tree about five feet from the rear wall of the cabin. One of its branches stuck out far enough that he could climb onto it and drop down onto the roof. As a boy, he had never been one for climbing trees—one just didn't do such things in Boston—but he thought that he could manage.

Climbing the tree proved to be harder than he expected, but he managed to reach the limb he wanted. Carefully, with his legs wrapped around the branch, he pulled himself along it until he could slide off. When he hung by his hands, his boots touched the rough wooden shingles on the roof. He let go. It seemed likely to him that whoever was inside didn't even know he was up there. The plan was working perfectly so far.

As quietly as possible, he moved over to the chimney and draped the blanket over the flue. He held it in place and waited to see what would happen.

He didn't have to wait very long. Someone began to cough heavily in the cabin below him. From the sound of the coughing, it was only one man. That didn't make any sense. There were a dozen horses in the corral, and Margaret MacTavish should have been inside the cabin, too.

Conrad suddenly had a bad feeling.

That feeling got worse when the cabin door slammed open and one man stumbled out, holding a bandanna over his mouth and nose as he coughed. He pulled his gun from its holster, aimed at the sky, and fired three fast shots. That had to be a signal.

But a signal for what?

"Damn it!" Conrad breathed as guns began to roar up on the ridge. Those shots weren't being directed at the cabin. They probably weren't even being fired by James MacTavish, Dave Whitfield, and Whitfield's men.

The ambush they had been waiting for was finally there.

He palmed out his Colt, thinking that the man who had just given the signal would be turning the gun toward him next. Instead, the man dashed into the trees. The move took Conrad so much by surprise that he didn't fire a shot.

Whatever happened next, Conrad didn't want to be stuck up there on the roof. He would be a sitting duck if anyone decided to line their sights on him. He holstered his gun, then hurried to the rear of the cabin, where he sat down, slid off the edge, hung by his hands for a second, and dropped the rest of the way to the ground.

The gunfire was still going on atop the ridge, but the shots seemed to be dying away. That couldn't be good, Conrad thought. He drew his Colt again and hurried into the trees. Maybe he could circle around and get back up there to see what was going on without the bushwhackers spotting him.

Making his way up the slope wasn't easy. It was steep and thick brush covered most of it. He had climbed only a few yards when the shooting stopped, leaving an eerie silence hanging over the depression along with the thickening shadows of approaching night.

Then a man's voice called, "Browning! Browning, you hear me, you son of a bitch?"

Conrad's breath hissed between his teeth as he recognized the voice. *Trace!* The son of a bitch had somehow double-crossed them after all. Conrad had been right not to trust him.

But that knowledge came a little bit late, he thought bitterly.

"I know you're down there somewhere," Trace went on. "Come on out in the open, in front of the cabin. You've got my word that you won't be hurt if you do!"

Conrad wondered why Trace thought such a promise would mean anything to him. He stayed where he was in the brush and didn't move. His brain worked furiously, trying to figure out some way he could get back to his horse and return to the spot where they'd left Pamela before any of the others could get to her.

It was probably too late for James MacTavish and Whitfield. Chances were, they'd been killed in the ambush. That thought put a bitter, sour taste in Conrad's mouth.

"I know you hear me, Browning! But just in case you ain't payin' attention . . ."

A woman screamed.

Conrad didn't necessarily hear pain in her voice, but she sounded utterly terrified. He wasn't sure if the voice belonged to Pamela or to Meggie MacTavish, but then a second later, the scream stopped and she cried, "Conrad! Oh, God, help me, Conrad! You have to do what they say!"

The world spun crazily around Conrad. *Again. Again. Again.* The word beat like a madman's drum in his head. He didn't love Pamela anymore, but he did care about her, and she was in deadly danger because of him. Sure, it had been her own choice to follow him, but if she hadn't known him in the first place, she never would have experienced so much tragedy in her life, never would have found her life threatened that way. The same was true of Meggie MacTavish.

Was this his fate? To bring death and suffering to every young woman who crossed his path?

"In front of the cabin, Browning! Now!"

Conrad took a deep breath and shouted toward the top of the ridge, "All right! Just hold on!"

A fusillade of shots didn't greet his response, so he figured that maybe they didn't plan to kill him off hand. Anthony Tarleton had more in mind than simply killing him. That lunatic would want to torture him some more first.

Conrad moved through the brush and broke out into the open. He walked toward the cabin. The sky above Big Hatchet Mountain still held a faint rosy hue, the last afterglow of the vanished sun, but there most of the light was gone.

Conrad saw two burning brands flare into life. The men who came down from the ridge needed torches to light their way. He stood in front of the cabin, his arms at his sides, the Colt still gripped in his right hand, and watched as the torchbearers descended the slope. When the two men reached the bottom, they separated so that the rest of the group could move between them and walk toward the cabin. Conrad saw Jack Trace and another man leading the way. He recognized the second man from Pamela's description.

He was looking at Anthony Tarleton, the man responsible for Rebel's death, and for all the other deaths that had followed in the past few months.

Tarleton was a big man, as Pamela had said, and

he wore a smug smile on his broad, florid face. He carried a rifle and wore the sort of clothes a rich man might wear on a hunting trip.

Conrad could see between Trace and Tarleton and was startled to spot Dave Whitfield and James MacTavish. He had figured that both men were dead. Whitfield clutched a bloody left arm but seemed to be all right otherwise.

James didn't appear to have any fresh wounds at all. He had his arm around a redheaded young woman who huddled against him as they made their way along slowly. *Meggie,* Conrad thought as he recognized her and relief went through him. They were still in a very dangerous spot, but he was glad to see that Meggie was alive and apparently unharmed.

Several men he hadn't seen before followed the prisoners with drawn guns. Covered and outnumbered as they were, Whitfield and James couldn't do anything except cooperate. Judging by the amount of shooting that had gone on a few minutes earlier, Conrad had a strong hunch that the rest of Whitfield's men were dead, but for some reason Tarleton had spared the rancher and the young brother and sister.

That left only one person unaccounted for. Conrad's eyes searched desperately for her. He knew she was alive because he had heard her cry out to him moments earlier.

The garish, flickering light from the torches

washed over the area in front of the cabin as the group came to a stop. Anthony Tarleton chuckled as he looked at Conrad.

"Conrad Browning," he said. "I've wanted to meet you for a long time, boy."

"No longer than I've wanted to meet you," Conrad grated. He fought down the impulse to jerk his gun up and put a bullet between Tarleton's eyes. He knew he was fast enough to do it before any of the others could stop him, even Jack Trace. At least he could die knowing that he had sent Rebel's murderer to Hell.

But that would leave Pamela at the mercy of Trace and the other killers, and he couldn't do that. He went on, "Where is she? Where's Pamela?"

"My dear niece?" Tarleton asked with a leer. He turned his head. "Come here, Pamela. Browning wants to see you for himself, to make sure you're all right."

The group of gunmen watching the prisoners parted. Pamela stepped through the gap and walked forward. Relief washed through Conrad again as he saw that she appeared to be all right. They hadn't hurt her when they captured her.

But then he realized that something was wrong, after all. Something that sent his heart plummeting and ripped the hide off what was left of his soul. Pamela was smiling as she asked, "Why wouldn't I be all right, Uncle Anthony?"

Then she looked at Conrad—and *laughed.*

Chapter 18

"Oh, Conrad," Pamela said. "You were too easy, my dear. Simply too easy. You believed everything I told you, you poor fool."

Conrad felt like the world was crashing down around him. His head spun, and reality seemed to be slipping away from him. He couldn't be seeing and hearing these things, he told himself. He just couldn't. The pain was too unbearable.

But it was real, he told himself. Pamela had betrayed him. Worse than that, actually, he thought. She had never been on his side. The whole thing had been a lie.

"Your uncle never held you prisoner, did he?" he choked out.

That question brought a harsh laugh from Anthony Tarleton. "Held her prisoner? The whole thing was her idea, you stupid son of a bitch!"

Tarleton was right about one thing. He was stupid.

Trace's revolver came up. "Drop the gun, Browning. I don't want you gettin' any crazy ideas." He grinned. "I'm gonna enjoy what these two have in mind for you, so I don't want to have to kill you too soon."

For a couple of heartbeats Conrad debated with himself. Forcing them to put him out of his misery quickly held some appeal. He had suffered enough, and now the already shaky underpinnings of his heart and soul had been yanked out.

But Frank Morgan had never quit just because the odds were against him. Although Frank didn't know it, Conrad had looked into his father's past. He knew that Frank had lost not only Vivian Browning, but also a woman called Dixie who had been his wife for a time years later. Following Dixie's death, Frank had descended into a morass of grief, self-doubt, and whiskey, only to pull himself out of it and become stronger than ever. (There just wasn't any back-up in him.)

Conrad had never pretended to be the man his father was. But at that moment, he knew Frank wouldn't lose hope in a similar situation. As long as The Drifter drew breath, the will to fight against even overwhelming odds would be in him.

His son . . . Kid Morgan . . . could do no less.

So it was, at that moment, that Conrad Browning died for all time.

Circumstances might force him to wear the clothes or even to use the name. But it would be a pose, nothing more. Back in San Francisco, Claudius Turnbuckle had referred to Kid Morgan as a masquerade. Now it was just the opposite. Conrad Browning was the masquerade. Kid Morgan was the truth.

The Kid bent over, placed the gun on the ground, stepped back and lifted his hands.

Anthony Tarleton jerked the rifle toward the prisoners and ordered, "Take them in the cabin." He sneered at The Kid. "All of them."

A couple of Tarleton's gunmen came forward to grab The Kid's arms and shove him toward the cabin. One of them was the albino, Loomis. He gave Conrad an ugly grin.

The rest of the hired killers, including Trace and Hogan, herded James, Meggie, and Whitfield ahead of them. Everyone went into the cabin.

Smoke still clogged the air inside, although some of it had drifted out through the open door. "Somebody get that damned blanket off the chimney!" Tarleton said. He held his rifle in one hand and waved the other in front of his face to clear away some of the smoke. One of the men went back outside.

A minute later, The Kid heard the man's boots thumping on the roof. The smoke stopped coiling out of the fireplace and started going up the chimney.

Inside, the cabin was divided into two rooms. Tarleton nodded toward the open door between them and said, "Take the others back there and tie them up. You can leave Browning in here."

Tarleton, Hogan, and Trace kept their guns on The Kid while the rest went into the other room—except for Pamela, who stood to one side with that maddening smile on her face as she looked at The

Kid. When the five of them were alone, Pamela said, "I'll bet you're just dying to hear all about it, aren't you, Conrad?"

The Kid kept his face as impassive as he could and said, "You're going to tell me anyway, aren't you?"

"Oh, yes. It's too delicious not to."

He made a little gesture with his hand as if being generous. "Then go ahead."

His nonchalant attitude irritated her, as he intended. He saw a flash of it in her eyes and in the tightening of her lips. She said, "I've been planning this for years, Conrad, ever since you abandoned me for that little frontier girl of yours and caused my father's death."

"I had nothing to do with your father's death."

"He wouldn't have been in jail and been murdered if not for you and your father," Pamela snapped. She took a step toward him. He thought she was about to slap him, but she controlled herself and went on, "I lost everything."

"Except your money."

She smiled again. "Yes, and I was glad of that, because it meant I could afford to have my revenge on you. I thought long and hard about what would hurt you the most. I knew that money didn't mean all that much to you. But Rebel did."

Red rage roared to life inside him. He stuffed it back down and kept his face stony.

"I paid Clay Lasswell to put together a group of

men and kidnap your wife," Pamela went on. "He was to arrange things so that you'd be there to witness it when he killed her. I wanted you to see your precious Rebel die, no matter what you did to try to save her."

He wondered fleetingly how he could have ever thought that Pamela had really changed. She was the same proud, bitter, spiteful bitch she had always been, made even worse now by her all-consuming hatred.

"Even before that, though, Uncle Anthony had come back to this country from South America, and he and I agreed to work together to make you pay for what you'd done."

Tarleton said, "How we went about it was all this little girl's idea." He chuckled, like any uncle proud of an exceptionally bright niece. The Kid felt a little tingle of revulsion go through him.

Pamela moved closer to him and lifted a hand to stroke his arm. The Kid forced himself not to jerk away.

"After that night, we thought you were dead," she went on. "Everyone believed that you died when your house in Carson City burned down. The stories in the newspapers even hinted that you might have killed yourself before starting the fire. Whose body was that they found in the rubble, Conrad?"

The Kid refused to answer, but then decided it couldn't do any harm. "One of Lasswell's men. He followed me there because I'd killed his brother in Black Rock Canyon."

"I always knew you could be a smart man," Pamela murmured. "So you let everyone think the body was yours. You wanted to lie low until you could figure out who had come after you."

The Kid didn't say anything. Pamela was figuring things out for herself just fine.

"Uncle Anthony and I kept track of Lasswell and the men he'd hired. When they started dying, killed by some mysterious man no one could identify, I began to wonder . . . When Lasswell himself was killed, I knew."

"So you came to Val Verde."

"That's right," she said. "I knew if you really *were* still alive, you couldn't stay away from your wife's grave. You'd have to go there sooner or later. We were waiting. I thought the mysterious woman putting flowers on Rebel's grave was a nice touch, don't you?" Her face twisted. "Even though what I really wanted to do was spit on it."

The Kid felt his muscles tremble. He wanted to slap Pamela as she stood so close to him, hissing out her hatred, but he didn't do it. He kept himself under control.

"Why the big show?" he asked. "Why not just kill me and be done with it?"

"Because that would have been too easy. You wouldn't have suffered enough if we'd done that."

That was the answer he'd been expecting. He had

no doubts about it now—Pamela Tarleton's hatred for him had driven her insane.

"So you see, that ambush at the cemetery was never meant to finish you off. It was just the beginning. And it was that stupid priest's own fault that he was wounded. He stepped in front of a bullet that was intended to miss you, Conrad."

"All so that you could pretend to escape and worm your way back into my affections?"

A jagged laugh came from her. "Exactly! I thought perhaps you'd turn to me again, after all this time, and I could pretend to love you once more . . . so it would hurt that much worse when you found out the truth."

Slowly, The Kid shook his head. "You were wrong about that. Nothing could ever hurt me more than what you did to Rebel."

"Good!" she said through clenched teeth. "I wanted to put you through hell, Conrad Browning, and I did!"

He couldn't deny that. But he wasn't going to give her the satisfaction of admitting it. He said, "How did the MacTavishes get mixed up in your sick little scheme, Pamela?"

"That was just pure luck. Bad luck for them, I suppose you'd say. Hogan happened to see Jack Trace on the street in Val Verde and recognized him. They had ridden together a few years ago in a range war or some such nonsense. Hogan thought that Mr. Trace might be a good addition to our little group, so he managed to talk to him privately in town and invited him to join us. Mr. Trace told him about your connection with those Scottish people, and once I heard about that, I realized it would make another good weapon to use against you."

"You'd gun down a man and kidnap his daughter just to help you get back at me?"

"Of course," she answered without hesitation. "I'd do anything to make you suffer, Conrad."

"Including riding for two days so you could pretend you followed us to *help* me."

"Well . . . it wouldn't be a proper revenge if I wasn't here to see it for myself, now would it?"

A proper revenge . . . That was all this was to her. That was all Rebel's death meant. To Pamela, Rebel wasn't a living, breathing human being with loves and hopes and dreams who'd had all that cruelly snatched away from her. She was just a means to an end as far as Pamela was concerned. A weapon to use against him, as Pamela had called it.

The Kid knew about weapons. He just preferred those made of iron and steel and lead, not flesh and blood.

"Bourland was telling the truth about you, wasn't he? You lured him into your bedroll and then screamed."

"Lured?" Again the brittle laugh. "Conrad, you make me sound like some sort of . . . I don't know, spider spinning my web." She paused. "You know, I rather like that."

"Why?" he asked. "Why did you do that?"

"Well, that was one less man we had to deal with today, wasn't it? I knew that Mr. Trace could be counted on to side with us, but I wasn't sure about any of the others. It never hurts to tilt the odds as far in your favor as you can, you know. Besides, I wanted to see just how eager you were to believe everything I told you. I guess I found out, didn't I?"

The Kid wasn't going to lose any sleep over Bourland's death. The man had been a hired killer with plenty of blood on his own hands. But he hated the way Pamela had manipulated him. He hated even worse the way he had gone right along with her, making it easy for her to fool him.

"I suppose when Trace finally deserted, he told you all about our plan to take the cabin?"

Trace laughed and answered instead of Pamela. "It was a pretty good plan," he said. "Might've even worked, if we hadn't been waitin' for you."

Hogan spoke up. The Kid knew it was him because of the scar that marred an otherwise handsome face. Pamela had told the truth about that much, anyway. "We left one man here to keep throwing wood on the fire so you'd think we were all in here. The rest of us took the girl and hid out in the brush until we were ready to circle around behind Whitfield's men and bushwhack them."

The Kid looked at Anthony Tarleton and asked, "Aren't you going to get in on this boasting, too?"

Tarleton grinned and shook his head. "I don't

need to do any boasting. I got what I wanted. At least, I will have once I've watched you die screaming."

"Don't think it won't happen, too," Hogan said. "Loomis in there is mighty good at torture. He was down in Mexico a few years ago when some Apaches grabbed him. They didn't kill him because they'd never seen anybody like him before. They just kept him a while, practically made him one of them. Taught him everything they knew about makin' a man wish he was dead, and that's considerable."

The Kid knew that was true. It was a toss-up which tribe was the cruelest, the Apache or the Yaqui. If Loomis had spent time with the Apaches, he would know every trick there was to make a man scream in agony. The Kid was human. He felt a twinge of fear.

But he didn't let it show. Nor did he allow surprise to appear on his face when Pamela sidled over to Hogan and slipped an arm around him.

"I just love to hear you talk like that, honey," she said.

He shouldn't have been surprised, The Kid thought. Of course, Pamela had found herself a new man. Her biggest talent was wrapping men around her finger and getting them to do what she wanted. Obviously, she had been willing to give herself to Hogan in exchange for him helping her achieve her twisted goals.

"Why did you spare the lives of James and Meggie and Whitfield?" The Kid asked. The longer he kept Pamela talking, the better.

"I know how stubborn you can be, Conrad," she said. "It was just possible you wouldn't surrender even if you thought I was in danger. But I knew you wouldn't be able to stand it if we turned Loomis loose on the girl and she started screaming. As for MacTavish and Whitfield, you seemed to be friendly with both of them. An extra hostage or two never hurt anything." Pamela waved a hand. "Anyway, they're not really a threat. An old man and a boy . . . they're no match for Hogan and Mr. Trace and the others."

Unfortunately, that was true. Pamela had a dozen professional killers at her beck and call. If James and Whitfield tried anything, those gun-wolves would just shoot them down. They were expendable.

"That's enough talk," Tarleton said with impatience in his voice. "Let's get to it. I want to see Browning suffer."

Hogan gave Pamela an affectionate squeeze. "I'll tie him in a chair, and then Loomis can go to work on him."

A strange light shone in Pamela's eyes. Her breasts rose and fell as her breathing quickened. "Yes," she said. "It's time."

The Kid stiffened as Hogan approached him. At the same time, Trace closed in from the other side.

Both men had their guns out, menacing the prisoner.

The Kid knew that if he allowed them to tie him down, he would probably never get up alive. They might keep him alive for hours, or even a day or two, while Loomis tortured him, but in the end, he would die. And so would James and Meggie MacTavish and Dave Whitfield.

The time had come for desperate measures.

The Kid's knees buckled as Hogan and Trace approached him. He fell to the floor and cried, "Oh, God, no! Don't do it, please! I'll pay you . . . I have money . . ."

Pamela laughed. "So do I, Conrad. Anyway, there's not enough money in the world to save you."

Tarleton jerked the barrel of his rifle toward The Kid. "Get him up from there," he growled at Hogan and Trace.

The Kid covered his face with his hands and hunched over. His shoulders shook as if he were sobbing as he wailed, "Please don't kill me! Please!"

He heard one of the gunmen snort in contempt. "Cryin' like a baby," Trace said. They reached down, each of them taking hold of one of The Kid's arms.

His left hand shot up. He grabbed the front of Hogan's shirt and swung the man hard to the right, sending him stumbling into Trace. At the same time, The Kid surged to his feet, moving to his left so that the two gunmen were between him and Tarleton. He slammed the heel of his boot into Hogan's knee and heard the bone pop. Hogan screeched in pain and let his Colt slip through his fingers.

The Kid caught the gun before it hit the floor.

He didn't fire, though. He couldn't survive a shootout with a dozen hardened killers. Instead, as Tarleton yelled, "Stop him! Stop him!", The Kid lunged at Pamela. She was too stunned by the sudden eruption of action to move. He looped his left arm around her waist and jerked her off her feet. She screamed as he threw her over his left shoulder and rammed his right against the door.

It flew open. Shots roared. Bullets chewed splinters from the wall and the doorjamb as The Kid ducked through the opening.

"Don't shoot!" Tarleton shouted. "You'll hit Pamela!"

The Kid was counting on her being in the line of fire to make them hesitate, rather than just blazing away at him. He hated to leave Meggie, James, and Whitfield behind, but the odds were just too high against him in the cabin's cramped quarters. If he was going to be able to help them, he needed to be out where he had room to move.

And had a hostage of his own.

Pamela started squirming and struggling in his grip. The vilest obscenities poured from her mouth.

The Kid tightened his hold on her and raced around the corner of the cabin. He had to get to the corral.

As he reached the pole enclosure, he holstered the Colt and swung Pamela down from his shoulder. She screamed, "You bastard!", but those were the last words she got out before his fist cracked into her jaw. He hit her hard enough to stun her, but not to do any real damage.

The men poured out of the cabin, hot on his trail. "Grab him!" Tarleton yelled somewhere in the darkness. "Don't let him get away with my niece!"

The Kid yanked the loop up that held the corral gate closed. The commotion already had the horses spooked. A couple of them bolted toward the gate as he pulled it open. With one arm around Pamela's limp body, he twisted aside to avoid the horses. He grabbed the mane of another animal and held it still long enough to sling Pamela over its back. Then he put a foot on a corral rail and vaulted up onto the horse himself.

"Hyyaaah!" he shouted as he held on to Pamela with one hand and the horse's mane with the other. "Hyyaaah!"

His shouts sent all the horses stampeding out of the corral. He rode among them, clinging precariously to both Pamela and the horse. The gunmen had to scramble out of the way to avoid being trampled. One of the men ran out of the house carrying a burning branch from the fireplace to use as a torch. The Kid palmed out the Colt and shot the man as he rode past. The torch spun through the air and went out when it hit the ground.

Then the cabin was behind them. Tarleton was still shouting orders at the rest of the men, telling some of them to go after The Kid while the others stayed to guard the rest of the prisoners. Tarleton might be evil, but he wasn't a fool. He already realized what The Kid intended to do. The plan had sprung almost fully formed into The Kid's mind, brought to life by desperation and acted upon instantly, without hesitation.

If he had hesitated, he would have died. He knew that.

Now, he had a chance to live.

More importantly, he had another chance to settle the score for Rebel.

The Kid rode hard into the night.

Chapter 19

He could only go so far at a gallop. The circular depression was less than half a mile wide. Night had fallen and it was difficult to be sure where he was going, but he thought he was headed toward the ridge where Whitfield and the others had been ambushed. Maybe the horses were still somewhere on the other side of it. He knew that Pamela's hired guns hadn't brought them in to the corral yet.

He wanted to find the buckskin.

The horse he had grabbed in the corral was hard to control. When they reached the slope, the animal shied away from it. The Kid banged his heels against the horse's flanks and tightened his grip on its mane.

"Up, you bastard!" he grated. "Up you go!"

The horse went up the slope. Reluctantly, to be sure, but The Kid was able to force it through the brush.

He looked back over his shoulder but couldn't see much. He heard plenty of yelling as the men tried to catch and saddle their mounts. With any luck, The Kid still had a few minutes before any serious pursuit could begin.

The horse fought its way to the top of the slope. Pamela suddenly twisted in The Kid's grip and he realized she'd been pretending to still be stunned. Her hand came up toward him, clutching the little pistol she had pointed at him the day before.

He let go of the horse's mane to swat the gun aside just as Pamela pulled the trigger. The weapon went off with a wicked crack. The Kid felt the heat of the muzzle flame as it licked past his face. The bullet whined by his ear.

The shot so close to its head sent the already panicky horse over the edge. Neighing shrilly, it reared up and pawed at the air. The Kid didn't have hold of anything except Pamela and both of them toppled off the horse.

He managed to hang on to Pamela as they hit the ground and he found his hands full of hissing, spitting, fighting wildcat. He rolled and threw her off him. He didn't want to hit her again . . .

Then he thought of Rebel and slugged Pamela hard enough to knock her out cold this time.

He climbed to his feet, then bent down and picked her up. With her cradled in his arms, he began stumbling through the brush. Further down the slope, branches crackled as the gunmen forced their way uphill. The Kid knew he had only moments to spare.

He whistled, hoping the buckskin was close enough to hear it and would respond. As he felt the far side of the ridge slant under his feet, he whistled again. Despair nibbled at the edges of his brain, but he ignored it.

He was Kid Morgan now. And Kid Morgan didn't give up.

Suddenly, a large shape loomed up out of the darkness at his side. The horse nudged his shoulder as he came to a stop. "Thank God," The Kid breathed. He had found the buckskin. Or rather, the buckskin had found him.

Once again, he lifted Pamela onto the back of a horse. This time, though, the buckskin was saddled and ready to ride, and a lot steadier than the mount The Kid had liberated from the corral. He got his foot in the stirrup and swung up into the saddle.

They weren't going to catch him. He knew it in his bones.

But there was still the problem of how to free James and Meggie and Whitfield. They were in danger because of Pamela's mad scheme of revenge directed at him, and he wasn't going to abandon them. He had a bargaining chip of his own—

A beautiful but thoroughly evil bargaining chip named Pamela Tarleton.

The Kid heeled the buckskin into motion. He didn't flee northeast toward the desert, the way they had come.

Instead, he followed the ridge for half a mile and then cut southwest, climbing higher into the mountains that hung darkly above them. He knew that Tarleton and the others would come after him.

And when they did, he wanted the high ground.

• • •

Several times that night, The Kid heard shouts in the distance as the killers searched for him. He pushed on, despite worrying about what might be happening to the three people he'd been forced to leave behind.

He didn't think Tarleton would hurt them. The man was smart enough to know that The Kid would want to bargain with him, and all he had to trade were the lives of the prisoners.

When Pamela began to stir, The Kid reined in and helped her sit up in front of him. When she started to curse again, he said, "Stop it." His voice was hard and flat. Pamela fell silent.

But only for a moment. Then she said, "What are you going to do, Conrad? You're not going to . . . hurt me, are you?"

"Hurt you? I ought to kill you for what you've done." He paused as she gasped. He didn't know if her reaction was feigned or not. He didn't care. "But I won't," he went on. "You're my ticket to getting the MacTavishes and Whitfield away from your uncle."

Pamela shook her head. The night was so dark that he sensed the movement as much as saw it.

"He'll never let them go, not as long as he thinks he can use them against you." She laughed coldly. "He hates you almost as much as I do, Conrad."

"Well, at least you're smart enough not to try to play up to me again. I'm not a complete fool."

"It wouldn't do any good, would it?" Pamela shifted slightly, so that her breasts pressed against him.

It was The Kid's turn to give a cold laugh. "Not one damn bit," he said.

She shrugged. "All right."

Then she opened her mouth and screamed as loud as she could.

The Kid's hand clamped over her mouth after only a couple of seconds, cutting off the sound. He reached into his pocket with his other hand and pulled out a handkerchief. As he did that, Pamela tried to bite him. He pulled his hand away. Before she could scream again, he crammed the handkerchief into her mouth so that she could only make angry, muffled sounds.

"You actually just did me a favor," The Kid said with a chuckle. "If any of your uncle's men were close enough to hear that, they'll tell him about it. Maybe it'll help convince him he'd better try to negotiate with me."

Because of the gag, he couldn't quite make out what she said in response, but he thought she was saying that Tarleton would never do anything except kill him.

"We'll see about that," The Kid said. He rode on, keeping one arm locked around Pamela like an iron band.

He didn't stop again until the gray of false dawn lightened the eastern sky. By that time, exhaustion had claimed Pamela. She sagged against him in a half-sleep, half-stupor. Her head rested on his shoulder.

He reined the buckskin to a halt as they emerged from a winding trail onto a narrow bench that jutted out from the side of the mountain. It wasn't Big Hatchet Mountain. They were a little north of that point. He could see the other peak looming in the darkness to his left, cutting off some of the starlight.

During the flight from Tarleton's men, The Kid hadn't even tried to hide his trail. He wanted his enemies to be able to follow him, come morning. A showdown was inevitable. But The Kid intended to control the details of that showdown.

Carefully, he dismounted and then lowered Pamela from the back of the horse. She didn't wake up. Or at least, she didn't appear to. He hadn't forgotten the way she had pretended to be unconscious earlier, and then tried to kill him. Clucking for the buckskin to follow him, he carried Pamela over to a tree and set her on the ground at its base, leaning her against the trunk.

He reached up quickly, snagged the coiled rope that was attached to his saddle, and wrapped it around her, tying her to the tree.

She hadn't been pretending this time, he realized. But she came awake as he was wrapping the rope around her and the tree trunk. The makeshift gag had loosened enough for her to spit it out. She did so, and followed it with more curses.

The Kid tied a knot in the rope, securing her. He stepped back as she continued to heap verbal abuse on his head.

"Go ahead and curse me all you want," he said. "It won't change anything."

"We'll see how smug you are when you're dying from a bullet in your gut," she said as she struggled against the rope. She couldn't loosen it, though. How to tie a good knot was something else Frank Morgan had taught him, The Kid realized, even though he hadn't really thought much about it at the time.

Satisfied that Pamela wasn't going anywhere, The Kid led his horse around to the other side of the tree. Once she couldn't see him anymore—not that she could have seen much, anyway, in the predawn gloom—he took his other clothes out of the saddlebags. It felt good to discard the trappings of Conrad Browning and pull on the clothes of Kid Morgan. He strapped on the gunbelt with its buscadero holster and slid the Colt .45 he had taken from Hogan into it. The revolver was the same model as the one he normally carried, so he knew his ammunition would fit it.

He settled the wide-brimmed brown hat on his head and walked back around the tree. The false dawn had faded and the real thing was approaching. Enough light came from the glow in the eastern sky for Pamela to see him. She gasped in surprise at her first sight of The Kid.

"Conrad?" she said.

"Used to be," he drawled. "The name now is Kid Morgan."

"My God," Pamela said softly. "*You're* the one who killed Lasswell and all those other men?"

"That's right."

"When I heard the description of the man, it never occurred to me that it might actually be you. I thought that you had hired some gunman to track them down . . ." A sneer twisted her mouth. "But no, you decided to become a gunfighter like your father, is that it?"

"Something like that." She would never really understand, he thought, so he wasn't going to waste his time trying to explain it to her.

She leaned her head back against the tree trunk and laughed. "You're mad, do you know that? You're insane. You're Conrad Browning! There is no Kid Morgan!"

"That's where you're wrong," he whispered. He turned away from her.

"Fine! Play your little game. See if I care. But you can't bring Rebel back, no matter who or what you pretend to be."

The Kid swung back around. He fought down the impulse to draw his gun and shoot her. He was a killer more than a dozen times over, but he was no murderer. Pamela would face justice for what she had done . . . justice from the law. James and Meggie MacTavish and Dave Whitfield had been in the other room. They could testify to what they had heard in the cabin. Pamela would go to jail for the rest of her life, which was probably the worst punishment of all for a woman like her.

Tight-lipped, he said, "Sorry I can't offer you a fancy breakfast. I can give you a piece of jerky and a sip of water from my canteen, though."

"Go to hell," she snapped. "I don't want anything from you."

He shrugged. "Have it your way." He got some jerky from the saddlebags and went over to hunker on his heels at the top of the trail.

From there, he could see for miles over the arid landscape of southern New Mexico Territory. Closer at hand, as the sky lightened more, the small, brush-covered foothills below became visible where they folded in on each other. Closer still, the slopes became more rugged, with less vegetation. His eyes searched them, looking for any sign of the pursuit he knew must be down there.

After a few minutes, he spotted movement in several places. The gunmen had spread out to search for him and Pamela. They were traveling in pairs, he saw, and the closest two men were riding through some mesquites about a quarter of a mile below him.

That wasn't far from where he had stumbled over the game trail that led him to this bench. He stood up and walked quickly back to the tree where he'd left Pamela.

She gave him a sullen look and said, "I guess I am pretty hungry, after all. I'll take a piece of that jerky."

"Sorry," The Kid said. "You're too late."

"What are you talking—"

She didn't get any further because he knelt in front of her and crammed the handkerchief in her mouth again. This time he took off his bandanna and used it to tie the gag in place, so she couldn't work it out and start yelling. He didn't want Tarleton's men finding either of them just yet.

Not until he'd had a chance to whittle down the odds a little.

To that end, he went back to the buckskin, took a sheathed knife from the saddlebags, and attached it to his belt on the left side. The knife had belonged to Phillip Bearpaw. After the Paiute was wounded, he had insisted that The Kid take it, along with the old Sharps carbine that Bearpaw carried.

The Kid intended to put the knife to good use.

He loped past the tree where he had tied Pamela and ignored her muffled grunts of protest. When he reached the top of the trail, he started down it, staying low so that the brush flanking the path gave him some cover. In the still, clear mountain air, he heard the slow, steady hoofbeats of the horses below him as their riders searched for his trail.

The Kid left the path and made his way into the brush where it was particularly thick. He stretched out on the ground and waited. He knew it was only a matter of time before the men found the tracks the buckskin had left.

Sure enough, in less than ten minutes he heard the horses coming closer. A minute after that, he heard voices.

"—still think we should signal the others," one of the men was saying.

"Don't you reckon Tarleton will be even more grateful if we bring back Browning and the girl by ourselves?" the other man asked. "And I reckon the girl might be *real* grateful if we was to rescue her."

The first man snorted. "You're dreamin', Quint. That gal ain't ever gonna give you the time of day. She's too rich and snobby for that. Not to mention a mite loco."

That hombre had Pamela pegged, all right, The Kid thought. She was everything he'd just said.

The Kid didn't recognize either voice, so he knew the men had to be some of the hired guns Anthony Tarleton had gathered. He stayed where he was, letting the men come closer. The trail grew narrower here, which was another reason he had picked that spot. As the riders came in sight, the brush closing in on either side forced them to climb the trail in single file.

The Kid didn't move, didn't even breathe, as they went past him. When one of them started to say something, the other shushed him, whispering, "We might be gettin' close now."

They didn't know how close they were, The Kid thought.

Close to death.

He waited until both men had gone past him, then slid out of the brush almost noiselessly, drawing the knife as he did so. He leaped onto the back of the second horse, behind the rider, and looped his left arm around the man's neck as he plunged the knife into his back. The man stiffened in shock and pain and made a little noise as the blade went into him. The Kid pulled it free, then drove it in again.

The man in the lead started to hip around in his saddle. "You say somethin', Quint?" he asked.

He saw Quint's face contorting in its death agony, with The Kid peering over his shoulder. The man yelped in surprise and clawed at the gun on his hip.

The Kid had practiced quite a bit with the knife while he was on his way to New Mexico Territory. He wasn't as good with it as he was with a gun, but he pulled the knife out of the dying man's back and threw it with swift, unerring accuracy. It thudded into the second man's chest.

The hombre had his gun out by then and got a shot off, his finger contracting involuntarily on the trigger as he started to topple off his horse. The revolver roared and bucked. The bullet screamed off harmlessly into the sky.

The sound of the shot rolled through the morning air, echoing from the mountains and the foothills. It was only one shot, not the usual three that formed a signal, but that didn't matter. It would still be enough to bring the rest of Tarleton's men in their direction.

The Kid would have preferred to eliminate at least a couple more of them before the showdown came, but that wasn't the way the cards had fallen.

He let go of the man he'd been holding and slid down from the horse. The corpse hit the ground. The other man had fallen off his mount as well, but he was still alive. He struggled to raise his gun. The Kid stepped over to him as both horses, spooked by the sudden smell of fresh blood, rattled their hocks toward the top of the trail.

The Kid reached down and twisted the Colt out of the man's hand. He didn't have much time, but there were a few things he wanted to know. He hunkered beside the man and asked, "What's your name?"

"My . . . my name?"

"That's right."

"J-Jess. Jess Winger. Who . . . who the hell are you? You ain't . . ." Recognition dawned in the killer's pain-wracked eyes. "You're him! You're Browning!"

The Kid shook his head. "Not anymore. The name's Kid Morgan."

"K-Kid . . . Morgan? Hell, I . . . I heard of you . . . They say you've killed . . . half a dozen men."

"More than that," The Kid said. "And two more

now. Quint's dead, and you're about to be, Jess. How many more men does Tarleton have?"

"G-go . . . to . . . hell."

The Kid grasped the knife and pulled it out of the man's chest. Winger hissed in pain.

"Die quick or bleed to death slow," The Kid said. "Your choice."

"They're gonna . . . kill you."

"Then what does it matter if you answer my question?"

Jess Winger couldn't argue with that logic. "There are . . . thirteen men . . . countin' Tarleton . . . and that fella Trace. Hogan's not much good, though. You . . . busted his knee. He can't walk. Can barely ride."

"I'll bet he can still shoot, though."

"You'll . . . find out." Winger raised a hand and pawed at The Kid's arm. "Don't kill me," he pleaded. "Just . . . drag me off in the brush. I won't . . . say nothin' . . . won't warn—"

His head fell back. His mouth hung open. Blood formed a red bubble in it, a bubble that burst a second later.

The Kid had heard the whistling sound from the chest wound and knew that the knife had penetrated one of Winger's lungs. He had known that the gunman had only moments to live, no matter what he did.

He wiped the blood from the blade on Winger's shirt, then straightened to his feet. He bent and grasped Winger under the arms. Winger had said to drag him off into the brush, and that was what The Kid did. He concealed Quint's body the same way. Then he kicked some dirt over the blood that had spilled in the trail.

Hoofbeats sounded faintly in the distance. The rest of Tarleton's men were on their way.

The Kid turned and hurried up the trail to get ready for them.

Chapter 20

Pamela's eyes were wide as she watched The Kid walk toward her. Both horses had reached the bench and run off toward the cliff that formed the rear wall of the small level space. He saw them cropping grass. They had settled down in a hurry once they got away from the smell of blood.

The Kid knelt beside her and drew his knife. Pamela's eyes bugged out even more.

"Don't worry. I'm not going to kill you." He used the blade to cut the rope that held her to the tree. His other hand closed around her arm. "Come on."

He lifted her to her feet. She swung a punch at his head. He moved out of the way of the blow with ease and caught hold of her wrist. He sheathed the knife and grasped her other wrist, then moved them together and held them in one hand. Stooping, he picked up the rope and looped it around her wrists, quickly tying it in place and then cutting off the extra. He coiled the lariat on the saddle again.

Pamela made noises at him. "You want me to take out that gag?" The Kid asked.

She nodded.

"Sorry. It stays for now. Let's go."

Holding on to the short length of rope that dangled from her bound wrists, he led her toward the cliff. It wasn't sheer. He had already noticed a ledge that led up to it, zigzagging back and forth.

He hoped it was wide enough for the buckskin. He would hate to have to leave the horse behind. He'd never had a better mount.

Whistling for the buckskin to follow him, he started up the ledge, which was about a yard wide. The buckskin followed after hesitating for a second. The Kid wouldn't have wanted the ledge to be any narrower, but if it stayed like this all the way to the top, he thought that they could make it.

Pamela continued to make muffled sounds of complaint through the gag. The Kid continued to ignore them. He wished there had been time to reconnoiter at the top of the cliff. He didn't know what he'd find up there. But he knew he had to keep moving higher.

Eventually, of course, he would run out of places to go.

Then it would be time for the showdown.

The ledge took them to the top of the cliff, where they came out on another bench, even smaller than the first one. Twenty yards deep, maybe forty yards long, it backed up to another cliff, and this one *was* sheer.

The rock wall had an opening in it—the black mouth of a cave. The Kid led Pamela toward it. She pulled back on the rope and made more noises, sounding frightened rather than angry. He understood that. The cave mouth had a sinister aspect to it. Pamela didn't want to be forced to go in there.

But Rebel hadn't wanted to be kidnapped and murdered, either, he reminded himself. He couldn't allow himself to feel any sympathy for the woman who had ordered that.

"Get inside," he told her as they reached the cave mouth.

Pamela hung back and shook her head emphatically.

"There's nothing in there," The Kid said. Of course, he didn't know that. The black hole in the cliff might be a bear's den, or there might be a nest of rattlesnakes inside. He relented and fished a match from his pocket, snapped it to life with his thumbnail.

The match flared up and cast a harsh light into the cave, which was shallow enough that The Kid could see all the way to the back of it. There was nothing inside except dust and a few broken branches that lay near a charred spot where a fire had once been . . .

And the picked-clean skeleton of a dead man, also lying next to the old fire.

Pamela managed to scream even through the gag. The Kid stepped back, his mouth tightening. Chances were, the bones belonged to an old Indian who had climbed up here to die. From the looks of the skeleton, it had been here for years, maybe even decades.

"All right, settle down," The Kid told Pamela. "I reckon you don't have to go in there after all. Just sit down there with your back against the rock. And don't move."

She sat about ten feet to the right of the cave mouth. She kept cutting her eyes in that direction, but at least she had stopped screaming.

The Kid took the Winchester from the saddle boot and went back to the place where the ledge ended at this smaller bench. From there, he had a good view of the slopes below them, including the spot where the trail emerged onto the lower bench. He stretched out on the ground and trained the rifle on that spot.

It was just a matter of waiting.

The hoofbeats weren't long in coming. They stopped before they reached the top of the trail. Somebody in Tarleton's bunch was smart enough to realize that it would be a mistake to ride out into the open without knowing what was waiting for them.

After a moment, Jack Trace's voice floated up to The Kid. "Browning! You up there, Browning?"

There was no point in denying it. The Kid called back, "Come on up, Trace!"

The gunman laughed. "And ride right into a bullet? I don't reckon I'll do that. Why don't you send Miss Tarleton down here, and then we'll talk about what happens next."

"I don't reckon *I'll* do *that,*" The Kid replied. "If I turn her over to you, I won't be long in dying. Or maybe I will, if that fella Loomis has his way."

"Well, you're probably right about that," Trace admitted. "But where are you gonna go? There's no way out for you up there!"

"How do you know that?"

Trace didn't answer. The silence told The Kid that he had scored a point. Trace, Tarleton, and the others *didn't* know what was up there. There could be another trail leading out. They had to be careful.

When Trace spoke again, it was to voice a threat. "Give us Miss Tarleton, or we'll kill one of the prisoners."

"If you hurt any of them, I'll kill her," The Kid shot back.

That brought another laugh from Trace. "We got three chips, you just got one. You sure you want to throw everything into the pot first thing, Browning?"

The Kid grimaced. Trace was right, damn it. He was at a disadvantage, so he couldn't afford to wait.

"We'll make a trade," he proposed. "Miss Tarleton for all three hostages."

"That ain't hardly fair, three for one. How about we just trade gals?"

"All or nothing," The Kid responded coldly. "That's the way it has to be."

Trace didn't say anything. The Kid figured he was talking it over with Tarleton. He took advantage of the opportunity to study his surroundings a little better.

There was no trail up the cliff at the back of this bench, but he noticed a ledge farther up the side of the mountain that led off to the north and then angled down. That might be a path out of the Hatchets, The Kid realized, if there was any way to get to it.

He peered up at the face of the cliff and saw a place where a fang-like rock jutted out. If he could throw a loop over that rock, he could climb up to it, use it for a foothold, and reach up to grasp the ledge, which was only about four feet higher. He was confident he could make that climb up the rope, but could James and Meggie and Whitfield?

They might be able to, if they had some time. It would be dangerous, but worth the risk, especially if the alternative was certain death at the hands of lunatics and hired killers.

Someone would have to cover their escape, though, he realized.

That would be his job.

Suddenly, Trace called from below, "How do you want to work this swap?"

"You mean you agree to it?"

"Mr. Tarleton wants his niece back safe and sound. He's willin' to let all of you go in return."

The Kid didn't believe that for a second. Tarleton was up to some sort of trick. But The Kid didn't see any option except to play along for the moment.

"I'll send Miss Tarleton down the ledge to the lower bench," he called. "You send all three prisoners up. I'll have my rifle on Miss Tarleton until the MacTavishes and Whitfield are up here with me."

Again there was no response for several moments. Then Trace said, "All right. But you'd damned well better not be trying any tricks, Browning! Our guns will be pointed at the three of them, too."

"All right. Give me a minute."

The Kid eased back from the edge, not standing up until he was out of the line of fire of the gunmen hidden in the brush. He went over to Pamela, reached down to grasp her arm, and helped her to her feet.

"I know you heard all that," he told her. "You're going back to your uncle."

She made angry noises at him, but her eyes glinted in triumph. She thought she had won.

She didn't realize that all he was trying to do right now was secure the freedom of the MacTavishes and Whitfield. Once the three of them were safe, he would be going after her and Tarleton and the rest of them. Actually, he figured it was likely they would rush him, and he would make a final stand on this lonely, windswept bench high in the Hatchet Mountains.

That was all right. He would trade his life to avenge Rebel, if that was what it took.

But if he did that, Pamela would probably escape justice, he realized. He couldn't afford to die yet.

He couldn't stand by and allow the prisoners to be tortured or murdered, and he had no doubt that was what would happen if he didn't go through with the swap. Circumstances had maneuvered him into a bad spot.

Or call it fate, destiny, what have you. When you came right down to it, he had to try to save the hostages.

That was what Rebel would want him to do.

"Come on," he said as he steered Pamela toward the ledge. "I'm not going to untie you or take that gag out. Your uncle and your friends can do that for you once you're back with them."

He stopped short of the ledge and let go of Pamela's arm.

"Go ahead," he told her. "But take it slow and easy."

She cast one last, hate-filled glance over her shoulder at him and then stepped out onto the ledge. She started down, moving slowly as he had told her.

The Kid stretched out again in a cluster of several small rocks that gave him some added cover and thrust the Winchester's barrel over the edge. He couldn't see Pamela as she descended the ledge, but he'd be able to track her with the rifle as soon as she stepped out onto the lower bench.

"Miss Tarleton's on her way down!" he called. "Send the hostages up!"

"Hang on!" Trace replied.

The Kid felt a surge of anger. "Damn it, you'd better not be backing out on the deal now!"

"Take it easy," Trace said. "Here they come."

A moment later, James and Meggie MacTavish appeared on the trail that led through the heavy brush. James had his arm around his sister's shoulders. Behind them, Dave Whitfield trudged along the path. The rancher looked gray and exhausted. None of them were tied up.

They moved onto the lower bench. Their steps were stiff. The Kid figured they had to know that several rifles were trained on them at that moment. They walked across the bench toward the spot where the ledge began.

Pamela reached the bottom of the ledge and moved out so that The Kid could see her again. She walked toward the three hostages, moving a little faster than they were. It took only a minute for her to reach them.

"Hold it!" The Kid shouted. "Pamela, you stay there!"

For the first time since this standoff began, Anthony Tarleton spoke up. "Like you said, it's too late to change the rules, Browning! Let Pamela go, or I'll have my men kill those prisoners right now!"

"I'll put a bullet in her head at the first shot!" The Kid yelled back. "I'm not backing out of the deal! I just want the others up here first!"

Pamela shook her head and made noises through the gag, as if urging her uncle not to go along with it. But after a tense moment, Tarleton said, "All right. Just wait right there, Pamela. You'll be back with us shortly."

The prisoners moved on past Pamela. As they approached the ledge, The Kid couldn't see them anymore. He kept the Winchester's barrel rock-steady as he aimed it at Pamela.

Would he pull the trigger if Tarleton tried a double-cross? Could he? Killing some of those gunmen without giving them a chance didn't bother him. They were cold-blooded murderers with plenty of blood on their hands. They had chosen to live by the gun. They knew that the odds were they would die by it as well.

Pamela was different. She had probably never carried out an act of real, personal, face-to-face violence in her life. But she had plotted Rebel's kidnapping and murder, as well as everything else that had happened to torment The Kid in the past few months. She had ordered someone's death, more than once. Was that the same as committing murder herself? Was it actually *worse?*

The Kid didn't know the answers to those questions. He didn't know if he would pull the trigger, either. He reckoned he wouldn't know until the time came, if it ever did.

He heard the scuff of footsteps on the ledge. The prisoners were moving faster now as they approached freedom. Suddenly James MacTavish reached the top of the ledge and came hurrying onto the upper bench, practically dragging Meggie with him. Dave Whitfield puffed along behind them, out of breath from the climb. He wasn't a young man anymore.

"Get back there by the cave," The Kid told them without taking his eyes off Pamela. "They can't get a shot at you once you're there." Then he raised his voice. "All right, Pamela, go on down."

She glanced back at him, but she was far enough away that he couldn't really make out the expression on her face. Especially with the bandanna tied across the lower half of it to keep the gag in. He would have bet a hat, though, that she was seething with anger and hatred.

She strode toward the brush, moving faster. After a moment, she reached the trail and stepped down onto it. He watched as she disappeared from his view.

A pang of loss went through him. He was back to where he'd started, trying to avenge Rebel's death. He had had the person responsible for that atrocity in his hands, and he had chosen to let her go.

It hadn't really been much of a choice. Whitfield and the MacTavishes didn't deserve to die because they had gotten caught in Pamela's vicious plot against him.

The Kid kept his rifle trained on the opening in the brush. He heard people moving around down there, as well as the faint sound of voices. But he couldn't make out any of the words. He expected

Tarleton's men to start taking potshots at him, but so far nothing had happened.

"James," he called softly, "get the rope off my horse and see if you can throw a loop over that rock that's sticking out up there."

Instead of doing as he was told, James said, "What are you dressed up for, Browning? You look like some sort of dime novel gunslinger."

As a matter of fact, Conrad Browning had taken some of the inspiration for his new identity of Kid Morgan from the fanciful dime novels that had been written about his father, Frank Morgan. But that wasn't the time or place to explain. He snapped, "Just do what I told you."

"Are you thinkin' we can climb up to that ledge?" Whitfield asked. "Hell, there's a better way to get out of here than that."

The rancher's comment was so unexpected that it prompted The Kid to look around. "What are you talking about?"

Whitfield used a blunt thumb to point toward the dark hole in the cliff face. "That's Dead Injun Cave. In the back of it, there's a little crack—a chimney, I guess you'd call it—that runs all the way to the top of this mountain. It ain't the easiest climb in the world, but it's easier than tryin' to shinny up a rope on a cliff while somebody's shootin' at you."

"How do you know about that chimney?" The Kid asked.

"I told you, I've hunted in these mountains, and dodged Apaches, too. They chased me into that very cave about fifteen years ago. I figured I was a goner, but then I found that crack and climbed out through it. The 'Paches don't know it's there. They won't come anywhere near the cave because of those old bones in it. Bad medicine, they call it."

That made sense. The Kid felt his pulse quicken as he realized that Whitfield might be on to something.

"All right, Whitfield, lead the way. Get those two youngsters out of here. I'll stay behind to cover you."

"No!" Meggie cried. "You have to come, too, Mr. Browning."

"Somebody's got to stay," James said. "Otherwise, those killers will just rush up here and shoot us while we're trying to climb out."

"Your brother's right, Meggie," The Kid told her. "Go with him. Show them the chimney, Whitfield."

The rancher nodded. "Come on, you two." As he led them toward the cave, with James practically dragging Meggie, Whitfield added, "Don't pay no never-mind to that ol' skeleton in there. He's fifty years or more past bein' able to hurt anybody."

As the three of them disappeared into the cave, The Kid settled down to wait for the inevitable battle. The taut silence had already hung over the mountainside for longer than he expected.

268

For that reason, he wasn't surprised when shots began to ring out.

What surprised him was the direction they came from.

Above him.

Chapter 21

The Kid rolled over onto his back as a slug whipped past his ear and slammed into the ground beside him, kicking up dirt and rock chips. Some of the dirt got in his eyes and blurred his sight.

More bullets whined around him like angry bees. He didn't have to see perfectly to know the shots were coming from the ledge he had considered using as an escape route. Aiming in that general direction, he cranked off three rounds from the rifle as fast as he could work the lever, then jackknifed up off the ground and ran toward the cliff.

Slugs kicked up dust at his feet, but he was moving too fast for the riflemen to draw a good bead on him. He knew what had happened. One of his enemies down below had spotted that ledge and realized that anyone who managed to climb onto it would have a good shot down at him. Tarleton had split his forces, sending some of the hired killers to work their way around and get onto the ledge.

If The Kid had sent Whitfield and the MacTavishes up the rope, as he'd intended, they would have been climbing right into the gunsights of Tarleton's men.

The Kid reached the cliff and pressed his back against the rock face. The shots fired by the men on the ledge couldn't reach him there—but he couldn't hit them, either. Even worse, he couldn't keep the rest of Tarleton's men from getting to the lower bench and coming up *that* ledge.

A grimace twisted The Kid's face. They had backed him into a corner, all right. All he could do now was go down fighting.

"Browning!"

The low-voiced call came from the cave mouth. The Kid glanced over, saw Dave Whitfield emerge from the dark hole in the cliff.

"What are you doing here?" The Kid snapped. "You're supposed to be helping James and Meggie escape."

"I got 'em started up that chimney," Whitfield said. He was still breathing hard from the climb, and his haggard features held an even more pronounced gray tinge. "It's about a three hundred yard climb, and it's steep and tight. It'll take 'em a while. There ain't nothin' else I can do to help them now. But I can still play a hand down here."

The Kid shook his head. "No, get on up there while you still can. I'll hold off Tarleton and his men from inside the cave. They'll be here any time now."

"Damn right they will, but you ain't gonna hold 'em off." Whitfield reached out and closed his hand around The Kid's Winchester. "I am."

"This is my fight—"

"Yeah, it is," the rancher broke in, "but I sat in on the game. And now I'm cashin' out, Browning. My ticker's shot."

The Kid frowned. "Your heart?"

"That's right." A look of pain passed over Whitfield's rugged face. "Something's busted inside. I felt it when it happened. So I know I ain't goin' home. If those two kids have any chance o' gettin' out of this alive . . . it's you."

The Kid's mind reeled. He knew Whitfield was telling the truth. It was obvious by looking at him that something was very wrong.

"Damn it . . . ," The Kid began softly.

Whitfield shook his head. "There ain't time to go on about anything. Come on. I'll show you the way out of here."

The Kid finally let go of the Winchester. Whitfield nodded toward the cave, and they both hurried into its dark maw.

They had to step around the ancient skeleton to reach the back of the cave. The sun was high enough now so that its rays slanted into the gloom. Whitfield gestured toward the low-hanging ceiling and said, "Up here."

The Kid moved closer and saw the narrow slit in the rock that he hadn't noticed before. It started from the rear wall, ascended at a steep angle, and was so dark he couldn't see more than a couple of feet up it. When he leaned closer to it, he heard faint scraping noises that came from Meggie and James struggling to reach the top.

"You're sure it still goes all the way through?" he asked Whitfield.

The rancher grunted. "Well, if it don't, then you and them other two are pure-dee in a bad fix. But if you stay here, you *know* you'll end up dead."

The Kid nodded. Whitfield was right.

The opening was so narrow that The Kid wasn't sure if his shoulders would fit through it. But the brawny James MacTavish had made it, so he supposed he could, too. He turned to Whitfield and held out his hand.

"They call you Devil Dave," he said, "but I reckon—"

"Oh, hell, I told you not to start goin' on," Whitfield said as he gripped The Kid's hand. "Chances are, I'm just as bad as the MacTavishes made me out to be." He sighed. "Damn, I hope ol' Hamish pulls through, anyway. And one more thing . . . if you get outta this mess alive, Browning, I'd sure be beholden to you if you'd tell my daughter that I love her. Help her out any way you can, will you?"

"Sure, Dave," The Kid answered without hesitation. "You have my word on it."

"I reckon that'll do, then." Whitfield gestured curtly with the rifle. "Get the hell outta here while you still got a chance. I think I hear 'em comin' out there."

The Kid nodded, reached into the chimney, and pulled himself up until he could get a foothold and push himself higher. The stone walls closed in around him, scraping his shoulders and threatening to take his breath away. His heart pounded heavily in his chest. He crawled upward into the pitch blackness inside the mountain.

He hadn't gone very far when he heard a sudden blast of gunfire. The shots echoed up the crack in the rock and were so loud that he winced as they assaulted his ears. After a few seconds, the fusillade died away for a moment. The Kid heard Dave Whitfield yell, "Come on, you mangy polecats! I'll kill ever' damn one of you!"

From his voice, there was no way to tell that Whitfield was already dying. The Kid had seen it in the rancher's eyes. Whitfield was sacrificing what little was left of his life to give him and the MacTavishes a chance to escape.

The Kid kept climbing. He had to press his feet against the sides of the shaft to keep from sliding back down and pull himself higher with his arms and shoulders. It was grinding, exhausting work. The darkness surrounded him like a black shroud, and from time to time, he had trouble catching his breath. If he could see just a flicker of light above him, he thought, so that he would know he was climbing toward freedom, it might make the ordeal easier.

Only moments after that thought went through his head, he saw a faint glimmer in front of his eyes. He thought at first he was imagining it, but then he realized it was really there. From somewhere high above him, a tiny ray of light had penetrated into the mountain. It shone on a bit of metallic rock wedged into the side of the chimney. A fleck of gold or silver, maybe. A grim smile tugged at The Kid's mouth. He might be climbing right through a bonanza and not even know it— although it was more likely the rock was mere quartz or something like that.

The shots came in bunches below. The Kid couldn't hear Whitfield shouting anymore, but he knew the rancher was still alive. If he wasn't, the shooting would be over.

The Kid tilted his head back and peered upward. He could see an actual opening now, with a bit of blue sky in it, but it was no bigger than his thumbnail. The sight encouraged him. The fact that he could see it told him that James and Meggie had made it to the top and gotten out of the chimney. If they could make it, he told himself, so could he.

Below him, the gunfire had stopped, although it was a moment or two before The Kid realized it wasn't starting up again. He paused, just for a second, and closed his eyes. *Vaya con Dios*, he thought.

He resumed climbing, forcing himself up the shaft as quickly as he could. Once Tarleton and his hired killers realized that The Kid, James, and Meggie were gone, they would start looking around. It wouldn't take them long to find the chimney leading up from the cave. Unlike the

Apaches, they wouldn't be afraid to venture into the final resting place of that old Indian.

The little opening above him grew larger, though it still seemed maddeningly far away. The Kid gritted his teeth as he heard voices below him. The killers were in the cave. If they found the escape route, all they'd have to do was stick a couple of revolvers up the chimney and empty them. There was no place in there for him to hide.

He couldn't control what they did down there. All he could do was keep climbing. The opening was fifty feet above him, he estimated. Then forty, then thirty, then twenty . . . The shaft narrowed even more, so that he could barely force himself through it. One of his feet slipped, and he drove his elbows against the sides to keep himself from sliding back down. Even through the buckskin, the rough rock scraped his skin raw.

After catching himself, The Kid started climbing again. Ten feet to go. He reached up, caught hold of a small projection, pulled up and shoved with his feet at the same time. Five feet. A few more seconds and he'd be able to reach up and grab the edge of the opening. Then it would be a simple matter to pull himself out.

". . . must've gone up there!"

The shouted words rose up the shaft. One of Tarleton's men must have stuck his head right into the chimney before he yelled the news of his discovery.

"Shoot up there, you fools! Shoot!"

That was Tarleton. The Kid grimaced and tried to scramble the few remaining feet.

That was when something suddenly blocked out the light from above. The Kid looked up and saw James MacTavish looming in the opening, stretching an arm down toward him.

"Grab my hand!" James urged.

The Kid lunged upward and caught hold of James's wrist. The brawny young man hauled him upward. The Kid's booted feet pushed against the sides of the chimney at the same time. His head came out into the open air. Then his shoulders caught and wouldn't budge. James grunted with effort as he wrapped both arms around The Kid's right arm and heaved. The Kid felt like that arm was about to pop out of its socket.

But instead, his shoulders popped free of the shaft's narrow opening. Still hanging on to The Kid's arm, James toppled backward. The rest of The Kid's body emerged from the chimney. He rolled away from the opening just as guns began to roar at the other end. Bullets ricocheted madly back and forth against the chimney's walls. Some of them made it all the way to the top and whined off into the air.

The Kid jerked out his Colt, and as soon as the shooting stopped below, he thrust it into the opening and triggered three fast shots. He wasn't really trying to hit anything. He just wanted them to think twice before they started climbing up the chimney themselves.

He looked around and saw that James and Meggie appeared to be all right except for a few bloody places where the rock walls had scraped them as they were climbing. Relieved to see that, The Kid studied their surroundings. Just as Whitfield had said, they were at the top of the mountain. Big Hatchet Mountain, a half-mile or so to the south, was the only one in the range that was taller. The slopes of the peak were tufted with grass and fell away fairly steeply, but The Kid saw several places where he and the MacTavishes could start making their way down.

"Come on," he said as he pushed himself to his feet. "We need to get moving. Tarleton's not going to let us live if he can prevent it. He and his men will be looking for us soon."

"We just got out of that hole," James complained. "We need to rest for a few minutes."

Meggie asked, "Where's Mr. Whitfield?"

The stricken look on her face told The Kid that she already knew the answer to that question, whether she wanted to admit it or not.

"He stayed below to give us more time to get away," The Kid said. "We can't let what he did go to waste. Come on."

This time, James got to his feet, although he groaned about it. He took his sister's arm and said, "Let me help you, Meggie."

"I'm all right," she said. "You're the one who's wounded."

James shook his head. "Just scratches. Nothin' to worry about."

The Kid got them moving down the far side of the slope away from the benches where the showdown had taken place. He wanted to put as much distance as he could between them and Tarleton's bunch.

But sooner or later, he would have to confront them again, he thought as he glanced back. He had left the buckskin on the upper bench, and James and Meggie didn't have horses, either. Tarleton and his hired killers had the only mounts.

Which meant that The Kid would have to take some away from them.

James addressed that very issue as the three of them made their way down the slope. "How are we gonna get away from them?" he asked. "We don't have any horses. Even if we manage to give them the slip, we'll starve to death before we can walk all the way back home."

The Kid wasn't worried about starving to death. There was game out there—rabbits, prairie dogs, the occasional deer or antelope—and anyway, it took a long time for someone to die from starvation. Water was a much greater concern. A person on foot could die of thirst in just a few days.

"We're not going to walk all the way back," he said. "We'll get our hands on some horses."

"How?"

"Let me worry about that."

"Like you've worried about everything else?"

The Kid laughed and shook his head. "You never change, do you, James? You have to complain about everything."

The young man scowled. "If I hadn't pulled you out of that hole, those fellas would've ventilated you for sure."

"Yes, they would have," The Kid said with a nod. "And I'm glad you reminded me of that. I forgot to say thank you. I'm obliged to you for your help, James."

"Forget it."

"No. I won't do that. I won't forget what Dave Whitfield did for us, either. When we *do* get back, there's going to be peace between the MacTavishes and the Circle D."

Meggie nodded. "That's right, James. There won't be any more feuding."

"But Pa—"

"I said, *there won't be any more feuding.*" The firm tone of Meggie's voice made it clear she wasn't going to put up with any argument, even though James was older than her. The Kid figured she had enough iron in her spine to back it up, too. She had gone through hell, and she hadn't fallen apart yet.

The descent was actually easier on the western side of the mountain range than it would have been on the eastern side. They didn't encounter any cliffs. Some of the slopes were steep enough so that they had to turn around and back down them, clinging to rocks and bushes and clumps of grass to keep their balance, but that was the worst of it. By late morning, they were in the lower canyons.

Another stretch of desert rolled off to the west. A range of mountains that looked to be about the same size as the Hatchets lay in that direction, ten to twenty miles away. The heat was already getting bad as the sun rose higher in the sky. The Kid knew he and his companions couldn't walk that far during the day.

Heading for those other mountains wouldn't do them any good, anyway. Tarleton, Pamela, and the hired killers would spot them easily out there in that vast open area. What he really needed, The Kid thought, was somewhere he could leave the MacTavishes while he tried to get his hands on some horses.

He found just the place a short time later. It was a little canyon with a narrow opening, no more than thirty feet across, and thick brush closed off most of that. The Kid just happened to notice it, and he thought it was possible men on horseback might ride right on past without giving it a second look.

He led James and Meggie through the brush, James complaining as usual when it clawed and scratched at him. Beyond the brush, the canyon ran for about fifty yards before coming to an end at a tumbled mass of boulders that must have fallen down from higher on the mountain sometime in the past.

"The two of you stay here," he told the MacTavishes. "There's some shade in those rocks, so the heat and sun shouldn't be too bad."

"There's no water here," James said. "No food."

"That's true, but by sometime tonight, I'm hoping you'll be on your way back to Val Verde with enough supplies and canteens to get you there safely."

"You expect those things to fall down from the sky?" James asked, ignoring the warning glare that Meggie sent in his direction.

"No," The Kid replied with a shake of his head, "I expect to steal them from those varmints who've been trying to kill us."

Chapter 22

By the time dusk began to settle again over the Hatchet Mountains, a tired, sunburned, hungry, and footsore Kid Morgan had located his quarry. It made sense that Tarleton and Pamela would order their gunmen to spread out and search for the three fugitives. With less than a dozen men, though, there was only so much ground the killers could cover. Because of that, The Kid couldn't just sit back and wait for some of them—and more importantly, their horses—to come to him. He had had to find them.

So once again, the hunters had become the hunted.

The Kid crouched behind a rock and watched two men on horseback sit at the mouth of a canyon and debate whether or not they ought to ride up into it and carry on the search.

"I don't like it," one of the gunmen said. "It's already too dark and shadowy up there. I say we ought to go back to camp and wait there for the others."

"What are you worried about?" the other hardcase asked. "There are just three of 'em, and they ain't armed."

The first man shook his head. "That's not true. Browning's got a pistol, accordin' to what Miss Tarleton told her uncle."

A snort of contempt came from the other man. "Some Eastern dude playin' gunfighter! You afraid he's gonna ambush us, Carlin?"

"It could happen. A bullet fired by an Eastern dude can kill you just as dead."

That was true, The Kid thought. He had proven it on numerous occasions.

Carlin's companion hitched his horse into motion. "Well, I'm goin' to take a look up this canyon. You can stay here if you want, but if I catch those three, then I'll get all the credit."

"All right, all right," Carlin grumbled as he started his horse forward, too. "I'm coming."

The Kid knew they wouldn't find anything in the canyon. He waited until they were out of sight, then hurried after them, using every rock and tree and bush for cover.

Their mention of the group's camp intrigued him. That would be the best target for a raid. He couldn't follow them back to it on foot, though. He needed to find out its location *and* get his hands on at least one horse right now. That might be a tall order.

The sound of hoofbeats suddenly coming closer made him scramble for cover behind a slab of rock leaning against the canyon wall. The two gunmen hadn't gone very far before running into a dead end and were returning.

The Kid began climbing onto the rock, quickly formulating a plan as he did so. He waited on the side where they couldn't see him until they rode past. As they did that, he launched himself in a diving tackle from the top of the rock at the gunman nearest to him.

The man let out a startled yell as The Kid crashed into him and drove him out of the saddle. Both men landed heavily on the ground, but The Kid was on top and the impact stunned the gunman momentarily. The Kid rolled away and came up with his Colt in his hand as the other man fired at him. The bullet whined past The Kid's ear. He triggered his revolver and sent a slug into the killer's chest. The man slewed halfway around in the saddle, tried to hang on, but toppled off his horse anyway.

The first man groaned and stirred as his wits started to come back to him. The Kid reversed the gun in his hand and slammed the butt against the man's head, knocking him out cold. He hurried over to check the man he had shot. He knew he didn't have much time.

The second man was dead, drilled through the heart. As soon as The Kid was sure of that, he swung around and grabbed the horses before they could bolt.

The pair of shots would draw the attention of the other searchers, he was sure. He wanted to be well away from there before any of them could show up to see what had happened. He lifted the man he had knocked out, slung him over the saddle on one of the horses, and lashed him into place with a rope that was on the saddle. He tied the man's hands and feet together under the horse's belly. Then he swung up onto the other mount and rode away into the dusk, leading the horse with its unconscious burden.

He had two horses, but that wasn't enough. If he went straight back to the canyon where he'd left James and Meggie, someone would have to ride double, which would slow them down enough that the pursuit was bound to catch them. The Kid had an idea what to do about that, but it would take some more work on his part.

Gun work, more than likely.

He put some distance between himself and the site of the brief gunfight, heading south now, around Big Hatchet Mountain. As the shadows thickened, he listened intently, because the sound of hoofbeats might well be the only warning he got if he was about to run into more of Tarleton's men.

When he had gone about a mile, he reined in. The man on the other horse let out a groan and struggled against the rope that held him on the saddle. The Kid dismounted, stepped over to the other horse, and pressed the muzzle of his Colt against the man's head. That made the hombre freeze right away.

"Browning?" he croaked.

"Never mind who I am," The Kid said. The explanation was too complicated to get into. Instead, he went on, "Tell me where the camp is."

"Get me off this horse first. My head hangin' upside-down like this is makin' me—"

He didn't finish the sentence. Because the next second he threw up. The Kid stepped back to avoid being splattered. He didn't worry about a trick. Throwing up was something a fella couldn't really fake.

When the gunman's spasms subsided, he groaned again. "Son of a bitch," he muttered. "Come on, Browning. Give me a break here."

"Like you gave a break to those men of Whitfield's you massacred?"

"They were hired guns, too! Hell, they knew what they were gettin' into."

The man was right about that. It didn't make him any less of a cold-blooded killer. The Kid pointed the Colt at him again and said, "Talk."

"You want to know where the camp is? Fine, I'll tell you. You gotta let me loose first. And give me my horse back, so I can get out of here. After Hogan and the others kill you, I'd just as soon they think I'm dead, so they won't come after me for double-crossing them."

What the gunman said actually made sense, in a way, but The Kid wasn't going along with it. "You're not going to double-cross *me*," he said. "You're taking me to the camp."

"Go to hell!"

The Kid thrust the gun barrel against the man's temple again. "I've already reduced the odds against me by one. Knocking them down one more can't hurt anything."

"Wait, wait! Hold on! Don't shoot, mister. We can work something out."

"Damn right we can. Where's the camp?"

"You remember the place you left the girl? Miss Tarleton? That's where her uncle said we'd all rendezvous."

That made sense. There was water there, and it was at the base of Big Hatchet Mountain, which meant it was about in the center of the range on the eastern side. Straight across the mountain from where he was right now, The Kid thought.

He wondered if there was a trail that would let him reach the place without having to go all the way around. That would certainly make things simpler.

Assuming, of course, that his prisoner was telling the truth.

"You're still coming with me," he said as he stepped back and holstered his gun. "That way, if you're lying you'll regret it."

"Mister, I already regret ever signin' on with this bunch. I'm sick, I tell you. At least untie me so I can sit up in the saddle."

"Sorry," The Kid said, even though he really wasn't.

Not for a second.

Gagging the prisoner was an obvious precaution. The Kid ripped pieces off the gunman's shirt to serve as the gag and tied it in place. Then he set off up the slopes in the dark, hoping to find a pass to the other side.

The Kid had discovered that he had a natural sense of direction, something else he had inherited from Frank Morgan. Even though natural obstacles forced him to take a twisting path through the mountains, he always had a general idea which direction he was going and which way he needed to go. After several hours, he had managed to reach the eastern side of the Hatchet range.

The prisoner, who had tried to yell and curse through the gag at first, just like Pamela, had fallen silent after a while. When The Kid figured he was within half a mile of the camp—if the captive gunman was telling the truth—he reined in, dismounted, and cut the man loose, letting him fall to the ground. A low moan came from the man, telling The Kid that he was still alive.

The Kid hunkered next to the prisoner and used the pieces of rope to tie his hands and feet. "You're staying right here," he said quietly as he straightened to his feet. "If you weren't lying to me, I'll come back to turn you loose later. If I get killed . . ." The Kid grinned down coldly at the gunman. "Well, you'd better hope no wolves or anything like that come along, I guess."

The man made muffled noises of complaint as The Kid turned away. He had left the ropes loose enough so that the man could work his way free eventually, although it might take him hours to do so. The hombre would figure that out sooner or later, when The Kid didn't come back for him.

Leading the horses, The Kid worked his way closer to the little pool at the edge of the foothills. He caught the scent of woodsmoke and knew he was smelling a campfire. So the man he'd captured hadn't lied to him after all. Tarleton, Pamela, and the others really were camped here. If what Jess Winger had told him earlier in the day was true, there were only eleven of them left, counting Tarleton and Trace. Still bad odds, but getting better all the time, The Kid told himself with a grim smile.

He left the horses tied to a mesquite tree and approached the camp as carefully and quietly as he could. Through a screen of brush, he caught sight of the flickering flames of the campfire. The Kid bellied down and went the rest of the way in a crawl.

When he got close enough to part the brush and peer through the tiny gap, he saw that no one was talking around the campfire. It was late enough so that at least some of the group would be asleep. One man was sitting up by the fire, standing guard while everyone else was rolled up in blankets. The lone sentry had his back to the flames so that they wouldn't ruin his night vision.

On the other side of the pool, the horses were gathered in a makeshift corral formed by stringing ropes between some of the pines. The Kid had his eye on them, but he waited patiently until he was sure that each of the bedrolls actually contained a sleeping body. He didn't move until he saw each of them shift around a little in slumber to be certain there was only one guard. Tarleton must have felt confident that they were in no danger. If he'd been in charge, The Kid thought, he would have posted at least a couple of men out from the camp a little way.

Once he was satisfied, he crawled around the pool toward the horses. His heart gave a little leap when he spotted the buckskin among them. The bastards hadn't even had the decency to unsaddle him. They would regret that. Their casual cruelty was just going to make it easier for The Kid to steal him back. The gunmen were using the other saddles for pillows, another thing they had in common with working cowboys.

The saddlebags from the other horses were piled up just outside the corral. The Kid figured those saddlebags had some supplies in them, so he planned to grab as many as he could before he left there.

The horses stirred a little as he slipped into the makeshift corral. The guard glanced toward them, but The Kid was stooped low enough that the man couldn't see him. The horses shielded him from view. He waited until the guard turned around again before he used his knife to cut the rope between two of the pines.

Then he grabbed the buckskin's reins, vaulted into the saddle, and let out a bloodcurdling yell as he yanked his hat off and slapped it against the rumps of several horses. The panicky animals stampeded straight ahead. Some of them splashed through the shallow pool. Others circled it. Either way, their route took them right through the sleeping gunmen.

The Kid had noticed two bedrolls off to the side and figured they belonged to Tarleton and Pamela. The horses missed those as they bolted, but The Kid didn't take the time to see if his guess was right. Instead he leaned down, scooped up as many of the saddlebags as he could, slung them over the buckskin's back, and sent the horse lunging ahead in the wake of the others, drawing his Colt as he did so.

Even though they had been startled out of a sound sleep, Tarleton's men were professionals. They came out of their blankets alert, with guns in their hands. The Kid swept his Colt in an arc toward them, triggering four swift shots before they could fire.

Two of the men tumbled backward, driven off their feet by The Kid's slugs smashing into them. Another doubled over, clutching his belly as he staggered to the side. Yet another man was down as well, probably trampled by the stampeding horses.

Then The Kid was through the camp, flashing past the remaining gunmen. He bent low over the neck of the galloping buckskin as the men still on their feet opened fire. Hot lead clawed through the night, searching for him, but none of it found him. The buckskin didn't break stride, so The Kid was confident that his horse hadn't been hit.

The rest of the horses were still in front of him. The Kid shouted at them to keep them running. They veered toward the desert, and he let them go, firing the remaining two rounds in his gun over their backs to speed them on their way. Chances were, they would keep running for miles before they stopped. It would take Tarleton's men most of the next day to round them up, if they were even able to find all the horses. In one bold stroke, The Kid had crippled his enemies.

The fight wasn't over yet. And he had to get James and Meggie MacTavish started on their way to safety.

He picked up the two saddled horses he had left tied up, then used the same pass he had found earlier and made his way back over Big Hatchet Mountain. The stars told him it was long after midnight before he approached the canyon where he had left James and Meggie. He hoped he was in the right place. The night was so dark he couldn't be sure. The MacTavishes were probably sleeping the sleep of exhaustion by then. He called, "James! Meggie! Can you hear me?"

He had to call several more times before James responded, "Browning! Over here!"

The Kid followed his voice, and a minute later came up to the brush-choked opening of the canyon. James and Meggie hurried out. When The Kid swung down from the saddle and then turned toward them, Meggie took him by surprise and threw her arms around him.

"Mr. Browning, are you all right? We thought we heard some shooting a few hours ago, but it was a long way off."

"That was me," The Kid said, "but I'm fine. And I have horses and supplies for you now. You can start back to Val Verde."

"Don't we need to wait until morning?" James asked as Meggie stepped back.

The Kid glanced at the sky. "It'll be light in another couple of hours, but I don't see any reason to wait that long. I've started to learn my way around these mountains. I think you should head due north. That'll take you back to the Southern Pacific line, and when you hit it, you can follow it all the way to Val Verde."

"What about Tarleton and those hired guns?"

"I scattered their horses pretty good. I think you'll be halfway back to town before they could start after you, even if they wanted to. Which they won't."

"Why not?" Meggie asked. Then, before he could answer, she said, "You're not coming with us, are you?"

The Kid smiled and shook his head. "Like I said,

I'll point you in the right direction. Both of those horses have rifles in the saddle boot, so you'll have guns and food. There's some water in those canteens, but if you come to a creek or a spring, it'd be a good idea to fill them up. You'll make it through just fine."

"And what are you going to do?" Meggie asked tensely.

"I'm not finished here yet," The Kid said.

Chapter 23

By the time dawn grayed the eastern sky, The Kid had taken James and Meggie to the northern tip of the Hatchet range, pointed them in the right direction, and said farewell to them. Meggie hugged him again, and James shook hands and said with grudging gratitude, "Thanks for everything you've done, Browning. You never gave up on gettin' us away from those—" He glanced at his sister and finished, "Varmints. I just wish . . . well, shoot, I can't believe I'm sayin' this . . . I wish ol' Devil Dave had made it out, too."

"So do I," The Kid agreed with a nod as he shook James's hand. "Keep your eyes open, find the railroad, head east. You'll be all right."

James nodded. "I reckon we will be."

The Kid watched them ride off, then turned and headed south again, riding along the eastern slope of the mountains with the rugged peaks to his right. He was alone again, and that was the way he liked it. No more innocents would get hurt as he finished what he'd set out to do.

The sun peeked over the horizon a short time later, spilling orange and gold light over the land. The Kid kept an eye on the desert, thinking that he might spot some of Tarleton's men searching for their horses. It wasn't long before he noticed a couple of dark specks out there that quickly resolved themselves into the figures of two men trudging along. He circled around so that he could come at them out of the sun, then trotted the buckskin toward them.

They must have taken him for one of their group, because they stopped and just stood there as he approached, shading their eyes in an effort to make him out against the glare of the rising sun. He was within twenty yards of them before they realized their mistake.

One of the men howled, "That's Browning!" and they both slapped leather.

The Kid reined in, pulling the buckskin to the side. His gun came smoothly out of its holster. He had reloaded, filling all six chambers in the cylinder since he had plenty of ammunition. In little more than the blink of an eye, the Colt roared three times, the reports blending in with the single shot each of the gunmen got off before The Kid's lead smashed them off their feet.

Neither of those return shots came anywhere close to The Kid. He threw his left leg over the buckskin's back and slid down to the ground on the horse's right side. Keeping the revolver in his hand trained on the fallen men, he walked toward the sprawled shapes.

One of the men was already dead. Blood leaked from the mouth of the other one as he looked up at The Kid and tried to talk. All he managed to get out was a curse before his eyes rolled up in their sockets and his head fell to the side. A final breath rattled in his throat as his bloody chest stopped rising and falling.

The Kid thumbed fresh cartridges into the Colt to replace the expended ones, then turned back to the buckskin and caught up the reins. He swung into the saddle and rode on, leaving the two dead gun-wolves where they had fallen.

His destination was the little oasis where the killers had made their camp the night before. He suspected that he'd find Tarleton and Pamela there, since he couldn't see either of them walking through the desert looking for the scattered horses. They would rely on the men they were paying to bring their mounts back to them.

With his injured leg, Hogan wouldn't be tramping around the desert, either, which meant only two men were left out there, plus Trace. Slowly but surely, he was taking care of them. If he could live a while longer, soon the only ones left would be the two people most responsible for what happened to Rebel.

He would take them back and turn them over to the law, he told himself. He wasn't a cold-blooded murderer, despite what had happened in the past.

Dust spiraling up into the air off to his left caught his eye. He turned and saw two men on horseback galloping toward him. A couple of the hired guns had caught their horses faster than he'd expected them to. That guess was confirmed a second later when powdersmoke spurted from the riders and bullets began kicking up dust not far away.

The Kid leaped out of the saddle and pulled his horse into a tight turn. He hauled down on the reins. The buckskin lay down. The Kid stretched out on the ground behind the horse. He hated using the buckskin for cover, but there was nothing else out there on those flats. He pulled the Winchester from the saddle boot, feeling the buckskin's quivering flank as he did so.

"Take it easy, boy," he said. He lay the rifle's barrel across the buckskin's body, drew a bead on one of the charging gunmen, and fired.

Unfortunately, the two men veered away from each other, splitting up just as The Kid pulled the trigger, so his first shot passed harmlessly between them. That was a smart move. He wouldn't have time to get both of them before they were on top of him. He rolled away from the buckskin and slapped the horse on the rump.

"Get out of here!" he shouted. He wanted the buckskin out of the line of fire.

The horse lunged to its feet and raced off. The Kid wound up prone. Bullets struck the ground close enough to spray dirt and gravel over him. He braced himself on his elbows, aimed the Winchester at the man on his right, and pulled the trigger again.

This time his shot was true. The gunman flung

his arms out to the sides as the bullet drove deep in his chest. He turned a backward somersault off the horse.

The Kid quickly levered the Winchester and shifted his aim, but he didn't have time to fire. The second rider was only a few feet away. In desperation, The Kid rolled to his left, away from the flashing hooves. Shots slammed out as the gunman raced past. A fiery finger traced a burning path along The Kid's side as one of the slugs grazed him.

One of the horse's rear legs struck the Winchester's barrel and sent the rifle spinning out of The Kid's hands. He forced his brain and body to ignore the pain of the wound in his side as he shoved himself up on one knee and palmed out the Colt. The rider twisted around, realizing he had overrun his enemy, and managed to get one more shot off before The Kid's revolver blasted twice.

Both bullets ripped into the man's right side. He folded up and toppled out of the saddle as his horse started to run again. With a foot caught in the stirrup, the wounded man bounced along behind the horse. After a hundred yards or so, that foot slipped free. The horse kept going, leaving its wounded rider behind.

The Kid climbed to his feet and looked around. His buckskin had gone about two hundred yards and then stopped. The horse looked at him quizzically. The Kid whistled, unsure the sound would carry that far. It did, and the buckskin responded immediately, trotting toward him.

While he waited for the horse, The Kid grimaced and lifted his shirt to take a look at the wound in his side. The bullet had plowed a very shallow furrow, not much more than a burn. A little blood welled from it. The injury was painful but not serious, he decided.

He reloaded the Colt, slid a couple of rounds into the Winchester's loading gate, and checked the first man he'd shot. The hired gun was dead.

The buckskin trotted up to The Kid and nuzzled his shoulder. The Kid patted the animal's shoulder and said, "Sorry about using you for cover, fella." He grasped the reins and led the buckskin over to the man who'd been dragged by the stirrup. That one was dead, too, bloody and battered almost beyond recognition.

Not so much so, however, that The Kid couldn't tell who he was. Or rather, who he wasn't. So far, The Kid hadn't seen any sign of Jack Trace among the men he'd encountered. He really wanted to catch up to the little gunslinger. If Trace hadn't betrayed Dave Whitfield, things might not have played out as they had. The rancher might even still be alive if not for Trace's treachery.

Trace was either still out there on the desert somewhere, or back at the camp with Tarleton and Pamela. The Kid mounted up painfully and headed toward the foothills. He had chopped the odds down far enough to go ahead and confront the two masterminds behind all the hell he had gone through.

He entered the hills a good distance north of the campsite he had raided the night before. He rode into the mountains and began working his way around so that he could come at the camp from above.

When he was close, he dismounted and went the rest of the way on foot, pausing on a little ridge that overlooked the pool surrounded by pine trees and grass. A man sat in the shade of the trees, and after a moment The Kid was able to see him well enough to recognize the gunman called Hogan. The man's right leg stuck out straight in front of him. Someone had tied a couple of branches onto it to serve as crude splints. Hogan's head leaned back against the trunk. It looked like he was asleep.

That wasn't the case, though, because after a moment, Hogan's left hand came into view as he lifted a bottle of whiskey to his mouth. He took a long swig, then lowered the bottle to his side again.

The Kid didn't see any sign of Tarleton or Pamela.

A frown creased his forehead as he studied the camp. He'd been convinced that the two of them would be there. The idea of them tramping around the desert looking for the runaway horses just didn't ring true for him. They were the sort of people who relied on others to do any physical labor for them.

After a few minutes, The Kid accepted the evidence of his own eyes. Hogan was alone.

Carefully, The Kid moved closer. He drew his gun and leveled it at Hogan as he stepped out of the brush.

The gunman didn't seem surprised to see him. In fact, Hogan chuckled and said, "I was wonderin' when you'd get here, Browning."

"Where are the others?"

"Gone." Hogan lifted the bottle again and waved it at the campsite. "You don't see 'em anywhere around here, do you?"

"They just left you here?"

Hogan took another pull on the bottle, which was almost empty. "I can't very well walk, not with this leg you busted for me." A bleak bitterness filled his voice.

"So they abandoned you." Actually, the idea wasn't that hard to accept, now that he thought about it. Pamela and Tarleton weren't the sort to take pity on anyone, especially when that person was no longer useful to them. "I thought they'd wait here until the others rounded up the horses and brought them back."

"What others? They're all dead except for Pamela and Tarleton and Trace. I reckon you killed the ones who went lookin' for the horses, since you're here and still alive."

The Kid frowned again. "Wait a minute. The numbers don't add up. There should be at least one more man out there somewhere."

Hogan shook his head. "No, the other fella— name of Horrigan, if that matters—died early this morning from being busted up when you stampeded those horses through the camp. You killed two men, and Loomis got run over and had his head stove in, then and there." More of the whiskey gurgled down Hogan's throat. "You pretty near wiped us out, Browning. Any normal man would've given up when he saw the odds against him, but you just kept on comin' until nearly everybody was dead."

The Kid nodded, willing to accept what Hogan told him. The man was too drunk to be lying, he decided.

"So Pamela and Tarleton decided to go with Trace and hunt for the horses?"

"Yeah." Hogan laughed humorlessly and shook his head. "She said she loved me, but once she saw I was crippled, it didn't take her any time at all to realize she'd been wrong about that. She started playin' up to Trace instead."

"That doesn't surprise me." The Kid moved so that he could look around the tree where Hogan was sitting. "They didn't even leave you a gun?"

"Nope. Just this bottle. Hell of a note, ain't it?"

"Once I get back to civilization, I'll send somebody out here to find you."

Hogan drained the last of the booze from the bottle and then slung the empty across the camp. "The hell with that!" he said as he leaned forward. "I'll be dead by then, and you know it. Kill me, Browning." He tapped his forehead. "One shot, right here. Get it over with, damn you. Finish what you started."

The Kid had lowered his gun. He shook his head. "I can't do that."

"Why not? Too merciful for you, you son of a bitch?"

"That leg of yours will heal. You might not ever walk right again, but it won't kill you. You won't die of thirst, either, with that pool right there. I'll leave enough supplies to hold you for a few days. You'll get hungry, but you won't starve to death."

"Forget it. You know how much my life'll be worth once word gets around that I'm a cripple? I got enemies. They'll come for me."

The Kid shook his head again. "Sorry."

Hogan closed his eyes, tilted his head back, and groaned. The Kid pouched his iron and started to back away. Hogan sat up again, twisted around, and grabbed hold of the tree. He used it as support and struggled to pull himself to his feet.

"Damn it, Browning, kill me!" he raged.

The Kid turned and walked away.

Hogan started after him, stumping along on his one good leg and the splinted, injured one. He whimpered in pain from the shattered knee. After making it only a couple of steps, he stumbled and fell, landing on his belly. His fingers clawed at the ground.

"Damn you, Browning! Damn you!"

"Too late," The Kid said without turning around.

He heard Hogan yelling for a while as he rode out into the desert, but then the sounds faded. Maybe Hogan would make it, maybe he wouldn't. It was out of The Kid's hands now.

Quite a few tracks led away from the campsite, but there was only one set of three. Those footprints had to belong to Pamela, Tarleton, and Trace. The Kid followed them, knowing that it wouldn't take him long to catch up since he was on horseback and they were afoot.

Half an hour later he saw something lying on the ground up ahead. As he kicked the buckskin into a fast trot, he realized the shape was that of a man lying facedown. The hombre was too big to be Jack Trace, and as The Kid came closer, he recognized the dark suit that Anthony Tarleton had been wearing.

Tarleton didn't move as The Kid approached. He had to be either dead or unconscious. Otherwise, he would have heard the hoofbeats. The Kid reined to a halt about twenty feet away and drew his gun. He didn't think Tarleton was trying some sort of trick, but he couldn't rule out the possibility.

Keeping an eye on the motionless shape, The Kid

dismounted and moved closer on foot. Tarleton still didn't move. The Kid hooked a toe under the man's shoulder and rolled him onto his back.

A large, dark red bloodstain spread over the front of Tarleton's shirt. It looked like he'd been shot at least twice. At first, The Kid thought he was dead, but then he saw Tarleton's chest moving. The man's eyelids fluttered as the bright sunlight struck them.

The Kid moved so that his shadow fell over Tarleton's face. Tarleton's eyes opened and peered up at him, but The Kid wasn't sure Tarleton really saw anything. He seemed more dead than alive. The Kid hunkered on his heels and said, "Tarleton? Can you hear me?"

The man's dry, cracked lips moved. "B-Browning? Is . . . is that . . ."

"Yes, it's me," The Kid said. Tarleton's eyes moved back and forth but seemed unable to lock onto anything. "What happened to you?"

"P . . . Pamela . . . she . . . she did this . . ."

"Pamela shot you? Your own niece?"

"There were only . . . two horses."

"Ah," The Kid said. It made sense. He looked around and spotted the hoofprints leading east. The three of them had come upon two of the horses, and neither Pamela nor Trace had been willing to ride double and take a chance on the mount giving out.

So Pamela had made the logical decision, based on which of her two companions might be able to do more for her in the future, and shot her uncle.

Somehow, The Kid wasn't the least bit surprised.

"Browning," Tarleton went on, "ev . . . everything that happened . . . to your wife . . . was Pamela's idea. You have to . . . help me."

"There's nothing I can do for you," The Kid said. "You're dying, Tarleton. I'm surprised you're not dead already."

"Then you've got to . . . settle the score . . . with that bitch. They're headed for . . . Val Verde . . . Don't let her . . . get away with . . ."

"I don't plan to let her get away with anything."

Tarleton didn't hear what The Kid said. His eyes had already glazed over. His plea for vengeance on his niece had been his dying words.

The Kid straightened. He'd told the truth. He didn't intend to let Pamela get away with everything she had done. He wouldn't be settling any scores for Anthony Tarleton, though. The man had brought his own doom upon him by allying himself with Pamela.

Taking the buckskin's reins in his hand, The Kid mounted up and pointed the horse's head northeast, following the trail left by Pamela and Trace. Just the two of them left for him to deal with. They were an hour, maybe an hour and a half ahead of him.

But he was in no hurry to catch up.

The showdown, when it came, would be in Val Verde.

The same place Rebel was laid to rest.

Chapter 24

"Mr. Browning! Mr. Browning! Is that you?"

The excited shouts made The Kid look over toward the hotel. He saw Rory MacTavish standing there waving at him and turned the buckskin in that direction.

The Kid put a weary smile on his face as he reined to a stop in front of the hotel porch. "Howdy, Rory," he said.

"I *thought* that was you," the boy said. "You look . . . different."

"Never mind that," The Kid said. "How's your father? Did he pull through?"

Rory nodded. "Yeah. Doc Churchill said it was touch and go for a while, but now he thinks Pa's gonna be all right."

The Kid felt relief wash through him at that news. He was glad Hamish MacTavish hadn't died because of Pamela's twisted need for vengeance.

"What about your brother and sister? Are they here?"

Again, Rory nodded. "They rode in this morning. I was never so glad to see anybody in my life. I was afraid they wouldn't make it back." The youngster rested his hands on the porch railing. "They said they wouldn't have, if it hadn't been for you, Mr. Browning."

"Just call me Kid. Conrad Browning's not really here anymore."

Rory looked puzzled by that, but he didn't question it. He just said, "James and Meggie aren't the only ones who rode in today. That gunfighter who worked for Mr. Whitfield, Jack Trace, is in town, too. I saw him go into the saloon a little while ago."

"What about Miss Tarleton?"

Rory frowned and shook his head. "I haven't seen her."

That surprised The Kid. He wondered where Pamela was.

But there was still Trace to deal with. He swung down from the saddle and held out the reins toward Rory. "Would you mind taking my horse over to the livery stable? Tell the hostler to take mighty good care of him. He's been through a lot the past few days."

Eagerly, Rory took the reins. "Sure, I can do that. What are you going to do, Mr. Browning? Go in the hotel and clean up?"

"Not just yet," The Kid said. He turned and walked toward the saloon.

Behind him, Rory said, "Holy cow! I gotta get back so I can *see* this!"

The Kid had taken it easy during the day-and-a-half ride back to Val Verde, not moving any faster than his quarry. Despite that, a great weariness gripped him. The grief and strain of the past few months was like an unbearable weight on his shoulders, threatening to press him down until there was nothing left of him. There only was one way to lift that weight.

His side was stiff and sore where the bullet had creased him. His shirt stuck to the dried blood. His legs and back ached from the long hours in the saddle. But none of that mattered. He felt an irresistible force drawing him on toward the bat-winged entrance of the saloon. A hard desert wind sprang up, lifting the dust in the street. He stepped onto the low porch, pushed the batwings aside, and proceeded into the cool dimness of the place.

The drinkers at the bar and the card players at the tables began to scatter. How they knew what was coming, The Kid didn't know or care. They were like wild animals, fleeing instinctively before a natural disaster.

That left a lone, slender figure standing at the far end of the bar, his left hand raised halfway to his mouth with a shot glass of whiskey in it.

Jack Trace smiled. "I knew you'd make it out alive," he said. Then he brought the glass to his lips and tossed back the drink.

"Time to see who's faster, Trace," The Kid said.

"Damned well about time."

Trace dropped the empty glass at the same instant he spun toward The Kid, his hand flashing toward his gun. The Kid's eyes hadn't fully adjusted to the light inside the saloon. He relied on speed and instinct, muscle and blood, heart and soul. The Kid's gun was in his hand, sliding out of the holster and coming up level, so fast a normal man's eye could never follow it. So was Trace's, and flame spouted from the muzzle of his Colt just a hair ahead of The Kid's.

The revolver in The Kid's hand bucked against his palm. A split-instant later, he felt the hammer blow of a bullet striking him. He took a step back but caught himself before he fell. Down the bar, Jack Trace stood there smiling, smoke curling from the barrel of the gun he held.

"Like something out of a dime novel, ain't it?" Trace said.

Then blood slid from the corner of his mouth, and his fingers lost their grip on the gun. It thudded to the sawdust-littered floor at his feet. Trace made a half-turn and fell against the bar, then toppled away from it to land on his back, his arms outflung. A shudder went through his body, and then he lay still.

The Kid felt a hot weakness filling him. He lowered his gun and turned to stumble back out into the sunlight. He heard the men who had scrambled for cover inside the saloon coming out of their hiding places to see who had lived and who had died, but he paid no attention to them. With the wind in his face, he reeled across the boardwalk, caught hold of one of the posts supporting the awning. He leaned against it and tried to catch his breath as he looked down at himself and saw the fresh bloodstain on his left side. Every time he drew air into his lungs, pain stabbed through him. He knew Trace's slug must have broken a rib, at the very least.

He groaned through gritted teeth, but not from the pain. He hadn't found out from Trace where Pamela was, and now the gunman was dead. He would have to try to backtrack them . . .

The whistle of a train approaching Val Verde made him lift his head. That movement took his eyes along the street toward the mission. He blinked against the dust and the glare of the sun on the whitewashed adobe walls as he saw movement in the cemetery. A woman, her long skirt swishing around her legs as she walked . . . a shawl over her head, protecting her from the sun . . . Was he imagining things? Had the pain from his wound and the blood he'd lost sent him over the edge into madness?

No. She was really there. As she began to walk faster toward the depot, the shawl slipped back to reveal thick brown hair falling around her shoulders.

Pamela.

She was going to catch that train and ride away, out of his life, safe once again from the justice she so richly deserved.

That thought stiffened his spine. He stepped down to the street and staggered forward. The train station was between them. The Kid was a little closer to it, but all he could do was shamble along. Pamela saw him and stopped short for a second, then hurried toward the depot. The Kid forced himself to move faster as the train whistled again. He saw puffs of white smoke and steam rising from the engine as it rolled over the tracks just west of the settlement.

Agony stabbed through The Kid with every step, but he didn't slow down. He broke into an awkward run. He didn't go into the station itself but headed for the stairs at the end of the platform instead.

"Mr. Browning!"

He recognized Meggie MacTavish's voice and glanced over to see her, James, and Rory running toward the station from the hotel. He waved them back. Pamela was bound to have a gun, and she wouldn't hesitate to use it on anyone who got in her way.

He reached the steps and stumbled up them. As he careened onto the platform, the few people who were waiting to board the train or to meet someone getting off gasped in surprise at the bloody figure who was suddenly among them. At the sight of the gun in his hand, they backed off. Some of them turned and ran into the depot.

Pamela came up the steps at the far end of the platform and stopped as she saw him again. As the rumble of the approaching train grew louder, she cried, "Why won't you just die, you son of a bitch? Why won't you just *die!*"

"Not until you get what's coming to you," The Kid rasped as he started along the platform toward her.

She laughed. "I had to stop at the cemetery to tell your precious Rebel that you were dead. I hate anyone making a liar out of me, Conrad. Just like I hate anyone who takes me for a fool!"

Her hand came up, and sure enough, there was a pistol in it. The Kid knew he should lift his Colt and fire, but he couldn't do it. Even after all she had done, he couldn't bring himself to slam a bullet into her.

But he weaved to the side as she fired, the gun going off with a spiteful crack. He lunged forward, jerking backwards as her gun went off a second time. She stood there like an angel of death, tall and haughty, the long shawl slipping off one shoulder to flap in the wind. An angel's wing . . .

No, not an angel. Heaven had no place for the pure evil that was Pamela Tarleton.

He reached for her, knocked the gun aside as she fired again. She slashed the barrel across his face and twisted away from him.

"Damn you!" she screamed. "Damn you, Conrad Browning!" Her finger tightened on the trigger for another shot as the locomotive roared past right behind her.

The Kid never knew what Pamela's trailing

shawl caught on. All he knew was that one second he was looking into her hate-filled face, and the next she shrieked in terror as the shawl jerked tight around her neck and pulled her off the platform, under the wheels of the train. Her cry was lost in the hiss of escaping steam as the locomotive slowed.

"Oh, my God," Meggie MacTavish gasped in horror from behind him. He turned, and the world spun crazily around him. He would have fallen, but James and Rory were there to catch him.

"Come on, Mr. Browning," Rory urged. "Come on. There's nothing you can do here."

Rory was right. There was nothing more he could do. It was over at last. Justice had been done. Justice of a sort, anyway.

In this world, The Kid supposed, that was the most anybody could hope for.

A week later, The Kid stopped by the mission to say goodbye to Father Francisco, who was almost recovered from his wound. The Kid was feeling better, too, although Dr. Churchill had warned him it was too soon for him to be riding. The advice was probably good, but The Kid ignored it. He was ready to put Val Verde behind him.

For now. As long as Rebel was there, he would be back, from time to time.

There would be fresh flowers on her grave every month. He had already made those arrangements, including a sizable donation to the mission, with Father Francisco. Conrad Browning's money was good for something.

Hamish MacTavish and his children were back home, where Hamish continued to recuperate. The Kid had told Angeline Whitfield of her father's wish that the feud with the MacTavishes come to an end, and she had surprised him a little by agreeing. Grief had matured her, given her strength. It was a shame that it sometimes took a tragedy to make a person grow up, but The Kid knew that was true. Angeline planned to stay on and run the Circle D. Some of the ranch hands had taken wagons down to the Hatchets and recovered all the bodies, including Devil Dave's. After her father's funeral, Angeline had hinted to The Kid that she wouldn't mind if he stayed around, too. But he just wished her luck. That was all he could do.

He tied the buckskin to the hitching post in front of the mission. He had sold the buggy and the big black horse. They were left over from Conrad Browning's life, and he didn't need them anymore.

Father Francisco came out of the mission and greeted him with a smile. "Hello, my friend," the priest said. "You look like you're ready to travel."

"Ready as I'll ever be," The Kid said with a nod.

"Where are you going?"

A faint smile touched The Kid's lips. "Now, that's a good question, padre."

young man. You have time to find . . . whatever it is you are looking for."

"I hope you're right, Father." The Kid started walking along the path toward the cemetery. As the priest fell in beside him, he went on, "I couldn't leave without stopping by here one more time."

"They brought the new stone this morning, you know."

The Kid nodded. "I know."

Father Francisco stopped at the cemetery gate. "I'll let you go on alone. God's blessings upon you, my son."

"Thanks, Father."

Hat in hand, The Kid walked into the cemetery and stopped in front of Rebel's grave. He hadn't replaced the tombstone that her brothers had put up, but he'd had another stone made for the foot of the grave. It was flat and lay almost flush with the ground. The words engraved on it were simple.

REBEL
One Love, For All Time.

A few minutes later, Kid Morgan left the cemetery, mounted up, and rode out of Val Verde. A lone rider, headed north.

No reason. Just moving on.

Center Point Publishing
600 Brooks Road ● PO Box 1
Thorndike ME 04986-0001 USA

(207) 568-3717

US & Canada:
1 800 929-9108
www.centerpointlargeprint.com